John Esten Cooke

Her Majesty the Queen

A novel

John Esten Cooke

Her Majesty the Queen
A novel

ISBN/EAN: 9783337000660

Printed in Europe, USA, Canada, Australia, Japan

Cover: Foto ©Andreas Hilbeck / pixelio.de

More available books at **www.hansebooks.com**

HER MAJESTY THE QUEEN.

A NOVEL.

BY

JOHN ESTEN COOKE,

AUTHOR OF "DOCTOR VANDYKE," "SURRY OF EAGLE'S NEST," "THE VIR-
GINIA COMEDIANS," ETC.

PHILADELPHIA:

J. B. LIPPINCOTT & CO.

1873.

CONTENTS.

BOOK I.

(iii)

BOOK II.

BOOK III.

BOOK IV.

BOOK V.

HER MAJESTY THE QUEEN.

BOOK I.

I.

CECIL COURT.

My life has been so restless and adventurous that I go back with delight to my early years, spent at the old home of my family in Warwickshire, England.

Cecil Court was a peaceful, charming old place, on the banks of the Avon, low-pitched, built of brick, with Elizabethan windows, a flower-decorated terrace, and approached by a broad avenue overshadowed by lofty elms. You entered a large hall running from front to rear, with a winding staircase on the right, the balustrade, like the wainscoting, of heavy oak, carved and darkened by age. On the right was the sitting-room, with polished oak floor, tall-backed chairs, a wide fireplace with huge old andirons, a tall mantelpiece, and a dozen portraits on the walls. This apartment was, properly speaking, the dining-room, the drawing-rooms occupying the opposite wing, but in progress of time it had come to be used as the sitting-room, and our old neighbors invariably went thither unannounced to find my father. On the second floor were the chambers,

(7)

which were numerous and furnished in the style of the reign of Queen Elizabeth.

The family estate was by no means large, consisting indeed of but a few hundreds of acres, cultivated by two or three old tenants, grown gray-headed on the place. My father had never given his assent, however, to any diminution of the size of the old Cecil Court park,—an extensive chase of the freshest and greenest turf, dotted with century oaks, beneath which the cattle grazed undisturbed, and a few deer wandered, tame and confiding. Seen from a distance, through the waving foliage of its great trees, Cecil Court was a peaceful and attractive picture. On the right, beyond a green hillock, gleamed the still waters of a pond and the dancing waves of a little stream. The sylvan scene was calm and friendly, and you would have said that life here was as tranquil and serene as the slow movement of the white clouds floating over the blue sky.

Our household was small, consisting only of my father, my elder brother Harry, my younger sister Cicely, an old housekeeper, and a few old servants, whose heads had turned white in the service of the family, and who performed their duties with the regularity and more than the silence of machines. I often think now that a large part of the happiness of human beings depends upon the possession of such silent old household attendants. Never a word was uttered nor an order given. Comfort, kindness, and silence reigned, and the exact wine my father wished was placed at his elbow, without a word addressed to the old major-domo waiting, calm and silent, behind his chair.

Do not fancy from this picture, worthy reader, that the Cecils were very well-to-do in the world. We had barely enough; and although the country-people called my father "the Squire," and took off their hats to him with the profoundest deference, that was more a tribute to his kindly nature, which made all love him, than to his possessions. The estate had once been very large, but had dwindled away. Still, we had enough to live upon as gentlefolks, and my father's fondness for reading and study caused him to forget the narrowness of his fortunes. He was a very tall and distinguished-looking person, with long gray hair, which he powdered and tied with a ribbon, a broad and lofty forehead, blue eyes full of candor and simplicity, and lips wearing habitually a smile of great sweetness. His dress was plain, but about his whole appearance there was an air of grace and distinction which never changed. His manner was the same to a peer of the realm and to a plowman,—his bow to the last as courteous as to the first. In a word, good reader, my father was a gentleman of extreme pride, simplicity, and naturalness,—thought himself, I dare say, as good as the peer, and perhaps in many things no better than the plowman.

I do not remember my dear mother, who died in my infancy, taking away with her, people said, much of the sunshine of my father's life,—for to the last they were more like young lovers than old married people. For her, my father kept his courtliest bows and his sweetest smiles. The great aim of his life seemed to be to make her happy; and when she died, the old neighbors said that he went about as though he had lost something without which he could not live. This, however, was before my time, and when I first remember him my father had regained his calmness, at least. His smile was full of sadness, but of great sweetness too, as I have said. Once I found him in tears, gazing at a withered flower my dear mother had given him upon their wedding-day; but such evidences of emotion were infrequent. I recall him now, most clearly, sitting in his great arm-chair, reading a folio containing the dramas of his friend and neighbor Mr. Shakspeare, whom he knew in his own younger days, and esteemed highly.

A few words will introduce my brother Harry and my sister Cicely. Harry was a year or two my senior, a brave, handsome youth, full of sunshine and gayety, who had hunted every fox in the county from his boyhood, and ended by entering that select company of young gentlemen, the Queen's Guardsmen, at Hampton Court. In doing so, he had consulted both his own wishes and his love for me. The revenues of Cecil Court were insufficient to send us both to Oxford, and, as I was destined for the law, Harry declared that I should go, he becoming a guardsman. I accordingly went to Oxford, and Harry to London,—I became a fellow-commoner of Baliol College, and he a gay young gallant. When this history opens, I had just returned to Cecil Court, and Harry was in the Guards.

Of Cicely, my little sister, I shall say nothing at this time, and scarce more of that important personage, the writer of these memoirs. The said gentleman, Edmund Cecil by name, was a country youth who fancied himself a great philosopher; liberal in politics, but a monarchist for all that, and by no means pleased with the near prospect of becoming a denizen of the Inns of Court at London. It would have pleased him far better to have remained at Cecil Court in idleness,—reading, dreaming, wandering about the old park, and shaping cloud-castles for his own entertainment. He was, in truth, a most useless and incapable person, content to let the current waft him, without using his oars, and asking only silence and liberty to peruse the pages of Mr. William Shakspeare, for whom he had inherited his father's fondness.

Such a life was impossible, however; and one day my father informed me that he had made every arrangement for my entrance at the Inns of Court. My lodgings had been engaged in Essex Court, with young Master John Evelyn, and nothing now prevented me from commencing the study of my future profession.

"'Tis the best career I can think of for my boy," my father said, with his sweet smile, now filled with tenderness. "Cecil Court goes to Harry, but perchance you will be Chief Justice some day, my son. So take the old sword yonder,—every gentleman should wear a sword,—the best horse in the stable, and Dick the hostler will ride with you to London."

My heart sank at the very phrase "Inns of Court," but there was some consolation in that magical word "London."

"I will be ready at daylight, sir," I said, taking my father's hand and kissing it.

"That is well, my boy; and I need give you few counsels. Be a good man, my dear; be honest and true. Study hard; for remember 'tis the educated brain

A*

that rules the world. Avoid as far as possible the political commotions just beginning; for neither on the king's side nor the parliament's is the full right. The Cecils must be of the royal party, if the issue comes; but his majesty construes his prerogative far too liberally for my views. With him you must side nevertheless, if honor will let you, and you side with either. But remember that the Cecil honor is above and before all,—even that of the king, who is, after all, but the first gentleman of his kingdom."

My father stopped, and laid his hand upon my head.

"God bless my boy!" he said, in a faltering voice; and, turning away, he went out of the room, leaving me in tears.

At daylight I set out for London. The whole household had assembled to bid me good-by, and the old servants uttered many earnest blessings, for in their eyes I was yet but a child. Then my father pressed my hand closely, Cicely put her arms around my neck and kissed me, her face wet with tears, I mounted, waved my hand, and, followed by joyous Dick the hostler, went forth into the future.

My father stood on the old porch until I was out of sight. Reaching an eminence distant half a mile from the hall, it again appeared, and my dear father was standing there still. My heart went back to him, and to all the familiar localities I was bidding farewell to. With something strange in my throat which seemed about to choke me, I gazed long from the hill on the fields and forests of my childhood; then, turning my horse's head, I set forward at a gallop,—Dick the hostler made his best effort to keep up with me,—and Cecil Court disappeared from my eyes.

I was afloat upon the surge of that ocean which is called the great world.

II.

MY ADVENTURE AT WENDOVER.

As though to indicate the adventurous character of the career I was to run, a singular incident befell me on this the first day of my journey.

But first I will attempt, reader, to present you with an outline of myself as I thus went forth from the family nest,—a callow fledgeling, scarce winged as yet, —gazing around me eagerly on the fertile lands, on the old minsters and castles, and the fields so soon to be trampled.

The Edmund Cecil who thus rode to seek his fortune, was a youth of twenty-three, slight, active, with brown eyes, and hair of the same color; and he wore a dark cloth riding-habit, chamois boots, a hat with a black feather, and the old family sword clattering against his hunting-spurs. A downy mustache and *royale*, after the fashion of the time, set off the face,— a face in which, I think, hope and happiness must have shone; for the youth found something charming in the idea of London, whither he was going, and bestrode with delight his favorite hunter from the Cecil Court stables. There were not many there now; the Cecils were poor; but what was poverty to the young knight-

2

errant ?   Youth was stronger,—youth, the source of
nearly every joy ; to return to which to-day, when my
pulse rarely throbs, I would give all the experience
and wisdom I have since acquired !   Experience?
Wisdom ?   The tints of autumn are charming, and the
sunset is of solemn beauty ; but spring is sweeter than
autumn, the dawn fresher than evening !   My old age
is happy, and I am content with it.   But oh for the
curls and roses, the eye and pulse, of twenty !

I passed Aylesbury, in Buckinghamshire, and slept at
the *Cat and Bagpipes*, an inn in the small town of Wendover.   I had just descended at sunrise, and was about
to resume my journey, when a traveling-carriage, coming from the north and drawn by four spirited horses,
rattled up to the door, and through the window I
caught sight of an exquisite face.   It was that of a
young lady apparently about twenty, her countenance half concealed by a cloak and hood.   I could
still discern its outlines, however ; and its rare beauty
was unmistakable.   The cheeks were rosy, the eyes
large and earnest, the lips mild and full of a charming
innocence and sweetness.   Such was the occupant of
the coach,—a woman, evidently her attendant, being
the sole other person visible.

The coach stopped, and the driver leaped down.

" Fresh horses for London !" he cried to the portly
landlord, who had hastened out.

At the sound of that voice I started, and my whole
attention was now concentrated upon the speaker.   He
was a mere coachman, at least in costume,—huge over-
all, plain beaver, a handkerchief bundled around his
throat, and heavy top-boots.   I went closer, and looked

under the low hat. The coachman was my brother Harry, of the Queen's Guardsmen !

Our eyes met, and he turned quickly, endeavoring to conceal his face. I began to laugh, and called out,—

"Don't you know me, Harry?"

Thereat the supposed coachman turned, and whispered,—

"'Ware hawks, Ned !—on secret service for her majesty !"

He said no more; but went to the coach and seemed to propose that the young lady should breakfast therein ; for, in compliance with a rapid order, food was brought, and she ate hastily.

Meanwhile fresh horses were rapidly attached ; the postilion mounted ; Harry cracked his whip with the air of a born Jehu, and the carriage set off, the horses going at a gallop.

Harry had carefully avoided a private interview. He had simply whispered, in passing me,—

"I will see you in London."

Ten minutes afterwards, the carriage had disappeared over the crest of a hill, leaving me standing in the middle of the street gazing after it.

I hastened to follow ; but it was half an hour before I got to saddle. I then rode on rapidly, but did not catch up with the carriage. It had disappeared like a dream,—a visionary equipage drawn by phantom horses.

III.

THE LADY OF WENDOVER AGAIN.

LONDON was visible, as I approached, from a great distance, with its canopy of smoke; and I cantered gayly into the famous city, making my way, after inquiries of wayfarers, towards Essex Court, where my lodgings had been engaged.

In front of the palace of Whitehall, with which I was familiar from one other visit in my boyhood to London, a very great crowd had assembled. So dense was the mass of human beings that I pushed my horse through it with difficulty, followed by Dick the hostler; and the appearance of this crowd was singular. It consisted, apparently, of apprentices of the various trades in the City, their hair cut extremely short; and almost all carried in their hands staves upon which were placards bearing the word "Liberty." The great mass of human beings uttered vociferous cries, and kept their eyes fixed upon the palace, in front of which I now saw a long row of carriages drawn up, with the royal arms upon the panels.

"What is the cause of this excitement, sir?" I said to a burly individual standing near me.

"The tyrant is about to fly with his family, and we are come to stop him," was the stern reply.

"The tyrant, sir?" I said.

"Others call him Charles the First of England."

"Good heavens, sir!" I exclaimed, "'tis not possible that violence is meant by his majesty's faithful subjects to his person and his family!"

My interlocutor looked fixedly at me, and, tightening the grasp on his stick, was apparently about to take the offensive, when a great wave bore him ten feet from me. A hand caught my bridle, and my horse was thrown on his haunches. A moment afterwards, hoof-strokes were heard: a detachment of the king's body-guard pushed their horses through the crowd, the procession of coaches filled with ladies followed, and another detachment brought up the rear.

I had been swept away, still on horseback, by the great wave, and was looking at the carriages, when I recognized in one of them the face of the young lady whom I had encountered at Wendover. She was clad in velvet and laces now, and was even more beautiful. I was gazing at the calm, proud face, conscious of little save her very great loveliness, when a man rushed up to the coach,—it was my burly friend with the staff,— thrust the "Liberty" placard into the young lady's face, and uttered some words apparently of insult; for the calm face quickly flushed. This proceeding enraged me; and, leaping to the ground, I grasped the person guilty of this indignity by one of his ears, dragging him violently back. He uttered a yell of anger at this unceremonious assault, turned, and caught me by the throat; and, although I had drawn and directed my sword's point towards his breast, I was about to be dragged down and trampled under foot by the crowd, when a voice near me cried,—

"Hold hard, Ned! We are coming."

It was the voice of Harry, who rode at the head of the detachment of horse in rear.

"You will please allow me to pass, good people," he said, in his loud, hearty voice. "I don't want to ride against anybody; and, as this gentleman is my brother——"

He pushed at my big opponent, struck him with his horse's chest, and drew me, hot and furious, towards him.

"'Ware hawks, Ned!" he said, laughing. "There's Dick brandishing his arms and holding your horse. Mount, and fall in with the Guards! or I think these worthies will eat you up!"

Dick had pushed through and reached my side, still clinging to my horse's bridle. I threw myself into the saddle, and took my place in the line,—Dick imitating me. No further violence was offered any one; and an hour afterwards the procession of coaches, containing, as I now ascertained, the queen, the royal family, and maids of honor, issued from London.

Then I saw rising before me the imposing walls of Hampton Court; the procession passed through the park; the Guards were drawn up in a double line, and between these walls of silk, plumes, and steel, the queen and the rest entered the palace.

I was looking with interest and admiration upon the bevy of beautiful young ladies as they passed in and disappeared, when the voice of Harry beside me said,—

"What was the trouble about yonder, Ned?"

I told him all.

"Oho! Well, that's like a Cecil! And it was the fair Miss Frances Villiers whose knight you became,"

"Is her name Frances Villiers?"

"Yes; her Majesty's favorite maid of honor."

"Well, I think I did right, Harry——"

"You won the right to enter the guards of her majesty; and I'll apply for your appointment before I sleep, Ned. Come on! follow me to the guard-room."

IV.

HOW HARRY HAD COME TO DRIVE A COACH ALL THE WAY TO SCOTLAND.

THE guard-room at Hampton Court was an apartment of large extent, with tables against the wall beneath the tall windows, and around these tables a number of the gay young gallants of the Guards were already engaged at dice,—laughing, jesting, and exchanging comments on the events of the morning.

Harry had just made me acquainted with some of his friends,—and I could see at a glance that he was a favorite with the mercurial young gentlemen of the Guards,—when an usher entered, glided to him, and spoke in a low tone.

"Wait here, Ned," he said. "I am sent for." And taking his gray beaver, with its floating plume, he followed the usher.

He was absent for a quarter of an hour, during which time the guard-room resounded with jests, laughter, the rattle of dice, and the clatter of flagons on the tables. I was gazing at this animated scene, when Harry touched me on the shoulder, made a sign to me to follow him, and, leading the way, conducted me through a long corridor to the left wing of the palace.

"You are about to enjoy the satisfaction of being thanked for your chivalric gallantry, Ned, by the prettiest pair of lips at the court of England," said my brother, laughing. "Come on! Be firm, but determined; modest, but devoted!"

And, still with his gay laugh, Harry opened a door, beyond which, in a small but richly-decorated apartment, I saw seated the young lady of the inn at Wendover.

"I have the honor of presenting my brother Edmund, Miss Villiers," Harry said, bowing low, with his plume trailing on the floor. "He begs to assure you of his very profound respect." And Harry discreetly fell back.

The young lady inclined her head graciously, in response to my low bow, and I observed in her bearing the same air of calmness and repose. Nothing seemed to shake this singular serenity.

"I fear you make quite a court ceremony of this interview with a simple maid of honor, Mr. Cecil," she said to Harry; and it is impossible to conceive anything sweeter and calmer than the accents of her voice. Raising her great, limpid eyes to my face, she added, "Mr. Cecil has informed me that it was yourself to whom I was indebted for assistance to-day, sir; and I thank you sincerely."

The beautiful girl abashed me. I could only bow low again, when Harry's gay voice interposed.

"Ned is overcome, Miss Villiers. In a word, accept the devotion of the Cecil family at large; and should you kindly take us under your ladyship's protection, secure my brother's appointment to a place in the Guards.''

I could not protest that I was about to become one of the long-robe fraternity,—to be frank, I was quite ashamed of the fact,—and, with a throb of satisfaction, remained silent.

''Mr. Cecil wishes an appointment?'' said Miss Villiers. ''I am sure he may secure that.''

''He is discreet as well as brave,'' Harry said, quietly. ''He saw and recognized me at Wendover.''

The young lady turned her head quickly, and a slight color came to her face.

''I am sorry, sir,'' she said, somewhat stiffly. ''I had hoped——''

''That no one save myself and her majesty was informed of that escapade? But think, Miss Villiers, I alone was to blame.''

He turned to me, and added, ''This is the best time and place to inform you frankly, Ned, of the meaning of that encounter. It is due to Miss Villiers, who has not ceased to cherish sentiments of displeasure towards me. Know, then, that Miss Villiers is confidential maid of honor to her majesty, and that her devotion knows no bounds. Well, her majesty desired, recently, to send an oral message to his majesty, who is in Scotland. The times are troubled and dangerous; written communications are liable to be intercepted: in a word, Miss Villiers offered to go to Scotland and convey the message in person. Am I right, Miss Villiers? and have I your permission to proceed?''

"Yes, sir," returned the young lady, with the slight color still in her cheeks. "I even desire that Mr. Cecil shall be informed of the meaning of that singular adventure."

"I see that your displeasure continues, madam," said Harry; "but I can only submit. Pardon me, I pray you, for still speaking of you in your presence as though you were absent."

He bowed, and went on, addressing himself to me.

"Her majesty accepted the offer of Miss Villiers, and it was arranged that she should travel with a lady's maid only, but the coach was to be driven by an old and trusted servitor. When it left London it was I, however, who drove, and for a simple reason. A young lady would necessarily be exposed, traveling thus alone, to peril; so I locked up the old servitor, mounted the seat of the coach, and it was only when it had proceeded a day's journey, nearly, that Miss Villiers perceived the ruse. I need not say that she was very angry, and perhaps justly angry. But the die was cast; the message was pressing. The coach continued its way, and beyond Doncaster the advantage of being driven by an able-bodied young man in place of an infirm old servitor became apparent, did it not, madam?"

And, with lurking enjoyment of his triumph in his handsome eyes, Harry turned to the young lady.

"Continue, sir," she said.

"Footpads, Ned!" Harry said, laughing. "The coach was attacked. The coachman heroically discharged his pistols and unhorsed one of the knights of the road; the rest fled. The coach imitated them, and we reached Scotland, to return speedily over the same ground London-ward. In traveling, no time was lost. The coach was driven on day and night, as you may understand from the fact that we reached Wendover as you were coming down to breakfast. *Peste !* as her majesty's French maids say, I have not yet caught up with my lost sleep. I nod in the saddle, and snore while rattling the dice! To conclude, Miss Villiers most generously made my peace with her majesty. I am becoming a court favorite, they tell me; and after the assault of the footpads I regained, and still enjoy, the luxury of a good conscience and an exalted opinion of myself."

It was impossible to resist Harry's gayety. A smile came to Miss Villiers's lips, and she said,—

"Mr. Cecil was born to be an advocate in the courts of law. He will end by forcing me to thank him for locking up the queen's servitor."

"No, madam," said Harry, bowing low, and speaking with an earnestness in strong contrast to his former levity; "I shall be content if you pardon a very audacious escapade——"

As he uttered the words, an usher summoned Miss Villiers to attend the queen. She rose, and for the first time I observed the queenly outline of her person. There was something regal in her; a slight bend in her neck gave her appearance an indescribable grace. She smiled faintly, inclined her head, and, gliding rather than walking, disappeared.

"By heavens, she's a queen!" exclaimed Harry. "Come, Ned, and rest easy; from this moment you are as good as one of her majesty's Guards. My pockets

are full of gold; I make you a present of your uniform! Long live her majesty—and her maids of
honor!"

———

V.

I ENTER THE QUEEN'S GUARDS.

I SHARED Harry's bed that night, and was waked by
the trumpet sounding reveillé.

The Guardsmen paraded in the court,—stiff, motionless, sitting their horses in line, and answering gruffly
to their names as the roll was called. The gay gallants
of the guard-room were turned to wooden figures;
but at the order to return to quarters they again broke
forth into jests and laughter.

As Harry came in, his rapier rattling against his
boots, I saw that he held a paper in his hand.

"Here is what one of the queen's ushers has just
brought, Ned," he said.

I looked at the paper; it was my appointment to a
place in the queen's Guards.

"You see Miss Villiers stands by her friends, Ned,"
said Harry. "Come and don one of my old uniforms.
From this moment you are a Guardsman!"

He laughed, and put his arm round my neck. Of
all the faces I ever saw, Harry's came nearest sunshine
when he thus laughed.

The day passed in a round of excitement. I did not
reflect upon the scant respect paid my father in thus

cavalierly turning my back on the profession for which he had destined me. Had the eyes of Frances Villiers already worked their magic on me? I know not; but I hailed the change in my destiny with delight. Let me add here, as I shall pass soon to stirring events, that my dear father manifested no displeasure at the unceremonious step thus taken, but sent me his full approval; and I had no sooner received my appointment then I set about my arrangements. These were speedily made. The tailor of the Guardsmen, in Rosemary Lane, near the Tower, came and took my measure for my uniform,—in the mean while I donned an old one of Harry's;—Dick the hostler declared his strong wish to remain and attend to my horses, and so behold me suddenly a full-fledged guardsman of the queen!

I was to commence my duties more speedily than I supposed. I had just entered the guard-room, about noon, when Harry came in, and I could see that he was angry.

"What is the matter?" I said.

He drew my arm through his own, and dragged me rather than led me out.

"The matter is insolence and cruelty, Ned!" he said, with a sort of growl peculiar to him when anything moved him. "The crop-eared knaves in parliament have insulted her majesty!"

"Insulted?"

"Judge! Here comes to-day a messenger with a paper from that rascal Pym and the rest, that her majesty 'must surrender her young family into their hands during the absence of the king, lest she should take an opportunity of making papists of them.'"

"And her majesty has replied?"

"That her sons were under tuition of their governors, who were not papists: she obeyed the will of her husband that they should not be brought up in her religion. And this is not all!"

"What more, Harry?"

"Secret information has just arrived that a parliamentary order has been sent to a magistrate near Oatlands, where the royal family now are, to be ready with a part of the militia in the park of the palace to-night,—where he would be joined by a body of cavalry,—and await further orders."

"They mean to seize on the royal family!"

Harry burst out into such oaths as I will not record.

"At their peril!" he said. "I say no more now, but——"

The trumpet was heard without, sounding "Boots and Saddles," and the palace was in commotion. Harry was hastening out, when an usher came in, looking rapidly around.

"I am ordered to summon the first two gentlemen of the Guards I meet, to her majesty's presence," he said.

"Come on, Ned!"

Harry was already rushing after the usher. I followed. We passed along a great corridor, through a magnificent suite of apartments, then into an antechamber, where, at a sign from the usher, Harry paused, while we were being announced.

"Let them come in!" exclaimed a voice in a decided French accent.

A moment afterwards I had followed my brother

into a large apartment richly furnished and half filled
with maids of honor, among whom stood a lady clad
in black, with a pallid face and piercing eyes. This
lady, I heard afterwards, was the secret enemy of her
majesty, Lady Carlisle.

In one corner, near a *prie-dieu*, stood a father confessor in black robes. On the carpet gamboled a small
black dog, the famous Mitte, so intimately associated
with her majesty's wanderings and perils.

Lastly, at a table, where she wrote rapidly, sat the
queen.

VI.

HORSES FOR FRANCE.

HER majesty Queen Henrietta Maria—or "Mary,"
as King Charles and his followers always called her—
seemed to labor under great emotion.

She was a very beautiful person of about thirty,
of an exquisite clear brunette complexion, with glossy
brown hair, and large black eyes which sparkled like
stars. It was impossible not to admire her extreme
delicacy of features and the noble and imposing air
of her whole person. I am not skillful in costume, and
rarely recall what a human being wears, but I remember
the rich brocade the queen wore that day, the full lace
ruffles, the little cape, called a *berthe*, I think, and the
bodice finished around the bosom and at the waist
with a purple band. A string of pearls confined her

magnificent brown hair; on her bosom lay a cross suspended from a necklace: it was in this very costume, I think, that she was drawn by the great painter Vandyke, and inspired in Mr. Edmund Waller, the poet, the fine lines,—

> "Beauty hath crown'd you, and you must have been
> The whole world's mistress, other than a queen!"

When I first saw "the whole world's mistress," on that autumn day at Hampton Court, she was in a rage; the fine eyes flashed, and the clear brunette face was crimson with anger.

"The messengers!" she said, without looking up, and continuing to write rapidly.

The usher respectfully approached and uttered a few words. The queen raised her head, and one of her slender and beautiful hands went rapidly and nervously to the cross upon her bosom. She had opened her lips to speak, when a second usher entered and asked an audience for some one whose name I did not hear.

"The magistrate! the very one! Admit him!" came from the queen, quickly.

The usher hastened out, and soon returned with a portly, red-faced justice, who bowed low.

"I crave permission to lay this order before your majesty," said the justice. "It is from the parliament, and directs me to summon the militia and patrol Oatlands Park."

"Obey your order, sir!" exclaimed the queen.

"I must disobey your majesty. Nothing will ever

induce me to obey any order other than her own or the king's."

The queen rose with a brilliant flash of her proud eyes.

"Thanks, sir! thanks! His majesty shall know of this. But return and do exactly what the parliament has dictated, and be tranquil. We shall further explain this: at present return and obey your orders."

There was no room for reply. The magistrate left the apartment, and the queen resumed her seat and wrote a few more lines.

"This to Lord Digby, in London," she said, extending a paper towards Harry, who bowed low as he received it.

"This to its address," the queen added; and as she held out the paper her eyes met my own.

I thought I heard at the same moment a faint murmur from Miss Villiers, who stood near the queen.

"It is well; lose no time, Mr. Cecil."

I retired blushing with delight at this utterance of my name by the queen. She was so beautiful as she sat there with that ring of rose-buds, her maids of honor, around her, that the sternest Puritan, I think, would have flushed with pleasure as I did.

Harry and myself left the court-yard at the same moment, at a gallop.

"Huzza for Queen Mary!" he cried, as he disappeared.

The note to Lord Digby, as I afterwards ascertained, contained an urgent request that his lordship would muster his friends and proceed on that very night to Oatlands Park. The letter borne by myself was

addressed to a gentleman residing some miles from
Hampton Court, who possessed a stud of horses
famous for blood and speed,—the queen designing to
make use of them in bearing off her children, if necessary, to France.

I soon reached the old manor-house of the gentleman
in question,—Colonel Edward Cooke, of the royal
forces.   Colonel Cooke was a tall and stately old
cavalier, with piercing eyes, a stern expression, but
slightly ameliorated by the ghost of a smile, and the
bearing of a thorough soldier.

" Say to her majesty, sir," he said, with a bow, as
he read the note in his great hall, " that all I possess
is at her command,—including my heart and sword,—
both by day and by night."

With this reply, which I saw, from the sudden flash
of the eye, came from the speaker's heart, I returned
to Hampton Court ; and the response of Colonel Cooke
was conveyed to her majesty by Miss Frances Villiers,
who was installed in the antechamber as a sort of
adjutant-general.

" Her majesty bids me thank you, Mr. Cecil," the
young lady said, coming out again and gazing at me
with her great calm eyes. " I counsel you to sup now :
the Guards will move in half an hour."

As she spoke, the trumpet sounded " To horse !"
the Guards rapidly drew up in the court-yard ; and, with
a decided gnawing in his stomach, Mr. Edmund Cecil
took his place in the line.

Every man was fully armed, and an expedition of
some sort was evidently on the *tapis*.

VII.

WHAT TOOK PLACE BY MOONLIGHT IN OATLANDS PARK.

As night fell, an odd cavalcade left Hampton Court. It consisted of a number of coaches, containing her majesty and the ladies of her suite; behind these the Guards; and behind the Guards a motley rout of ushers, footmen, serving-men of every description, and even scullions from the kitchens,—all, with scarce an exception, bearing arms of some sort. So quaint was this armament, indeed, that it was difficult to restrain one's laughter. The serving-men carried cleavers and carving-knives, and the scullions had caught up the spits and other weapons more useful in peace than in war. Altogether, the spectacle was a comedy, whose fantastic humor still moves me, as it returns to my memory.

What did it mean, everybody asked himself, and whither was her majesty going? The reply was that she was "going to spend the evening in the park at Oatlands;" and doubtless it was her majesty's desire that her household should go too, as she had ordered their attendance, with the singular direction that every one should be armed!

No one of this generation will ever look upon Oatlands,—the ancient dower residence and favorite resort of the queens of England for so many reigns,—with its old walls, its moat and fosses, its shady park and secluded landscape. It was leveled to the ground during the civil wars, and is only a name now; but on that autumn evening of 1641 it was yet untouched. As the queen entered the vast park and drew near the ancient building, frowning from behind its moat and with the drawbridge up, the great oaks waved their variegated arms above the queer cavalcade,—their tops silvered by the first rays of the rising moon.

Suddenly the trumpet of the Guards rang out; and as the queen's coach stopped before the drawbridge, the palace front became alive with faces. Then the drawbridge was seen to descend, the coaches entered, and the Guards, followed by the motley rout, clattered over the bridge.

The queen was assisted from her coach by a tall and bland-looking gentleman of about sixty, richly clad,— Lord Harry Jermyn, as I soon discovered, her grand equerry and confidential secretary.

Lord Jermyn smiled, and uttered a few words.

"It is well, my lord," her majesty replied. "Have my palfrey saddled, and be ready to attend me."

The broad portals of the palace then swallowed the bevy of fair ladies; the Guards, followed by their nonde-script allies, recrossed the drawbridge, and were drawn up in the park; and, to return to myself, I remained for half an hour suffering the pangs of starvation.

Then, in the half-gloom, horses' hoofs were heard upon the drawbridge, a lady's scarf glimmered in the moonlight, and the queen appeared, mounted upon her palfrey, attended by Lord Jermyn, who rode at her side.

The queen rode straight to the officer commanding

her Guards, and gave him an order. He immediately turned, and ordered,—

"Attention! Form squads of three, passing off from the right, and patrol the park. If any suspicious characters are encountered, arrest them, and report with them here. March!"

At the word, the Guards separated into squads, and scattered in every direction. I followed with two companions a by-way winding through the densest portion of the park; and we were riding on, keeping a good lookout, when the trampling of hoofs was heard in front. I was in advance of my companions, and, drawing rein, ordered, "Halt!"

The tramp drew nearer, and in the moonlight I saw advancing a body of about one hundred horsemen. I repeated the order to halt, and drew my pistol, cocking it. The column halted, and a single horseman rode forward.

"This is a patrol?" the horseman said, in a commanding voice.

"Yes. What party is that?"

"Friends of the queen. Permit us to pass."

"Impossible, sir. I do not know you," I replied.

"Move aside!" was the response, in a haughty tone; and, as he spoke, the horseman advanced upon me.

"Halt, or you are dead!" I said, putting my pistol to his breast; whereat he paused, in some astonishment.

"I am Lord Digby, come hither by the queen's order," he said, gruffly.

"I do not know your lordship. You have, doubtless, your order on your person?"

"I have." And, drawing his sword with one hand,

B*

he presented with the other the queen's letter. A glance at it in the bright moonlight terminated every doubt.

"Pass, my lord," I said, bowing. "Your lordship will appreciate my course. Our orders are imperative to stop all persons."

"Your name, sir?"

"Edmund Cecil, of her majesty's Guards, my lord."

His lordship simply saluted, and ordered, "Forward!" as I rode into the wood with my companions. I had made an enemy of Lord Digby, it seemed; but then I had carefully obeyed orders; and, careless of the consequences, I continued to patrol the park with my two companions.

Nothing suspicious met our eyes, and we were returning in the direction of the palace, when I saw, through a vista in the trees, a party of about twenty horsemen. We rode at once towards them; and one of my companions demanded who they were. No reply was made; and I rode in advance, repeating the question. The group of horsemen grew agitated, and moved to and fro. The movement unmasked one of the party, who carried a fat buck across the saddle in front of him.

"You are poachers, assailing the king's deer!" I cried. "Halt, and give yourselves up!"

A shot replied. It issued from a sort of blunderbuss in the hands of one of the party, and the bullet passed through the rim of my gray beaver. I fired in return, and drove my horse at the owner of the blunderbuss, reached his side, closed in with him, and recognized the burly young man who had insulted Miss Villiers on the way to Hampton Court.

I had clutched him by the throat, and had nearly dragged him from the saddle, when he struck me a heavy blow on the temple, which threw me to the ground. As I fell, I heard cries and the trample of hoofs; the poachers fled; and I saw around me a confused crowd, in the midst of which the bright moonlight fell upon the flashing eyes and enraged face of the queen. It was the lioness, ready to protect her young,—to contend in person, if necessary, with those bent on robbing her of her children. The beautiful face was superb in its wrath and defiance: it towered above me for a moment, and then I lost consciousness.

I was lying on a couch in the palace when I regained my senses, and some one was bathing an ugly wound on my temple, which bled freely. As all traces of it, save a slight scar, have disappeared for thirty years or more, I will not weary the reader with a tedious account of this particular "broken head." One incident remains unalterably in my memory, however. A beautiful face appeared for an instant at the door, and a low, sweet voice said,—

"Her majesty desires to know if Mr. Cecil's hurt is dangerous."

The leech replied in the negative, and the face disappeared; but a blessed influence remained with me. It was the voice of Frances Villiers which had uttered those low words,—the eyes of the beautiful girl which had sent their healing balm into my heart. I fell asleep soon afterwards, and dreamed of the face. From that moment I seldom lost sight of it, waking or sleeping: in a word, Frances Villiers began to be, what she very soon became, the sole object of my waking thoughts and my dreams.

Such had been the events of the night in Oatlands Park. The lioness had mounted guard over her off-spring, defying her enemies; and the long moonlight night passed undisturbed.

VIII.

WHAT A PIE CONTAINED.

ON the next morning I got up, buckled on my sword, and reported for duty. Harry came up and hugged me with ardor.

"Here's the hero of the encounter!" he cried, "the only human being everybody talks of——"

"Even her majesty," said a grave and courtly voice behind me; and, turning round, I saw Lord Digby.

His lordship smiled with an air of great courtesy, and held out his hand.

"I have come to compliment your good soldiership, Mr. Cecil, in persistently halting me in the park last night," he said. "You serve her majesty as she ought to be served, and I offer you my compliments, sir."

He bowed, and passed on, leaving me charmed at my sudden importance! I seemed about to become some-body! A lucky accident had raised me from obscurity, and I had even attracted the attention of her majesty,—who from that moment, as the reader will perceive, remembered my name and honored me with her august regard.

The court returned on the same evening to Hampton Court; but before the cortége left Oatlands an incident of a very comic nature occurred,—one which made everybody laugh, and introduced an afterwards famous personage.

I had just risen from the mess-table in the guard-room, where I had dined, when shouts of laughter from the great hall of the palace, where her majesty was also dining, attracted our attention. So loud and unceremonious was this laughter that it drew us irresistibly towards the door. I hastened thither with the rest, glanced through the half-open door, and at first was almost unable to believe my eyesight.

Her majesty sat at table with her maids of honor and attendant lords, and on the broad board, immediately in front of her plate, knelt a figure scarce two feet in height,—a manikin clad in full cavalier costume, with top-boots, a minute sword at his side, with a plumed beaver in one hand, and the other hand upon his heart.

Behind the dwarf was seen a huge pie, from which he had popped up, I soon discovered, at the moment when the pastry was cut. The queen had started back in utter amazement, but the dwarf had respectfully stepped towards her plate. There he had stopped, fallen upon one knee, and offered his respectful homage to her majesty, his hand resting devotedly upon his heart.

As I reached the door and took in this odd spectacle, the shouts of laughter, defying all ceremony,

4

ceased. Her majesty turned towards Lord Jermyn, and said, in high good humor,—

"We owe this surprise to you, my lord."

Lord Jermyn, with his bland and courtly smile, returned,—

"Your majesty has concluded justly: the comedy comes after the *melodrame*. This little gentleman is one of your majesty's most faithful subjects, and, knowing your majesty's taste for small people, I have planned this surprise."

The queen gazed with suppressed smiles at the dwarf, and then at Lord Jermyn.

"Thanks, my lord. We accept your gift, and take into our service—how call you him?"

"Geoffrey Hudson, your majesty."

The queen extended her hand and drew the small sword of the manikin from its scabbard. With the same expression of struggling merriment, she then touched the dwarf's shoulder with the weapon, and said,—

"Rise, Sir Geoffrey Hudson: we take you into our service."

The manikin rose, and made a bow so profound that his head nearly touched the table. He was scarce two feet, as I have said, in height.

"I thank your majesty," he said, in a small, piping voice, "and will endeavor to serve her faithfully, however small my stature."

A great laugh saluted the words, and the dwarf's face flushed with anger, as he darted quick glances around him.

"I recommend caution to gentlemen who would

avoid Sir Geoffrey's sword-thrust !'' said Lord Jermyn, laughing.

And Sir Geoffrey having leaped nimbly to the floor, where he walked up and down with great gravity and dignity, the banquet proceeded and terminated.

When her majesty set out on her return to Hampton Court in the afternoon, I observed that the singular manikin had been furnished with a seat among the maids of honor in one of the coaches. The taste for such strange beings was at that epoch a passion almost: thus, the young ladies welcomed him warmly, instead of betraying any aversion ; and on the arrival of the queen at Hampton Court he was supplied with an apartment, and became formally a member of the royal household.

He will reappear more than once in the progress of these memoirs; and an event which I shall relate in its place will show that, small as this strange human insect might be, his sting was mortal.

IX.

I GO TO ROSEMARY LANE, AND MEET WITH AN UGLY ADVENTURE.

I WAS quite charmed with the new course which my life had now taken, and—thinking continuously of a young lady with great, calm eyes—grew sedulous of my personal appearance, and thought of my tailor.

Going to try on my new uniform, I met with two

personages, the one fantastic, the other terrible; and
of these I shall now speak.   .

The name of the tailor was Joyce, and his shop was
not far from the Tower. The gentlemen of the Guards
had made him the fashion, by a species of caprice:
he had sent to take my measure, on receiving a message from Harry; and the emissary, when leaving me,
requested with an air of importance that I would come
to his master's shop and try on the uniform "during
the process of its construction," as nothing caused Mr.
Joyce such pain as to supply gentlemen with ill-fitting
garments.

I hastened therefore, a day or two after the events
just described, to visit the shop of Mr. Joyce, tailor,
in Rosemary Lane. Leaving my horse in the Guardsmen's stables at Whitehall, I proceeded on foot; and it
was nearly evening when I at last reached Rosemary
Lane, where a tall house toppling forward was pointed
out to me as the shop of the tailor.

He was at work as I entered,—a small, important-
looking man, snipping viciously with a great pair of
shears,—and greeted me with a nonchalant air, very
unusual in a tradesman. Summoning an apprentice, he
gave him an order, and, taking no further notice of me,
strolled to the doorway. His hands were thrust beneath
his coat-skirts, he carried his nose in the air, and only
returned to the lower world, as 'twere, when his apprentice brought the half-finished coat.

At a sign from him the apprentice approached me.
I removed my coat, and tried on the new garment.
He of the elevated nose then walked around me and
surveyed me from all sides.

"Take up in the waist," he said to the apprentice. " More—more—not so much—more—there."

He then gazed at me from head to foot.

"If you would hold up your head," he said,— " there. The coat will fit. Be good enough to write your name here."

He laid a large ledger before me. I saw there the names of Ireton and Cromwell.

" So you are court and parliament tailor indifferently?" I remarked, laughing.

"Yes," said Mr. Joyce, carelessly. "I make for Guardsmen and parliament people, the court and the Roundhead class, as the new term has it."

" And your own politics?"

" Roundhead," said Mr. Joyce, coolly.

He then drew his hands from beneath his coat-skirts, informed me that my uniform would be sent me in three days, turned his back on me, and began snipping away again with his great shears.

Such was my first sight of this personage, who was to become historic. I went out of his shop, half angry and half amused. But night began to fall, I was far from Whitehall, and the narrow and winding street —a sort of ditch between the tall, toppling houses on each side—was far from presenting a very cheerful appearance. There was something decidedly cut-throatish about it; and footpads then swarmed in London. A dim lamp beginning to twinkle at long intervals, from the ropes suspended across the street, only rendered darkness visible, to use Mr. Milton's fine expression. So I determined to issue from this suspicious-looking

place as soon as possible, and set forward, walking
rapidly towards the Tower.

I had gone about two hundred paces, when a roystering party of apprentices apparently, armed with clubs,
came towards me, and, as they passed, one of them
jostled me rudely. As he did so, I looked at him;
our eyes met: it was the burly young man with whom
I had grappled in Oatlands Park.

"Fall on!" he shouted, suddenly. "I know this
popinjay, and you know him! He chased us in the
park,—and he pulled my ear, the fiend seize him!"

As he uttered these words, the speaker rushed upon
me, lifting his club to brain me.

"Hark! tackle to him, Hulet!" cried his friends;
"show him——"

A hoarse growl from my enemy drowned the rest.
He struck straight at me, and his associates closed in
on me at the same moment, reminding me of a pack of
hounds around a hare.

I was not precisely a hare, however, and I had my
rapier to meet the cudgel. With the determination to
give a good account of one or two of my assailants
at least, I lunged at the man called Hulet, and ran him
through the fleshy part of his arm. The wound seemed
to render him furious. He aimed a blow at my head
with his cudgel; I parried; the blow fell on my rapier,
and the treacherous iron snapped within a foot of the
hilt.

A loud cry followed; my assailants closed in upon
me, forced me to the wall, struck at me, keeping
out of reach of my sword-stump,—and I began to
realize that in a few moments I would probably be

knocked down and left senseless or dead on he paving-stones.

I looked hastily around. All the shops were closed. I was in front of a gloomy-looking house, whose windows were fast-barred, and against the door of this house my assailants had now forced me.

"Kill him, Hulet!" rose in a wrathful shout, and the whole party threw themselves upon me, aiming at my head with their clubs. I endeavored in vain to parry this storm of blows; my back was against the door of the gloomy house; I lunged with my sword-stump, shouting for the watch without result; then a heavy blow fell upon my forehead, and I staggered, dropping the stump of my weapon.

As I did so, the door against which I leaned opened suddenly, and I felt myself dragged in. As the apprentices rushed towards it, it was shut in their faces. I then heard a bar fall, and a chain drawn across the door. A voice said, "You are safe, sir,"—the voice of a woman; and, half conscious, half fainting, with a tremendous buzzing in my ears, I found myself led into an apartment, where there was an arm-chair: into this I fell, and the same voice said,—

"God be thanked! They have not killed you, sir!"

X.

A TERRIBLE PERSONAGE.

I RAISED my languid eyes and gazed at the speaker.
She was a girl of about twenty, evidently of the middle
or lower class, but pale,—I might say aristocratic,—and
with large blue eyes, which looked at me with womanly
sweetness and a sort of sad sympathy.

In her face this air of sadness predominated. A deep
melancholy seemed to weigh upon her, banishing all
her smiles and roses.

"You are safe, sir," she said, in the same low, sweet
voice. "These brawls are growing terribly common. If
I had not heard the noise of staves and the cries, you
might have been murdered."

"I had indeed scarce a chance of preserving my life,
I think," I returned; "but, thanks to your courage, I
am scarce hurt."

"Your head, sir——"

"'Tis nothing; a little faintness."

"I will prepare a reviving draught."

And, with deft fingers, the maiden busied herself in
mingling a flagon of wine, sugar, and spices, which she
presented to me with the same air of sad sweetness and
grace.

I had half emptied the draught, when a door in rear
of the apartment opened, and a man of tall stature,

carrying a little, curly-haired child upon his shoulder, came into the room. At sight of me he stopped, almost started, and seemed about to retire. Before he could do so, the maiden went forward hastily, and spoke to him in a low tone. Thereupon he bowed, and came forward, saying, in a deep, melancholy, and tremulous voice,—

"You are welcome, sir."

The man's whole demeanor agreed with the voice. Never have I seen a human being the victim, apparently, of such profound and hopeless depression. There was something sepulchral, almost, in the expression of his long, thin face, around which fell hair once black, but now threaded with silver. The eyes were sunken in their sockets and surrounded with dark rings. The thin lips wore an expression of utter discouragement. His dress was simple, and not striking in any particular,—that of a retired trader,—of dark and plain stuff. His manner in advancing was almost painfully hesitating and reluctant.

"My father, sir," said the maiden, whose sadness remained unchanged. "I have explained your presence; and now you must require food, sir. You shall have the best our poor house affords."

The maiden proceeded then to busy herself spreading food upon a small table, and, the man having taken his seat opposite me, we entered into conversation. Meanwhile, the child played about the room, turning everything upside down and laughing gleefully. The melancholy personage followed all these gambols with a glance of sorrowful affection, leaning back in his chair; when all at once I saw him rise quickly and hasten towards the child, who had half opened the door of a sort of closet in the wall.

The man dragged him back quickly, and hastily closed the door. As he did so, I caught what appeared to be the gleam of some bright steel object, and I know not what sombre influence this abrupt movement of the man exerted upon me. His pale face had flushed, his bosom heaved; and, glancing accidentally at the maiden, I saw that she was trembling and seemed about to burst into tears.

What was the meaning of this strange scene? I vainly asked myself that question. The man offered no explanation. Resuming his seat, and holding the boy on his knee now, he gradually grew composed again, and continued the conversation in which we had been engaged when he started up. It had related to the public events of the time, and the struggle going on between King Charles and his parliament.

"I know not which side you espouse, sir," said the man, in his melancholy and tremulous voice, "but I confess to you that my sympathies are with his majesty."

"And mine; but would he were well out of this dangerous conflict!"

"His majesty will not rid himself of his enemies until force is employed."

"Force? Ah! you mean the exercise of the royal right to try and punish. But that is perilous, 'tis said. The superior strength seems on the other side. Witness Strafford, on Tower Hill: these men tore him from the very arms of the king."

At the name of Strafford my host became as pale as a corpse.

"Yes," he said, in an almost inaudible voice.

" If they drank the blood of Strafford, that powerful and resolute enemy, any man's head in the kingdom may fall. 'Tis said that never was human being more resolute than he; and the story is that his eyes opened and his lips muttered some words even after his head was severed."

My host's pallor had become fearful.

" 'Tis true," he murmured. " I——saw him !"

" You were present at his execution ?"

" Yes."

" Sufficiently near to see plainly ?"

" Sufficiently near."

" Then this theory that life continues after decapitation is well founded ?"

" Yes."

The voice seemed to issue from some sepulchral vault. The man's eyes were fixed, almost stony.

"Life continues—for hours almost—after—decapitation," he said, in a slow, tremulous, monotonous voice, with a strange absent intonation, as though the speaker were soliloquizing. "The brain, when the neck is severed, is like a besieged fortress,—besieged, but not yet taken; the outposts are carried,—its communications are cut off,—but life is there still;—the facial muscles act,—the lips move,—the eyes open,—the volition is maimed, but not paralyzed,—the teeth snap,—the brows contract. I have—seen that !"

He stopped, his pale face bathed in cold sweat. At the same moment the maiden, whose cheeks were as wan almost as the speaker's, came to him, touched his shoulder, and said, in a faint voice,—

"There, father; you frighten our guest. Supper is ready."

The man uttered a sigh almost as profound as a groan. The maiden placed before me a small table, upon which food was arranged, and, looking at the man, added,—

"Your supper, father."

He shrank back. "No, Janet," he murmured; "it would be disgraceful thus to take advantage of——" He stopped.

"True," the maiden said, turning away with a quivering lip. "I had forgotten, father. I thought that kindness offered and accepted made us equal. Yes! yes! pardon me! We have no right to——"

The rest of the sentence was drowned in a sob. I could scarce swallow a few mouthfuls. The strange scene banished all desire for food. I rose, and said,—

"Thanks for your hospitality, sir; and yours, my kind, good friend. I have regained all my strength now, and will take my departure, with warm thanks. You have saved my life, I think, friends; and Heaven will reward you."

"God grant it!" came from the man, who rose, his hand resting tenderly and watchfully on the bright head of the child.

"Let me look and see if the street is safe before you go, sir," said the maiden.

She went to the door, and returned in a moment, informing me that she saw no one.

I put on my beaver, and, going to the door, said, "Thanks, friends, again; and now farewell."

As I spoke, I extended my hand towards the tall man, but he suddenly drew back.

" I cannot—touch your hand, sir !—As I could not sup with you——"

I gazed at him in astonishment.

" It would be—disgraceful !"

His tones were broken, and the words seemed forced from him.

" You do not know who I am,—and yet you came near knowing.—My dear child opened that terrible closet !"

"The closet?" I murmured, overcome with astonishment. "I saw nothing."

" Nothing ?"

" Save what appeared to be the gleam of steel."

The man half thrust me towards the door behind him. The maiden Janet bent down weeping, her face covered by her hands.

" That steel was——shall I tell you, sir ?"

A sort of convulsion passed over the speaker's face.

"Speak !" I said, almost trembling.

" It was the axe of the executioner ! I could not sit with you at table, or take your hand when you offered it. I am Gregory Brandon, the headsman of London !"

As he uttered these words in a hoarse and stifled voice, the headsman groaned. A moment afterwards he had closed the door: I was alone in the dim-lit thoroughfare : from behind the door I heard a second groan, with which mingled the sobs of a woman.

C   5

XI.

THE CAVALIER IN PURPLE VELVET.

I ISSUED from Rosemary Lane, passed beneath the shadow of the Tower, which rose grim and lugubrious above the houses, reached Whitehall, mounted, and returned towards Hampton Court, plunged in thought, and overcome by the strange scene which I had witnessed.

I had been the guest of the headsman! But for this terrible person's refusal to accept the hand I had offered, my own would have clasped the bloody palm which had severed so many necks.

I shuddered almost at the thought,—living over the whole scene again. The hand resting so tenderly on the bright curls of the child had struck off the proud head of Strafford! Within a few feet of me, there in that mysterious closet, was the frightful instrument which had so often cut through flesh, blood-vessels, and vertebræ, from whose keen, impassive edge human blood had so often been wiped! Seated opposite me in friendly talk, the talk of guest and host, was the grim human being who had entered the cell of the condemned as with the tramp of a fate, bound the firm or trembling arms, hobbled the feet with the inexorable cord, and, striking the victim on the shoulder when the moment came, had muttered, in his hoarse voice, "You belong to me now!"

All the way to Hampton Court I was thinking of my singular adventure; but as I came in front of the palace a figure, visible through one of the tall windows, banished every other thought. It was the figure of Frances Villiers, standing erect in the full light of the flambeaux flooding the apartment. She was clad in rich brocade, cut low, so that her exquisite neck was clearly revealed; the beautiful head, with the looped-up pearls, was bent towards one fair shoulder. She was smiling with her habitual expression of grave sweetness, and apparently listening to some one.

I drew rein, and, concealed beneath the shadow of a great oak, gazed long at the girl who had now become more dear to me than my life. In a day, an hour, as it were, I had come to love her with all the power of my being. She had waked up my slumbering heart, and henceforward I felt that she, and she alone, was my queen!

Pardon this gush of romance, friend,—'tis an old gray-head that indulges in it. Many decades have flown since then; I am aged, and the bloom of life is gone; but I remember, and will until I die, the beautiful figure I gazed on that night through the windows of the palace of Hampton Court.

I was still watching the exquisite figure, as it moved to and fro in attendance on the queen, when a sudden trampling was heard in the great avenue, and a party of horsemen, three or four in number, came on at headlong speed.

The incident aroused me from my reverie with something like a shock. Who were these horsemen who presumed to ride in so careless a manner towards the palace? It was *lèse-majesté*, almost, to pay this small respect to the queen. Could some partisans of the parliament design an insult, or a raid on the deer? Resolved to know, I spurred to meet them, and, interposing myself in the way, ordered them to halt.

No attention whatever was paid to my order. On the contrary, I was nearly ridden over. A cavalier, richly clad in purple velvet slashed with satin, a deep lace collar, and wearing a gray beaver with a feather, rushed by me at full speed; the rest followed. They all clattered to the great gateway, and then a sudden commotion followed, to ascertain the character of which I hastened to the palace.

The Guards were hastening to form line, and every sword was brought to the salute. The cavalier in the purple velvet habit had leaped to the ground. He was a person of middle age, with curling hair worn long, mustache and royale, large, mournful eyes, a long, thin face, and a very graceful person. There was something commanding in his air, and I was not long left in doubt as to his identity. The palace was in commotion; figures passed and repassed hurriedly in the queen's apartment, at which I had been gazing; then, as the cavalier of the velvet habit gave his bridle to one of his attendant gentlemen, the great staircase suddenly blazed, the flambeau-bearers descended, and in the midst of her maids of honor, gathered round her like a flock of doves, her majesty the queen was seen to come rapidly down the staircase.

As she came, the melancholy face of the cavalier filled with smiles. It was the expression of a husband who loves his wife and returns after long absence. He hastened towards her; they met in the full light of the flambeaux, and were clasped in a close embrace.

"Sweet heart!" exclaimed the cavalier, with glowing cheeks.

"Dear heart!" was the queen's response, in a murmur, and on the two faces I could see the sunshine of the heart.

They then drew back, as though to avoid the eyes of those around them, and passed up the great staircase between a double line of lords and ladies, her majesty leaning fondly on her companion's arm. The light of the flambeaux fell upon them in a sort of glory. They disappeared, and, as they were lost sight of, a great shout rose, rolling through the palace,—

"Long live their majesties!"

I had seen King Charles I. at last. He had left his escort on the road from Scotland, mounted his horse like a common cavalier, and, attended by only a few of his lords, had ridden straight to Hampton Court to see Queen Mary.

XII.

THE LITTLE QUEEN.

SCANDAL said that their majesties had not been always so devoted, or at least that furious storms had swept the matrimonial skies.

From London, the young king, just married by proxy, had hastened to Dover to meet the little queen of sixteen; caught her in his arms when she offered to kneel; and, in reply to her address, "Sire, I am come into this your majesty's country to be at your command," exclaimed, "You have not fallen into the hands of enemies and strangers, and I will be no longer master myself than while I am servant to you." And then what the French call *enfantillages* followed. The king, noticing that her head reached to his shoulder, glanced at her feet to ascertain if her height were not due to her high-heeled shoes. Whereupon the little queen drew aside her skirt, exhibited her small feet with all the *coquetterie* of a French girl, and said, "Sire, I stand on my own feet; I have no help from art: thus high am I, neither higher nor lower!"

This joy and laughter of the little daughter of the famous Henry of Navarre was truly a strange contrast to her after-woes. But then all was bright and smiling. The fatal conflicts of the future threw no shadows before. The youthful pair were greeted by great crowds upon the Thames, and fêted everywhere; and no raven croaked from the hollow tree to interrupt the joy, romance, and sunshine of their nuptials.

I have seen the portrait of Queen Henrietta at this period, painted by Vandyke, and the face and form are exquisite. In the picture she has a fair complexion, fine dark eyes, and hair of a chestnut color. The slight and delicate figure is clad in a dress of white satin, with a tightly-fitting bodice decorated with pink ribbon; the sleeves full, with ruffles; the arms encircled by bracelets. Around her neck she wears a fine pearl necklace; a red ribbon twisted with pearls is woven amid her glossy hair behind the head. 'Tis a gracious, smiling maiden, full of youth and joy, on whose forehead grief has never cast its shadow.

The shadow was approaching: private infelicities preceded the public; the fond lovers were to come to angry words, and criminations and recriminations.

All arose from the Catholic attendants of the queen, who fostered in every manner the religious differences between the pair, and went so far as openly to defy the king. Under this he was restive; and one morning his wrath burst forth. He came to the queen's apartments at Whitehall, and found the French ladies curveting and dancing in the presence of her majesty. The scene shocked his ideas of dignity and ceremony: he took the hand of the queen and conducted her to his own apartment, where he locked her majesty in; then he sent word by Lord Conway to the French ladies to leave Whitehall and repair to Somerset House, where they were to await his pleasure. Thereupon rose a grand lament and the din of angry female voices. Loud cries arose; defiant words were heard,— in the midst of which a guard appeared, and with little ceremony caused them to vacate the apartment, the door of which was inexorably locked behind them.

A sad scene ensued between their majesties thereupon. The queen ran to the window to bid her dear French attendants farewell. The king drew her back, saying, "Be satisfied; it must be so." The queen broke from him and rushed to the window, the panes of which she struck so violently with her clenched hands that the glass flew to pieces and crashed down into the court. The king succeeded at last in drawing her majesty away from the window,—the shocking

scene ended,—and the king wrote his grace the Duke
of Buckingham, "I command you to send all the
French away to-morrow out of the town,—if you can, by
fair means, but stick not long in disputing; otherwise
force them away, driving them away like so many wild
beasts, until you have shipped them, and so the devil
go with them."

The command was obeyed : in the midst of a great
mob, hooting at and cursing the Frenchwomen, the
ladies were ejected from Somerset House. They retreated, raging, scolding, gesticulating, and were sent
out of the country. The king had conquered.

There were other painful scenes. The king himself
related how, after retiring to bed with her majesty one
night, they had a passionate altercation as to the appointment of the queen's revenue-officers. Read the
narrative : 'tis painful. The king, falling into a rage,
bade her majesty "remember to whom she spoke!"
To which she replied, with passionate weeping, that
"she was not of such base quality as to be used so!"
There is a long distance, you see, reader, between this
state of things and the scene I witnessed at Hampton
Court. In the one case it is husband and wife squab-
bling and scolding like Jack and Gill fallen out; in
the other it is the fond pair embracing each other,
with "Dear heart!" "Sweet heart!" heard between
their kisses !

We old people have seen that often on our journey
through life! Alas! men and women grow angry,
are unjust and unkind, often; but happy are the married pairs who truly love and cherish each other. The
sunshine comes after the storm; all clouds disappear;

and even after that scene in which their majesties struggled at the broken window in Whitehall, 'tis said that the king and queen made friends speedily and "were very jocund together!"

XIII.

MY TRAVELING-COMPANION.

I was sent at daylight on the morning succeeding the king's arrival, to bear a dispatch to Woodstock Palace for her majesty, and, having fulfilled my duty, determined to gallop across country and spend an hour with my father at Cecil Court.

I shall not dwell upon this visit, which was a very great pleasure to me,—home events are not of interest to all,—but come to my first meeting with a very noble as well as a very famous man, whom I encountered on the highway, in Buckinghamshire, towards evening, on my way back to London.

I had just emerged from a belt of woods, and saw the sun setting across the beautiful fields, when a horseman riding in front of me attracted my attention, and I was very soon beside him.

He turned his head, and bade me good-day so courteously that I checked my horse's speed and rode on with him. He was a man of middle age, clad in a rich dark pourpoint, and wearing a black hat and excellent riding-boots. His figure was lofty and com-

c*

manding; his face very noble, and full of grave courtesy and sweetness. When he spoke, his voice had
an extraordinary calmness and simplicity, which simplicity was indeed plain in every detail of face, figure,
and bearing.

In ten minutes I felt entirely at my ease with the
stranger, and we rode on side by side, conversing
upon public events with perfect freedom.

"His majesty has returned from Scotland," said my
companion. "I am glad to know that: her majesty
will be made happy by seeing him again."

I smiled, and said, "You are plainly a royalist, and
not one of the new party, sir."

My companion smiled in his turn. "I am scarce a
royalist in the ordinary meaning of the term, sir; but
sure 'tis a pleasure to all honest men to know that a
good husband is safely restored to his wife, and to con-
template with satisfaction the little domestic picture
of their meeting."

"Assuredly; and, after all, the king is not perhaps so
black as he is painted."

"He is not, sir. It is the vice of partisan feeling to
drive men to extremes. His majesty, in my opinion,—
to be frank,—has committed very great faults. It is
scarce too harsh, I think, to say that his conceptions
of the royal prerogative, if carried out, would overturn all civil liberty; but that is no proof that he is
cruel or licentious, or a despot from love of despot-
ism." The words were uttered with great sadness.

"Shall I imitate your frankness, and utter my
thought plainly, sir?" I said.

"Surely."

" Were I his majesty, then, I should fear adversaries holding your views more than all the Pyms, Cromwells, and Hampdens in the world."

"The Hampdens?" asked the stranger, smiling. " Do you refer to Mr. John Hampden, the member from Buckinghamshire?"

" The same, sir."

" Is he so violent and dangerous a personage ?"

"I do not know Mr. Hampden, but such is his reputation."

The stranger rode on for some moments in silence.

" I had not supposed that Mr. Hampden bore so bad a character," he said, at length. "What are the grounds, I pray you, sir, of such an opinion of that gentleman?"

"His prominence in opposition to the levying of ship-money by his majesty. Mr. Hampden was the first person of high position who opposed the royal prerogative."

" True," the stranger said, somewhat sadly ; " and so the fellow-subjects of Mr. Hampden—honorable gentlemen—think him violent, and a demagogue ! Pity !—but may we not regard Mr. Hampden's motives as conscientious?"

" His friends do, doubtless,—not the adherents of his majesty."

" That sums up all, I fear, sir," the stranger returned ; " and I will not undertake a defense of Mr. Hampden,— of whom, however, it may be said with truth that he risked a good estate rather than pay twenty shillings without warrant of law for the exaction. Yes, his friends will defend him, his adversaries denounce him,

as you say.   To the first, he is a sincere lover of law
and liberty; to the second, a pestilent demagogue,
itching for notoriety and power.   So be it: one day
his true character will doubtless be known."

"Meanwhile, were I acquainted with Mr. Hampden,
I think I should give him some advice, sir," I said.

"And pray what would be the advice?" my companion said, smiling courteously.

"Not to act with Pym, Ireton, Cromwell, and other
extremists, who are ready to go all lengths."

"'All lengths' is a strong expression, sir," the
stranger returned, with his immovable grave sweetness.
"The gentlemen you name have the repute of aiming
only at a redress of grievances."

"They will not stop there."

"You would say——"

"That revolutions begin with the pen, and end with
the sword,—and shall I add something more terrible?"

"What?"

"With violence: the cup of the poisoner or the axe
of the headsman."

My companion started, and his countenance grew
cold and stern in an instant.   A flash darted from his
eyes, and his cheek became pale.

"That is a bitter charge against good men," he said.
"What induces you to believe that any living Englishman is ready to turn assassin?"

"The philosophy of revolutions," I returned, "and
the history I have read."

"And the political struggles of the period we live
in may result in the death of his majesty, you think,
by the hands of his own subjects?"

"'May' has many meanings, sir. 'Tis not impossible,—is it?"

My companion rode on without uttering a word. A mile at least was passed over thus, in profound silence. Then the stranger raised his head, which had been drooping. "You have broached a terrible idea," he said; "one which my mind never up to this time entertained. I will not discuss it. I shrink from the very thought with a species of horror. I can conceive that Mr. Cromwell and others might oppose the king,—even in open combat on the field of battle, perhaps; either side may inaugurate that struggle, and the other will accept the gage of defiance; but that the king's life can ever be threatened with poison or the executioner's axe on this soil of England,—that, sir, I will never believe,—never! the thought is too frightful!"

"I hope 'tis only my fancy."

"And I, sir. I cannot speak for others; but for one of those you have named I can answer without hesitation. He might oppose the king's adherents—even the king himself—in battle; but he would sooner lay down his own life than touch with a finger the person of his majesty. I can answer for that person, I say; and I have the best of all rights to do so,—for I am that John Hampden of whom we have spoken."

6

XIV.

I MAKE THE ACQUAINTANCE OF MR. CROMWELL.

I WAS so much astonished at this sudden revelation of the identity of my traveling-companion, that I gazed at him in stupid silence.

Thereupon the cordial smile returned to his fine face, and he said,—

"We have conversed under a mask, as 'twere, sir ; and I take no umbrage at the opinions you have expressed of a certain Mr. Hampden. I confess, even, that the maxim *noscitur a sociis* bears with some justice upon him, and perhaps justifies your views of him. But now let us abandon these mooted subjects. We differ in political views, but I dare to say that you are as true and honest an English gentleman as any. I would fain claim for myself the same character: I am called hospitable at least, and there is my house through the oaks. Will it please you, sir—see, the sun has set—to spend the night with me?"

I refused, and then accepted. There was something so gracious and noble in my companion's utterances that I could not resist.

"Thanks, Mr. Hampden," I said. "I accept your hospitality as cordially as you offer it. I am named Edmund Cecil,—a poor guardsman of the queen."

"Of the Cecils of Warwickshire?"

"The same."

"I know your father well, and esteem him highly, Mr. Cecil. But here is my poor house."

We entered a great park, and just at dusk came in front of a large and handsome manor-house, built in the Elizabethan style, and indicating wealth and consideration in its proprietor.

In the great drawing-room I was presented to Mr. Hampden's charming household; and in the faces which greeted me with smiles, as in all the appointments of the mansion, I observed that indefinable grace and distinction which never deceives.

I had just returned the hospitable greetings of the amiable family, when there came into the apartment a robust personage, clad in a dark cloth suit entirely without decoration, heavy boots covered with dust, and an old slouch hat discolored by sun and rain. This personage, despite the negligence of his attire, had yet something lofty and imposing in the carriage of his person: he advanced with an air of almost haughty independence,—absorbed, it would seem from the absent expression of his large eyes, in thoughts wholly disconnected from his surroundings.

"The terrible Mr. Cromwell!" said my host, in a low tone, smiling as he spoke. And I was presented to the personage who so completely justified afterwards the adjective now applied to him in jest.

Mr. Cromwell saluted me in an absent manner, and then removed his hat, which he seemed to have forgotten. I soon learned that he had just arrived from Huntingdon, riding out of his way, to accompany Mr. Hampden, his cousin, to London; and the evening passed in desultory conversation. What chiefly impressed me in this afterwards celebrated man was his rough earnestness, the pith and force of his utterances, which seemed to go right to the core of every subject, and the occasional employment of scriptural names and phrases in his conversation. I never before heard Ahab, Baal, Og, and other Biblical personages alluded to with such frequency or apparent gusto. And Mr. Cromwell never smiled; he was profoundly in earnest, and all his utterances were weighty. Even when relating how an ape had snatched him from his cradle, when an infant, and borne him, chattering, to the roof of his father's house, and how he had been rescued from drowning, when he had already sunk twice, and his nose and mouth were filled with water, he did not indulge in the faintest approach to a smile, but garnished those narratives, like the rest of his discourse, with names and allusions from the Old Testament Scriptures.

This culminated when at bedtime he offered up a prayer. It was an extraordinary prayer, deeply earnest and devout; I might almost say passionate in its evident outpouring from his inmost heart; but here too were the inevitable Old Testament names and references. When Mr. Cromwell rose from his knees, after his long and fervent prayer, his eyes were as dreamy as though fixed upon another world: he scarcely returned the addresses of the family, and retired from the room with the absent air of one who is walking in his sleep.

Such was the appearance of this extraordinary person on that evening. He was commonplace; he became terrible. He wore plain cloth; he came to wear royal velvet. He was then Mr. Cromwell, unknown save as

a country member ; he was to become known throughout the world as the slayer of King Charles I., the Lord
Protector of England, and one of the greatest sovereigns
that ever sat upon the English throne.

On the next morning I bade Mr. Hampden and his
excellent household farewell, and, riding rapidly to
make up for lost time, arrived late in the evening at
Hampton Court.

XV.

A COMBAT BY MOONLIGHT.

As I dismounted in the court-yard of the palace,
Harry came out and hugged me after the French
fashion introduced by the followers of her majesty.

"Here's a laggard!" cried Harry. "What was the
attraction at Woodstock, Ned? Did you lose yourself in the labyrinth built to hide Fair Rosamond?"

"I don't believe there is any labyrinth, Harry; and
I've been to Cecil Court."

I proceeded to give my brother news of home, and
to describe my meeting with Mr. Hampden; then,
seeing signs of unwonted activity in the palace, I asked
their meaning.

"His majesty is to make his royal entry into London to-morrow. You are just in time, Ned. We're
all going,—Guards, courtiers, maids of honor, dwarfs,
and all!"

"Dwarfs?"

"I mean that his worship Sir Geoffrey Hudson, now become a great favorite with her majesty, will grace the occasion with his presence, no less than the largest of us. And do you know, Ned, this little manikin and mere hop-o'-my-thumb is a decided character?"

"I should think as much."

"I mean that he is no mere plaything, weak in head as in body, like the rest of his pigmy species, but a man in feeling, and in brain too,—grave, serious, and courageous. His deformity is a source of deep mortification to him; and when the maids of honor caress him lap-dog fashion, he looks at them as though he would bite them, uttering a singular sort of snarl, and plainly resents their treatment of him as though he were a plaything."

"And towards the men?"

"He is stern and bitter. 'Tis the fashion to tease him; and that sallow-faced Coftangry of the Guards takes the lead. Hark! there they are in the guard-room now. I hear the piping voice of the dwarf and the gibing tones of Coftangry. Let us go see!"

We entered the guard-room, where a singular spectacle presented itself. Some young noblemen of the Guards—for half the company were lords—were standing in a circle around some object upon the floor, which I made out on a nearer approach to be the figure of the dwarf. The manikin, who was less than two feet in height, wore a very rich costume,—velvet cloak, plumed beaver, silk stockings, and high-heeled shoes with large rosettes. At his side hung a miniature dress sword, about the length of a knitting-needle; and his face flamed with anger, as he fixed his eyes spitefully upon a tall, sallow-faced young gentleman with a sneering expression of countenance, who was teasing the pigmy for the general amusement.

"Come, come, your knightship," said Coftangry, with a sneer; "dance a galliard for our entertainment. Hop, hop, Sir Hop-o'-my-thumb!"

"Were I a lady, sir," said the dwarf, in his thin, piping voice, "I know what I never should do."

"What is that, pray?"

"I should never hop in a galliard with such a tallow-faced anatomy as yourself!"

The retort raised a loud laugh. Coftangry was immensely unpopular, and the dwarf had touched his tender point,—his lath-like body and sallow complexion.

"'Twas but yesterday," piped the dwarf, "that I overheard two of her majesty's maids of honor conversing. One said, 'Who is this Coftangry, and how do such people get to court?' 'I know not,' returned the other, 'unless they are dug up and brought as curiosities.'"

A second laugh came from the group, and Coftangry grew furious.

"If you were not a wretched pigmy," he cried, losing his self-possession and giving way to anger, "I would chastise you upon the spot!"

The dwarf bounded with rage.

"Chastise me? You dare not attempt it! I wear a sword!" he shrilled.

"Ha, ha!" came from Coftangry, in forced merriment; "a skewer, you would say!"

The dwarf whipped out his weapon, and the circle suddenly widened.

"No fighting in the palace, gentlemen!" cried one of the young noblemen, with mock earnestness.

"True," the dwarf growled, returning his sword to its scabbard; "but this tallow-face has gibed at me, and I return his insult—thus!"

With incredible agility, the pigmy leaped upon a chair, thence to the long table near, and, before Coftangry divined his intention, bestowed a violent slap upon the Guardsman's face. It was delivered with all the energy of hatred, and rang through the apartment. Coftangry uttered a cry of rage.

"Woe to you, cur!" he shouted; and he was about to smite the erect and defiant dwarf to the earth, when a hand was laid on his shoulder, and Harry's voice said,—

"You don't mean to strike that little man, I hope, sir? You will exterminate him!"

"Who are you?" growled Coftangry, wheeling round.

"My name is Cecil, sir," was the reply.

"Well, I counsel you, Mr. Cecil, to attend to your own affairs!"

Harry flushed red, and went close to Coftangry.

"I make this my affair, sir," he said, "since 'tis always the business of a gentleman to protect the weak from outrage."

"You shall answer for this intrusion!"

"I am quite willing to do so, sir," said Harry, in a low tone. "The moon is shining; there is the park; five minutes' walk will take us out of view."

Coftangry had, apparently, not expected a proposition so sudden and direct. He was silent for a moment, and became very pale, but he saw that all eyes were fixed upon him. The consequence was that fifteen minutes afterwards Harry and himself were standing opposite each other, sword in hand, in a remote portion of the park, a number of the Guardsmen having accompanied the adversaries to witness the encounter.

Such affairs were at that time of every-day occurrence, and seldom resulted in more than a few scratches, when the friends of the parties would declare that honor was satisfied.

Such was the result on this occasion. It was a singular encounter,—a very burlesque. Harry lunged, expecting his opponent to parry. He did nothing of the sort, and Harry ran his sword-hand on Coftangry's point, wounding himself.

"'Tis plain you're no swordsman, sir; I will therefore disarm without hurting you," said my brother.

As he spoke, Coftangry's rapier flew twenty paces, and Harry coolly returned his sword to its scabbard.

"Take your life, sir," he said; "I have no use for it. Good-evening, sir."

And, winding a handkerchief around his bleeding hand, he left the spot, accompanied by his friends.

Such was the termination of the impromptu duel; beginning and ending in a few minutes, under the moonlight in Hampton Court park. I have spoken of it because it was the preface to a duel with more deadly results; but that incident will be narrated in its place.

I pass to the king's entry into London now, and to the great and unfortunate events which marked the few succeeding days.

XVI.

SIR THEODORE MAYHERNE.

THE royal entry into London was an imposing pageant.   The king rode in front on horseback, reining in his spirited charger, decorated with rich housings; and on his left hand rode the Prince of Wales, afterwards his majesty Charles II., at that time a handsome boy of eleven.

Behind the king came the queen, in her state-coach drawn by six white horses, their heads and backs surmounted by nodding plumes.   And in the royal coach also rode the children of her majesty, bright-faced little ones, looking with ardent interest upon the crowd. Then came the coaches, with the royal suite; behind, the Guards; last of all a vast multitude following, crowding close, and shouting, "God save the king!"

'Tis impossible to recall this scene, when that cry was heard for the last time, without sadness and a sinking of the heart.   Alas! the dark hours were coming, the shadow was even then descending upon those human beings.

The procession reached Whitehall and disappeared; then the crowd dispersed.

I was just unbuckling my sword, when Harry, who had entered the guard-room of the palace a moment before me, said,—

"This hand of mine hurts confoundedly, Ned! Serves me right for fighting with that awkward cub Coftangry! It is swelling. I wish you would go ask my friend Sir Theodore Mayherne to come look at it."

"Sir Theodore Mayherne, Harry? Who is he?"

"Their majesties' household physician, and a great friend of mine. He lives in Gray's Inn Lane, and is a perfect wolf, but an excellent surgeon and gentleman."

I set off at once to find the wolf, and soon reached Gray's Inn Lane, where I was directed to a handsome house and admitted by a servant in black. A moment afterwards, a portly personage, with long gray hair flying about his face, and the air of a lion interrupted in his repast, entered the room like a hurricane.

"Your pleasure, sir!" thundered the lion, wolf, or hurricane,—whichever the reader pleases.

"Sir Theodore Mayherne, I believe, sir?"

"An absurd question! Who else could I be?"

I smiled. "You might be a thunder-storm! if that response be not too unceremonious, Sir Theodore."

"Unceremonious? Not a bit! I hate ceremony! A thunder-storm? Ha! ha!" And the portly person shook. "That is the way I like people to talk to me," he added: "it's natural, expresses the thought. I'm sick of mincing and cant, and bowing and scraping, and French ways! What's your business?"

I saw that I had to do with an original who liked coming to the point.

"Harry Cecil, of the queen's guards, has hurt his
hand in a duel, and wishes you to come look at it."

"Harry Cecil!—a crack-brained jackanapes! What
the devil have I to do with Harry Cecil? 'Tis as much
as I can do to patch up her majesty's nerves, broken
down by her popish fasts and vigils and penances
and all the rest of their devil's inventions!"

I rose and bowed. "Thanks, Sir Theodore. I will
tell Harry you are coming, then." The thunder-storm
looked at me with a lurking smile. "He is at Whitehall," I added.

"Well, I'll come! These scatterbrains, with their
roystering and fighting, and drinking and swearing,—
mark my words, sir, the canting rascals of parliament
will clip their love-locks! Harry Cecil is one of the
worst of them,—your brother, from the likeness, no
doubt,—a pestilent rascal!" And, turning his back
upon me abruptly, Sir Theodore Mayherne, physician
to their majesties, disappeared from the apartment.

———

XVII.

I VISIT A GENTLEMAN AFTERWARDS FAMOUS THROUGH-
OUT THE WORLD.

I LEFT the house of the original character with whom
I had thus become acquainted, and was walking along
Gray's Inn Lane on my way back to Whitehall, when
there came forth from a handsome house a tall and

noble-looking gentleman, in whom I recognized at once my host of Buckinghamshire, Mr. Hampden.

"Give you good-day, Mr. Cecil," he said, grasping my hand with cordial regard: "it seems our fate to encounter each other. What brings you to Gray's Inn Lane, where I reside, on this chill morning?"

I explained my mission, and Mr. Hampden shook his head.

"You young gentlemen are too fond of that sword-amusement, I fear," he said; "but 'tis, unfortunately, out of my power to preach at length on this vice. I once practiced it."

"Is it possible?" I said, smiling; "the grave and serious Mr. Hampden, of the parliament?"

"He was once as bad as the worst, Mr. Cecil! Let us be honest! And I think even my good cousin Cromwell must plead guilty to the same charge."

"Mr. Cromwell! that enthusiast in matters of religion!"

"Was in his youth a roystering blade, fond of catches at midnight and the foam of flagons! Thus you see, Mr. Cecil, neither the grave Mr. Hampden nor the pious Mr. Cromwell can with a very good grace preach peace and order to the young gentlemen of this generation! I know but one person who seems to me immaculate,—a young man whose genius will render his name more famous than all others of his epoch. He lives in Aldersgate Street, and I am going to visit him. Will it please you to accompany me?"

"With great pleasure," I said; and ten minutes' walk brought us to a small house, set in a contracted garden. From within the house was heard the sound of an organ.

"Our friend is playing upon his organ: 'tis his favorite entertainment," said my companion. "I will use no ceremony, and enter, since he would never hear our knocking."

He opened the door as he spoke, and led the way to an apartment on the right of the entrance. It was poorly, almost meanly, furnished; in one corner stood a small erect organ with green hangings above, and at this organ sat a man of about thirty, playing a devotional piece, in which he was so absorbed as not to notice our entrance.

Mr. Hampden approached and touched him on the shoulder. He turned his head, and I never saw a face of more delicate beauty. The eyes were large and thoughtful; the lips thin, with an expression of grave austerity; the cheeks rosy, the high forehead as fair as a woman's, and around this beautiful countenance fell long fair hair, parted in the middle and reaching to the shoulders.

He rose, and bowed with grave courtesy, taking Mr. Hampden's offered hand.

"I have brought my friend Mr. Cecil to see you, Mr. Milton," said my companion.

Mr. Milton repeated his salute.

"Of her majesty's Guards, I believe, sir," he said, glancing at my uniform. "I witnessed the royal entry to-day,—a very imposing spectacle."

"You?" said Mr. Hampden. "Then wonders will never cease. I had supposed you safe at home here, composing your poems or treatises, Mr. Milton. What fancy now possesses you, and when will you carry out your design of writing your epic on paradise lost by our first parents?"

Mr. Milton shook his head somewhat sadly.

"Never, I fear," he replied.

"Are you afraid that our father Adam would not support you in your favorite theory?"

"What is that, Mr. Hampden?"

"Polygamy—that 'tis allowed in the Scriptures."

"Do you deny that it is therein taught? The proof is very easy," said Mr. Milton, quietly.

"And so you, Mr. Milton, I, and our friend Mr. Cecil have, each and all of us, the right to espouse two, or ten, or twenty wives, if we fancy?"

"Yes," said Mr. Milton; and he was going to open an Old Testament Scriptures, when his friend stopped him, smiling.

"I fear you will corrupt our consciences, my worthy sir. We are not of the line of the patriarchs. Let us leave polygamy and return to letters. You are engaged in composing something other than political, I trust. 'Tis so wearisome, that species of discussion. Ah! here are some sheets. Is it permitted me to look at them?"

Mr. Milton made a movement with his hand.

"'Tis only some rhymes of the woods and fields," he said. "I please myself in the din of this great city by thus returning to my youth in fancy."

Mr. Hampden had taken up the written sheets, and now read aloud in his deep and musical voice a truly exquisite passage from the afterwards celebrated poem styled "L'Allegro," a name no doubt bestowed upon it in consequence of Mr. Milton's fondness for the Italian tongue. The reader was plainly an expert in the difficult art of managing the human voice. A charming sweetness marked his intonation, and the glow upon his cheeks indicated the admiration with which the lines of the poet—yet unknown—inspired him.

The reading ended, and I, at least, was silent from admiration. I think Mr. Hampden was pleased with this expression of my face; for he said to me,—

"Is not that pure music, sir?"

He turned, as he spoke, to Mr. Milton, and said, in his deep rich voice,—

"'Tis truly like a breath from the fields of England, Mr. Milton, and the melody to my ear is wonderful. But

'Sweetest Shakspeare, fancy's child,
Warbles his native wood-notes wild,'

does injustice to greater men, I think,—to Mr. Beaumont, Mr. Fletcher, and rare Ben Jonson."

"Such, I know, is the common opinion, Mr. Hampden," said the other; "but I cannot share it. The brain that originated 'The Tempest' and conceived the wonderful tragedy of 'Hamlet, Prince of Denmark,' is, to my thinking, the greatest in our English letters. Others are tall; Shakspeare is a giant, methinks. I would be content, wellnigh, to have reached gray hairs could I have seen and talked with him."

I said with a smile, when my host thus spoke,—

"I think my father would exchange ages with you upon that understanding, Mr. Milton. We live near Stratford-on-Avon, and Mr. Shakspeare was a good friend of my father when the latter was young. He often came to Cecil Court, as our house is named, and was excellent company, and full of smiles and sweetness, I'm told. You cannot know him now, since he is long dead; but if you will visit us you shall sit in the chair he was accustomed to use, drink from his favorite cup, and see his name which he wrote with his own hand on a window-pane.''

''That would please me greatly, sir; but I am a prisoner here, I fear. I teach children for bread, and the birds have flown but recently. You must go?'' for I had risen some moments before. "Thanks for your visit, Mr. Cecil," said Mr. Milton; and, conducting me to the door, he made me a bow of much grace, in which he was imitated by Mr. Hampden, who remained.

Such was my first interview with the afterwards famous author of "Paradise Lost," a poem so grand that its fame must extend throughout the world. I afterwards read with wonder those august verses, and thought of the long-haired young author. His "Comus" and "L'Allegro" and "Il Penseroso" pleased me even more. The latter, published a few years afterwards, have a singular charm for me. In reading them, even now, a delightful freshness exhales from them; I fall to dreaming under the influence of that exquisite music, and forget the bitterness of the political partisan in my admiration of the sublimest of the English poets.

7*

XVIII.

A MOONLIGHT COLLOQUY, AND WHAT FOLLOWED IT.

I RETURNED to Whitehall; and on the same night occurred an incident which revealed to me the secret springs of one of those events which overturn monarchies.

It was nearly midnight, and I was passing beneath the trees of St. James's Park, near the palace, when the figures of two persons approached, and by the bright moonlight I could see that they were in animated conversation.

"I swear to your majesty that I speak upon sure information!" said the voice of Lord Digby. I recognized it without difficulty, though the speaker was greatly moved.

"'Tis impossible!" replied the voice of the king, which was equally unmistakable. "Impeach the queen? Wherefore? 'Twould be too infamous and absurd, Digby!"

"Infamous? Yes, your majesty! But absurd?"

"Have they aught against her?"

The other was silent.

"Speak!" the king said. "Whereon can impeachment of her majesty rest?"

"Will your majesty permit me to speak without ceremony?"

"Yes; speak plainly! You rack me, Digby! My

heart sinks. Speak! How and why should these people *impeach* my wife?"

"Her majesty is a papist, sire."

"Content!—but that is naught. What more?"

"She is striving to convert her husband!"

"'Tis false! She has never attempted any such thing!"

"They profess to believe it, no less, your majesty."

"They will profess to believe anything to my prejudice or hers! Aught more?"

"They declare that your alleged attacks on the privileges of parliament are in consequence of her majesty's arguments, and from the fact that you cannot resist her appeals."

"False! false! All false, Digby! Woe to these slanderers!"

"They are powerful, your majesty."

"I will show them that I too am powerful."

"Beware, sire! Let an humble subject speak plainly. They will crush you!"

"Crush me? 'Tis well, Digby. I will save them the trouble by first crushing *them!*"

I had drawn aside to permit the king and his companion to pass. Lost in the shadow, they did not perceive me; but I could see the king's expression of wrath, and Digby's unconcealed joy, as the moonlight fell upon their faces.

"I will strike at the leaders in this infamous scheme!" exclaimed the king. "I have the names here in my heart!" He struck his breast as he spoke. "From this moment I swear to strike them without mercy!"

As the king spoke, he passed beyond hearing, and a

moment afterwards the two figures had disappeared in the palace.*

Shall I relate what followed the incident in St. James's Park? This is not a history of the reign of King Charles I.; I would not repeat what is contained in the great histories,—above all, would not discuss the squab- bles of king and parliament. But a few words are necessary here, to explain after-events. It was King Charles who defied his enemies first, and in a manner most weak and imprudent.

In brief words, his majesty sent one of his household to prefer a charge of treason against five prominent members of the parliament. On the next day he de- manded the persons of the five; and, the parliament refusing to surrender them, the king proceeded at the head of an armed guard to arrest them in person.

It is said that the gods make lunatics of those whom they are going to destroy. His majesty was acting illegally, he was also acting madly. Time never was when a king of England was an irresponsible despot, unchecked by any law and competent to seize upon the persons of its representatives. As yet, however, respect for the kingly authority was great; and it was thought best by the parliament that the five members should escape. Time was given them for this by the intrigues of Lady Carlisle, the black-eyed Venus whom I had seen at Hampton Court. The king had just left

---

* Lingard, the parliamentary historian, alludes to the proposed im- peachment of the queen. He says, "Some hints had been dropped by the patriots of an impeachment of the queen; the information was conveyed to Charles, and urged him to the hazardous expedient of arresting the six members."—EDITOR.

Whitehall, and the queen in great agitation sat, watch in hand, with her eyes on the dial. The king had indicated an hour when—should no "ill news" come from him—all would be well; and, the hour having arrived, the queen exclaimed to Lady Carlisle,—

"Rejoice with me, for at this hour the king is, as I have reason to hope, master of his realm; for Pym and his confederates are arrested before now !"

The words are said to have caused Lady Carlisle to give a great start. She was a friend, secretly, of the enemies of the king. She invented some pretext now to leave the queen's apartment; hastened out, sent a messenger to warn the threatened members, and, owing to delay in the movements of the king, the messenger arrived in time.

When his majesty entered the Parliament House, the birds had thus flown. A violent scene ensued. Loud cries of "Privilege! privilege!" rang through the hall. The Speaker knelt to his majesty, but refused to pledge himself for the delivery of the accused, and the king retired, discomfited.

With this crow-bar King Charles I. overturned his throne. London suddenly blazed with rage at the attempted arrests. Great crowds escorted the members of parliament to the hall; the king retired ingloriously to Hampton Court, and from thence sent word that he would abandon the prosecution of the members and respect parliamentary privileges !

Oh, inglorious! He was brave, and not deficient in intelligence,—what made him thus act with such folly and timidity? 'Twas not conviction of having acted wrongfully: his majesty believed in his kingly pre-

D*

rogative always. Was it the spirit of intrigue, the intent to temporize?

A great sovereign, observant of ·the right, would never have begun that bad business. A resolute despot would have marched upon the malcontents and crushed them then and there. King Charles did neither. He struck the tiger with his whip, and, when the animal turned snarling, retreated before him. From that moment he was doomed, and was king only in name.

This occurred wellnigh half a century since. King and parliament are gone. I, an exile, am only musing and thinking, "How strange was all that!"

The royal family had all gone back to Hampton Court; and the queen was in despair, it is said, when she learned that her indiscretion had prevented the arrest of the members. Madame de Motteville, whom I knew well afterwards,—her majesty's intimate friend, —told me of the meeting of Charles and his queen after the attempted arrest. The queen threw herself into the king's arms, and with passionate tears upbraided herself for her fault. In narrating the scene to Madame de Motteville, she stopped, choked with tears, and sobbed out praises of her husband's unaltered tenderness. "Never did he treat me with less kindness," she faltered out, "than before it happened, though I had ruined him."

Events from this time rushed onward. It soon came to be whispered through the palace that her majesty was going on a visit to Holland, with the design of conducting the princess-royal, then a child, to her child-spouse the Prince of Orange.

The parliament had issued a circular to the nobility,

calling on them to arm and prevent the king from withdrawing farther than Hampton Court. Strange to say, however, they scarcely opposed the projected journey of the queen to Holland.

Before the queen's departure a singular event occurred, and this event I shall now relate.

XIX.

THE STING OF AN INSECT.

I WAS posted one night on guard in the anteroom to the queen's apartments, and, having been up very late on the preceding night, leaned against the doorway, half dozing.

From this condition I was aroused by a light footfall approaching along the corridor; and a moment afterwards the dwarf, Sir Geoffrey Hudson, made his appearance, laboring under great excitement.

My brother's espousal of his cause had made him the friend of the whole Cecil family; and, seeing me, he now stopped, and began to speak in a piping voice, which indicated both agitation and anger.

"I have discovered who did all the mischief," he squeaked.

"What mischief?" I asked.

"Warning the parliament people that his majesty was coming to arrest them."

"Ah? Tell me."

The dwarf looked guardedly around. Then he made

signs that I should sit down on a bench under one of the windows. I did so; and then the manikin mounted with surprising agility to the sill of the window, where his position enabled him to lean down close to my ear.

"Coftangry !" he whispered.

"Is it possible? One of the queen's guardsmen ! What object——"

"He was the tool only."

"The tool of whom ?"

"My lady Carlisle."

I stared at the small speaker. "It is not possible !" I said.

"I *know* it !" was the venomous ejaculation. "Coftangry is mad about her ladyship. Her eyes have turned his head. I saw them together, whispering hurriedly in one of the corridors, that day his majesty went to the parliament. I saw Coftangry hasten out,—lost sight of him,—but this evening discovered all.".

"In what manner?"

"I was lying beneath a couch in the antechamber to the blue-room. Her ladyship came in with Coftangry, and sat down on the couch. I heard every word they said; he is mad about her; and she made him betray the queen !"

It was impossible to doubt the sincerity of the speaker. He was passionately in earnest; his eyes blazed, and his small form trembled with excitement.

"An ugly affair !" I said; "and I will take prompt action in the matter. The queen's guardsmen shall not rest under the imputation of harboring a spy and traitor in their ranks."

"No," said the dwarf; "you must promise me to leave the affair in *my* hands."

"In your hands?"

"Yes. I exact that, Mr. Cecil,—for the moment, at least."

"What course have you determined upon?"

"That is my affair."

"I cannot make you any promise," I said. "This concerns her majesty."

The dwarf knit his brows, and reflected for a moment. At last he said,—

"When were you posted here, Mr. Cecil?"

"An hour and a half ago. But why do you ask?"

"What is the length of your watch?"

"Two hours. But how can that interest you?"

"It interests me greatly," was the cool reply of the dwarf. "And, as I have now told you all, Mr. Cecil, I will bid you good-evening."

As he uttered the words, he sprang to the floor with his habitual agility, made me a bow full of grave courtesy, and then hurried off in the direction of the ground-floor of the palace. I looked after him in some astonishment, unable to make out his design, and reflecting upon the tenor of his statement.

So the subtle and brilliant glances of my lady Carlisle had made Coftangry a traitor! Lured on by her caressing eyes and ruby lips, he had sold faith and honor! I was still meditating on this piteous exhibition of a man's weakness, when footsteps approached. It was the new guard coming to relieve me; and I was soon free to return to the guard-room.

As I descended and approached the door, I heard a

loud altercation. I hastened on, entered the guard-room, and saw Coftangry and the dwarf facing each other, both raging.

"You are a traitor! Are you a coward too?" came in piping tones, full of wrath, from Hudson.

"Is this pigmy to continue thus to insult the queen's guardsmen?" exclaimed Coftangry.

"This pigmy," hissed the dwarf, "is as well-born as you are!—is, moreover, a belted knight, which you are not, and defies you to single combat!"

The words raised a storm in the guard-room; but a large majority sided with the dwarf.

"He is right!" cried one. "Beware how you refuse him, Coftangry. You will dishonor her majesty, who has knighted him."

The tumult continued for fifteen minutes longer; then everything grew quiet. The dwarf had carried his point. On the next morning at daylight, Coftangry was to meet him in a secluded part of the park, each on horseback with pistols, in order to equalize the combatants.

I was a witness of the singular scene which duly followed this arrangement.

Just as the first streak of dawn was seen above the great oaks of the Hampton Court park, Coftangry and Sir Geoffrey Hudson, his diminutive opponent, made their appearance on horseback at the retired spot selected for the encounter. Each was accompanied by one friend; and a number of the Guardsmen who had followed them formed a group near.

The countenance of Coftangry wore a satirical and mocking expression, which, added to his sallow complexion, did not render him a very attractive spectacle. He seemed to regard the whole affair as an "excellent jest," and, drawing his cloak around him, took his place with an air of mingled amusement and disdain.

The dwarf was cool and determined. His eyes were fixed upon his adversary with an expression of cold menace. He wore a light velvet cloak, from beneath which protruded his minute sword; over his brow drooped a plumed hat. It seemed impossible that his short legs could enable him even to retain his seat on the big horse he rode; but he did retain it, holding the reins and directing the animal with the ease of a perfect horseman.

In five minutes all was arranged, and the adversaries were placed near and facing each other. Then the word was given, and the dwarf drew his pistol.

Coftangry, with a short laugh, drew—a *squirt*.

"Here is the weapon I have chosen to meet this chivalric paladin!" he said. "I feared lest a pistol-bullet might prove a cannon-ball to this sparrow!"

He raised the squirt, and, uttering a second laugh, aimed at the dwarf.

"Ready!" he said.

A flush of rage rose to the face of Hudson.

"Are you a gentleman, or a clodhopper?" he snapped. "Or simply a coward?"

"Come on!" cried Coftangry, with feigned laughter; though it was easy to see how much the dwarf's words stung him.

The dwarf looked towards his adversary's friend, and, lowering his pistol, pointed with the other hand to Coftangry. The gesture was full of such contempt that

Coftangry turned pale. The words of the Guardsman appearing as his second in the duel did not soothe him much.

"If you wish any further aid of mine, Mr. Coftangry," said his friend, "you must conform to the rules of combat, and meet Sir Geoffrey Hudson with the weapons of a gentleman."

"I have no pistol with me!" growled Coftangry, in reply.

The dwarf threw back his cloak, and drew a second pistol from his belt. He took both by the handles,— they were small, but exquisitely chased and mounted,— and, holding them out, said,—

"Here are pistols! Take one; I will take the other."

The words ended all further parley. It was not possible to make longer any opposition. A moment afterwards, Coftangry and the dwarf were sitting their horses at the distance of fifteen paces from each other, pistol in hand, and awaiting the word.

It was given, and a simultaneous report was heard,— the crack of a popgun it seemed,—accompanied by a puff of smoke.

The dwarf remained erect, curbing his startled horse with a firm hand. Coftangry reeled, dropped his rein, and fell from his horse.

All ran to him, and raised him up. The bullet had pierced his heart. Five minutes afterwards, whilst attempts were being made to stanch his wound, his head fell back, a gurgling sound escaped from his lips, and he expired.

Such was one of the most singular events I have

ever witnessed; and I have related all the details to afford some idea of the strange complexion of affairs at that epoch. The queen had taken into her household, as a plaything, this pigmy of only two feet in height: a full-grown man had mimicked him; he had demanded satisfaction for the wrong; pistols fired from horseback had equalized giant and pigmy; and it was the bullet from the dwarf's pistol which penetrated the full-grown man's heart. Such, I repeat, was this strange event,—not the result of my fancy, but an actual occurrence during the reign of his majesty Charles I. The moral, I think, is, Do not laugh at misfortune, and beware of the smallest insects, if their sting is mortal!

The death of Coftangry created a great excitement in the palace for two or three days. But there was no one to punish. The dwarf had set spurs to his horse,— if he wore spurs,—and disappeared. His unfortunate victim was buried, and the event passed from all minds. Memory of the dead is short in this world:—at courts, I think, it is shortest of all!

8*

XX.

GOOD-BY, SWEET-HEART!

THE queen's arrangements then in rapid progress for her journey to Holland contributed largely to banish the fate of Coftangry from all minds.

This proposed journey plunged me into veritable despair. It was understood speedily that her Guards would not accompany the queen,—that this body of *élite*, under Lord Bernard Stuart, would remain with the king. I was a member of the Guards, and must continue with them, and thus for weeks, months, years, it might be, would not see—Frances Villiers !

I fancy I see one of my grandchildren—some little maiden of seventeen, let us say—smiling archly as she reads the above words in her grandpapa's memoirs. She will have seen, perchance, the old gentleman who pens them, and will wonder if ever the flowers of love bloomed under the snow of his hair. Yes, little one ! that snow had not yet fallen at the time I write of : my life was in its springtime ; the first violets bloomed. I would have plucked all the world contained, could I have done so, to make a *bouquet du corsage* for Frances Villiers !

So I was really in despair when I thought I should see her no more for a long time : her tranquil smile which greeted me every day had become a sort of necessity of my life. Harry, too, seemed full of gloom.

"Hang it, Ned," he said, "how will I be able to sustain life, my boy, without a glance now and then from the eyes of the fair Frances?" And it was only long afterwards, as the reader will see, that I came to understand what was hidden under that jest.

Thus I moped, seeing my sunshine about to leave me; but 'tis certain that parting must take place in life, and I summoned all my philosophy. I think Miss Frances saw the gloom on the faces of the two Cecils; but she said nothing, remained quite calm, and one morning entered the coach which followed that bearing her majesty towards Dover, with entire composure, and naught more than her habitual composed sweetness.

The queen was thus *en route* for Holland, and King Charles, surrounded by a party of noblemen and followed by the queen's Guards, escorted the coach on horseback.

The journey was to be marked by one or two incidents,—affecting both his majesty and my humble self.

As the cortége came in sight of Dover, where a vessel awaited the queen, a party of horsemen was seen rapidly approaching from the direction of London. As the queen descended from her chariot on the jetty, the horsemen reached the spot, and a tall cavalier of dignified appearance, the leader apparently, dismounted, gave his bridle to a man, and approached the king, doffing his plain round hat as he did so.

His majesty looked at the new-comer over his shoulder, and with an expression which indicated little satisfaction. The dialogue which followed was brief and to the point.

"Sir William Strickland, I believe? Your good pleasure, sir?"

The tone of the king was imperious, haughty, and not a little disdainful.

"Your majesty will first permit me," returned the gentleman, "to assure your majesty of my very profound respect."

The king made a curt movement of the head.

"You come on the part of my parliament, doubtless, sir?"

"Yes, your majesty."

"Your errand, sir?"

"A very painful one, your majesty. I am commissioned by the parliament to beg that before the departure of her majesty the queen for Holland, the law excluding the bishops from sitting as peers in the House of Lords may receive your majesty's approval."

The king's brow darkened more and more.

"In other words, unless I permit this iniquitous scheme to become a law of the realm, the parliament will not permit her majesty to depart for Holland?"

Sir William Strickland was silent.

"Is it not so, sir?" exclaimed the king, with rising anger.

"I am unfortunate in being the bearer of a message displeasing to your majesty," was the diplomatic reply.

A flush of anger and disdain rose to the face of the king. Around him, all faces wore a similar expression.

The king hesitated. At that moment her majesty touched his arm, drew him aside, and for some minutes spoke with him in animated tones. The result was that the king, with an expression of suppressed displeasure, turned to Sir William Strickland, and said,—

"Be it as you and the parliament will, sir. You have doubtless the required form for the passage of the act by commission ?"

Sir William bowed low, and, drawing a paper from his breast, presented it with profound respect to the king. As he did so, a clerkish-looking individual of his party approached with pen and ink, which the emissary presented to the king with the same air of deference.

The king rapidly, and with a sort of flirt of the pen, affixed his signature to the paper, and Sir William received it from his hands with a low bow. The king scarcely acknowledged it,—turned his back,—and a few minutes afterwards the party of parliamentarians were riding away.

"So much for that," murmured the king. "Events seem hastening."

With these words, he seemed to dismiss the whole scene from his mind. In half an hour her majesty, with the princess and her suite, was on board the vessel which was to bear her away, and the king and queen parted from each other on the deck with a long embrace. The eyes of the queen were filled with tears, and the king's face flushed with emotion. A last embrace was exchanged ; the king went ashore again ; the vessel spread her sails.

The king, however, seemed unable to tear himself from the sight of the queen. He sat his horse, gazing at the vessel upon whose deck the queen stood erect, waving her handkerchief; and this salute he returned by raising and holding aloft his gray beaver, with its floating plume. The handkerchief continued to wave from the deck, and, as the course of the ship was along the shore, the king, surrounded by his noblemen and guards, rode along, keeping it in sight. In this manner his majesty passed over a distance of four leagues, ever keeping the ship in sight, and straining his eyes to see the white speck moving to and fro upon the deck.

At last a fresh breeze sprung up, and the bark flew like a sea gull towards the open channel. From a lofty cliff, and motionless in the keen winter's wind, the king looked his last. Slowly the vessel faded,—then it resembled a dark speck,—then it vanished. As it disappeared, the king drew a long and labored breath, let his head fall, and slowly turned his horse to retrace his steps.

I shall always remember that scene; and think to-day, as I thought then, that there is nothing more respectable than the faithful love of husband and wife. What are rank and power and wealth beside this? And all wandering loves,—how mean and poor they seem in presence of this beautiful and noble sentiment, on which I think the All-seeing smiles!

Doubtless King Charles I. committed terrible errors as a ruler; but for all that he was a good husband. A court full of frail beauties could never induce him to turn his eyes from the wife God had given him.

XXI.

HOW I WAS COMPELLED FOR A TIME TO TAKE NO FURTHER PART IN PUBLIC AFFAIRS.

AN irritating incident followed close upon this painful scene, and, as the reader will soon perceive, this incident seriously affected my own person.

The king had just turned his horse's head to ride back to London, when Sir William Strickland again came on at the head of his party of horsemen, and, reaching the spot, dismounted a second time, and approached the king with the same air of deep respect.

The eyes of the king filled with sudden fire.

"What now, sir?" he exclaimed, in accents so abrupt and haughty that they resembled a blow struck.

"I am deeply pained to offend your majesty," began Sir William Strickland.

"A truce to words and ceremony!" rejoined the king. "You are not here, sir, as my friend or loyal subject. Your business, sir! And I beg that you will dispatch it briefly, as we are not in the mood to be annoyed to-day."

The emissary bowed low again, and said,—

"I would fain spare your majesty annoyance. Briefly, a courier reached me on my way back to London, bearing the paper I hold in my hand, which is addressed to your majesty."

The king caught the paper with a movement of rage

almost. His eye ran over it: suddenly he crumpled it up and threw it upon the ground.

"Tell these people——" he began. Then he stopped, and seemed to realize how unbecoming his anger must appear. His eyes were fixed with a cold and haughty expression upon Sir William Strickland.

"Do you know the contents of that paper, sir?" he said.

"I do not, your majesty."

"It is a 'petition,'—everything is a 'petition' now,— in which the gentlemen of my parliament considerately ask that I will not deprive them of the charms of my company; they will be in despair if I absent myself from London, and will be plunged into melancholy if I even remove the Prince Charles from them. Will I therefore, they say, 'be pleased to reside nearer the metropolis, and not take the prince away from them'? It would afflict them, these tender-hearted gentlemen! 'Tis this that yonder paper contains, sir."

The emissary inclined his head before the royal displeasure, but was silent.

"The meaning is simple!" added the king, with disdain in eye and lip. "My good subjects of the parliament design making me and my son prisoners. They have assailed my prerogative, they would lay hands on my person. I am intractable, they would render me docile. 'Tis an ingenious device, sir,—is it not?—this humble 'petition' of my humble subjects?"

Sir William Strickland bowed profoundly; but I could see from the obstinate expression of his countenance that he was unmoved.

"You do not reply, sir," said the king, in the

same tone. "You do not think the device ingenious, then?"

"Your majesty will pardon me for declaring that I regard it as natural."

"That is the opinion of Sir William Strickland, Baronet?"

A slight color tinged the face of Sir William at these words. With sudden embarrassment he bowed low, but made no reply. The king gazed at him for a moment in silence, and then said, coolly,

"I will reply to this petition within three days, sir. Does that suffice, or am I compelled to respond here and now?"

"That will assuredly answer every purpose; and I now beg to take my leave of your majesty."

With these words, Sir William Strickland, who had begun to betray some signs of discomposure at the threatening faces around him, made the king a profound inclination, and, mounting his horse, rode away.

The king gazed after him for a moment, and said to a nobleman of his suite,—

"So pass away one's old friends to the enemy's standard! 'Tis scarce two years since I made this gentleman a baronet: I would not upbraid him with it, but he had the grace to blush as he remembered it. Well, a truce to all this. Things hasten more than ever! Before three days have passed——"

He suddenly stopped, and the sentence remained unfinished. Some scruple, if not some secret resolve, seemed to check him,—the latter, it appeared.

"That message to the parliament may involve the

appearance of trick," he muttered. "In *three days,* I said. The message must be modified."

He turned quickly to an officer of the Guard.

"Captain Hyde, take two or three gentlemen of the Guard, and ride after Sir William Strickland. Say on my part that I will make a *speedy reply*—use those words —to the petition of the parliament, if it be not made in three days."

Captain Hyde bowed low, and turned to select two or three of the Guard. I caught his eye, and he nodded; then he indicated one other. A moment afterwards we were all riding at full speed after Sir William Strickland, whose party was visible on the crest of a hill in our front.

The guardsmen of the queen possessed fine horses and were hard riders. We went on at a pace which would soon have borne us over the distance separating us from Sir William Strickland, but this very rapidity defeated our object: the emissary seemed to suspect something, and also pressed forward at a rapid gallop.

Thus it was that the affair became a chase. The king had followed us with the rest of his suite, and Sir William now plainly regarded the aspect of things as hostile. The war had begun!—the royal forces were pressing the retreating representatives of parliament!

The speed of the Guardsmen's horses at last enabled them to come up with the parliamentarians,—but I was not present at the scene: I was in fact unaware of my existence. My horse, a fine bay, had enabled me for some time to keep the lead of the pursuing party: an old fox-hunter, he went on at a thundering rush, when unfortunately a stone in the road caused him to stumble and fall. I rolled beneath him, his full weight fell upon me, and I dislocated my shoulder.

I only remember thereafter that the king stopped beside me, and raised my head: there was a group around; then I fainted. Half an hour afterwards I revived, and was dimly conscious that a surgeon was setting my shoulder. Then I fainted again—was aware that I was placed in a vehicle—the vehicle moved: when I opened my eyes next, I was lying on a couch in a lofty antechamber at Whitehall, and Harry was sitting beside me, holding my hand and gazing at me tenderly.

"So, Ned," he said, "here you are yourself at last again. How do you feel?"

"Badly, Harry; but not so very badly. This is Whitehall?"

"Yes; we brought you here, the king's affairs summoning him to London: arrived an hour since, just at sunset, and you were so weak that you were laid upon this couch. Better remain here, wrapped in your cloak, until morning: I will watch beside you. Meanwhile, Dick is riding post to Cecil Court to bring the coach. 'Twill doubtless come speedily, and you must go thither till your recovery."

As Harry spoke, his name was pronounced at the door: he was absent from my side a moment, and then, returning, said, with some annoyance,—

"I must go on post for two hours, Ned. Then I will return to you. Compose yourself to sleep: no one will disturb you in this part of the palace; and the moon through the oriel yonder will be sufficient light."

"Content, Harry; I will sleep," I said.

And, drawing my cloak around me with my well arm, I closed my eyes.

XXII.

THE PORTRAIT OF STRAFFORD.

NEARLY two hours had passed, I think, after Harry's disappearance, when I was aroused from my dreamy half-slumber by footsteps on a side corridor leading to the anteroom in which I lay. A moment afterwards the door opened, a figure slowly entered, and this figure paused in front of a portrait upon which the moonlight fell in a flood of light. A second glance told me that the new-comer was King Charles. He was clad in a dressing-gown of velvet; his head, with its long curling hair, was bare; and the pale, melancholy face, with an unhappy light in the dark eyes, was turned towards the portrait, upon which the king fixed a long and absorbed look. So intense indeed was that gaze that my eyes followed it and fell upon the portrait.

It represented a man past middle age, and the face was an extraordinary one. Dark, harsh features; eyes full of dauntless courage, mingled with a sort of stern severity, and mournful foreboding, as it were, of some approaching calamity; lips upon which were written an unshrinking resolve, a will all iron; and in the poise of the grand head something majestic, calm, and imposing;—such was the portrait which the moonlight fell upon, and at which the king now gazed, standing motionless as a statue in front of it.

At least ten minutes passed, and not a muscle of the king's figure stirred. Then I saw his bosom heave, a low groan issued from his lips, and he raised one hand to his eyes, as though to brush away tears.

Whose was this portrait which had aroused such terrible emotion? for the tears of kings are terrible, and burn as they fall. I knew not, but was soon to know. The king was still looking with the same absorbing gaze upon the picture, when another figure appeared at the door, remained there for a moment motionless, then entered the apartment, treading noiselessly, and stood beside the king. The shadow of the new-comer—a man—was thrown upon the wall. The king started, and turned with a wild look towards the man; then, drawing a long, deep breath, Charles exclaimed, in a broken voice,—

"Oh, Digby! methought that—— I am unnerved to-night, and this face——"

He turned again towards the portrait.

"The eyes haunt me," he murmured, "the mournful eyes of the man I sent to his death! Strafford! Strafford! Would to God I had died before I grew a coward and allowed cozening voices to persuade me to your death!"

The king pressed his thin white hand to his forehead as he spoke, and, interrupting Lord Digby, who essayed to speak, added, in the same broken voice,—

"There are deeds that brand men as cowards in history. I thought myself brave once, but I signed that terrible warrant! It was forced from me, they tell me

9*

to console me. I resisted, protested, refused, they say, but I signed at last! Well, that day, Digby, was the blackest of my life. I was a forsworn gentleman! I was a king, and I acted as a coward! I had the power to say no, and I said yes. Strafford was my friend,— faithful unto the death; and my return for all was to send him to that death with my own hand!"

The speaker's emotion was overpowering as he uttered these words. He covered his face with his hands, and sobbed like a child. His frame shook. A shudder passed through my own frame as I looked and listened.

Lord Digby seemed to experience the same emotion, and could scarce speak.

"I beseech your majesty," he said at last, "to cease this fearful talk, and retire from this apartment. What evil spirit counseled your majesty to come hither?"

"No evil spirit, Digby, but the conscience in my breast," murmured the king.

"Your majesty exaggerates the part borne by your-self in the death of Strafford. That signature to the death-warrant was forced by enemies; the very bishops counseled it: the good of the realm was paramount."

"No good comes out of evil: 'twas cruel cowardice, Digby, and has borne its fruits."

"Cowardice! that word again? Who will dare call your majesty a coward?"

"History!"

The word was uttered with a solemnity that thrilled through me.

"Let us banish all glosses and party passion from this question," said the king, gloomily. "For the opinions of this generation I care little, esteeming them but lightly. My reign is stormy and divides all minds; royal prerogative and democratic power are at issue: wonder not, then, that my bitter enemies charge me with untold crimes. I am a tyrant, a violator of my word, the author of the fearful Irish massacre; I am a despot, reigning by fraud and falsehood and duplicity; of all the monsters of history, Charles I. of England is the most monstrous. And these charges, Digby, are so bitterly insisted upon that all men's minds will soon be poisoned against me. Well, I care not. I never violated my word of gentleman yet. I claimed, as to tonnage and the rest, what I thought my just and im-memorial prerogative only. When I heard of the Irish murders, I shuddered like the most protestant of my subjects. In my own heart I am guiltless of all this; but history will bring against me another charge, and of this I am guilty!"

He spoke in a low tone, motioning to Lord Digby to be silent.

"I am guilty of that man's death," he said, raising his hand slowly, and pointing to the picture. "He worked for me, fought for me, served me faithfully. And I, who should have defended him, abandoned him to his enemies. Of fraud, falsehood, tyranny, I am guiltless: the charges pass me by as the idle wind. Of Strafford's blood I *am* guilty! When that head, that should have worn the crown, fell on Tower Hill, Charles, the first of the name, of England, was for-sworn!"

I could see in the moonlight that the king's fore-head was covered with drops of cold sweat. He had mastered himself by an immense effort, but the tears and agony of the outer man a moment before seemed, so to speak, to have struck inward. The wound bled internally and was past cure.

The king continued to gaze for a long time upon the portrait. At last his lips opened, and he muttered, in tones almost inaudible,—

"Farewell, Strafford! 'Twere better to have lost my crown than to have consented to your death! But the deed is done. I carry in my breast an ineradicable remorse! Smiles and happiness are not for me any longer on this earth! Yet I go to my work. I am king, and dare not shrink. You are no longer beside me, with your great brain and fearless soul, to be my strong tower of defense! I go on my path alone. Farewell! Something tells me that I will ere long rejoin you."

As he uttered these words, the king went towards the door, but, as though the great rugged head of the portrait, with its dark eyes, still fascinated him, looked over his shoulder at it as he moved away.

I shall never forget the face of the king as I saw it then in the moonlight. It was deadly pale, and in the eyes was that settled gloom which is seen in all his portraits.

A moment afterwards he was gone with Lord Digby, and the steps died away on the corridor.

XXIII.

I RETURN TO CECIL COURT.

On the morning succeeding this strange scene, I was removed to a bedchamber in the palace, and three days afterwards my father arrived in the family chariot, and I was borne from my couch to it.

My father followed; Harry bade me an affectionate farewell; and then the old coach, with its four horses, moved slowly away towards Cecil Court.

As I left the palace, I observed something which forcibly arrested my attention. In the great court-yard were drawn up the entire company of the queen's Guard, with the servants in rear; and near the great entrance stood grooms holding three horses, completely equipped,—one of which I knew to be the favorite riding-horse of the king. About the horses, the Guardsmen, their retainers, everything and everybody, there was something which indicated a long journey rather than a brief ride.

I was still gazing back through the window of the chariot at the line of Guardsmen, armed and ready, when a great shout arose in front, and I turned in the direction of the sound. The spectacle was striking. As far as the eye could see, the street was crammed with a great multitude, and in the centre of the thorough-fare moved a procession, first of men and then of women,—a procession strange, wild, fierce, with in-

E*

flamed faces, violent gestures—moving furies. As I afterwards discovered, they were the guild of porters, the watermen of the Thames, beggars,—then forming a distinct guild ; and the women were from the markets, brawny, masculine persons, with bare arms and furious visages, clad in little better costume than their non-descript associates. All were-marching to the Parliament House to offer their " petitions."

For a moment, it seemed that the chariot and the head of the great column would come in conflict. The coachman, directed by my father, drew to one side, however,—we were about to avoid the anticipated collision,—when one of the multitude, uttering a curse, caught the leaders by the bridle, and ordered the coachman to turn about and retrace his steps.

" Why, the movement is impossible, friend," said my father, in his calm voice. " Should my horses attempt to turn, they would trample upon some one."

" Hear him !" shouted the man, one of the " beggars," and clad in rags : " he says he will trample upon the people ! Down with them !"

The words aroused a sort of fury in the crowd. The horses were violently seized by the bridles; a rush was made upon the ponderous coach, beneath which it shook, and half turned over; in a moment it would have been broken to pieces, in all probability, and its inmates trampled under foot, when a commanding voice cried, " Hold !" and a plain-looking personage forced his way through the crowd.

His very appearance seemed to produce a magical effect.

" Pym !"

That name escaped from a hundred lips; and an instant afterwards, Mr. Pym by a simple gesture, it seemed, had cleared a space around the vehicle.

"Permit this gentleman to proceed on his way," said Mr. Pym. "No time is to be lost. Parliament awaits the worthy porters and the rest with their petitions."

A shout rose, and the crowd obeyed. The chariot was no longer molested, and Mr. Pym, whom I saw that day for the first and last time, disappeared. He died soon afterwards, and, 'tis said, regretted his part in the excesses of the parliament. I know not; but 'tis certain that he was disinterested in his course: he ruined his private fortune, and died poor.

The coach proceeded then without further molestation upon its way, and we had just reached the suburbs of London when the clatter of hoofs came behind and rapidly approached. I glanced through the window: it was the Guardsmen, moving at a quick trot. At their head rode the king, and beside him the Princes Charles and James, afterwards Charles II. and James II. All were richly clad,—the boys like their father,—but they wore their swords, and moved steadily forward.

A moment, and the cavalcade had passed, Harry waving his hand to me. We were now beyond the city, and, instead of towards Hampton Court, the king's party turned northward.

"Look! see the road his majesty takes, my son!" said my father.

"It is the road to——"

"York! From this moment civil war begins!"

My father's surmise was correct.   Finding himself a virtual prisoner at Whitehall or Hampton Court, the king had resolved to free himself, had mounted his horse in front of Whitehall, and, riding past the great procession, which saluted him with threatening murmurs, had left London, to take refuge at York.

I could take no part in the coming conflict.   I was in bed at Cecil Court, pale, feeble, wholly powerless indeed, with a compound fracture of the shoulder-blade.

BOOK II.

I.

DREAMS AT CECIL COURT.

MAY of this troubled year 1642 came into the world, and found me still weak and feeble,—scarce able, indeed, to rise from my bed. As June approached, however, I grew somewhat stronger, began to move about the grounds, and slowly my hurt healed,—with which came a sense of exquisite enjoyment.

I look back upon those summer days at Cecil Court as among the happiest of my life. Everything was charmingly fresh and buoyant; and my brief experience of the bustle of courts had only intensified a sentiment always powerful in me, my love for the scenes and occupations of our English country life.

It is certain that one is born with this sentiment and never loses it. I have seen all phases of life in my time,—the splendid court at Versailles, the rush and whirl of battle; have talked with dukes and countesses, flirted the fans of court beauties, and taken part in royal processions :—all the fine pageant of the life of cities has passed before me, with waving banners, triumphant music, gorgeous silks and velvets, and jewels, and floating plumes; but the whole has been for me a

mere phantasmagoria or idle picture. What I liked
better, and returned to with ever-increasing fondness,
was the calm, untroubled life of the fields and forests,—
the fields and forests of dear, ever-blessed England.

It was these fresh scenes that I looked on now from
the doorway of the old mansion of my fathers on the
banks of the Avon. My illness seemed to have sharpened every faculty of enjoyment. Through my very
pores I seemed to absorb the delightful influences of
the vernal season. The songs of the birds in the elms,
the daisies starring the turf, the skylark circling in
the clouds,—all were sources of the sweetest happiness ;
and I thrilled with an enjoyment which no words can
express.

The banks of the great river of Virginia, wherefrom
I write, are beautiful, and Virginia is surely a charming country; but, go where you will, friend, there is
no place like home. A kind heaven made my home in
Old England,—with green turf, and blooming hedges,
and great trees, and cawing rooks swarming in and
out of their nests on the summits of the lofty oaks,
beside the little sheet of water on which some swans
sailed serenely to and fro. Every spot around the old
house had some family incident or memory of my own
youth connected with it. There were the apple-trees
where I had gathered the ripe red fruit in autumn ;
there was the spot in the hedge where I had hung with
delight over the dove's nest, with its two milk-white
eggs ; there was the crotch in the great apple-tree,
where I had robbed the blackbird's nest of its speckled
treasure ; yonder the old pony had rolled me on the
grass, when an idle urchin; at the quiet nook in the

little stream where the grass hung over the shadowy pool, I had fished with a pin-hook and brought home in triumph my willow twig full of trout. Thus every locality was full of memories of my childhood. And boyhood had its souvenirs, no less vivid and delightful. The child had become a youth, and his heart had expanded amid these same scenes. The dreams of the great poets, the first vague thrills of romance, visions of beauties with great soft eyes and flowing hair,— these too were framed as it were by the green fields and woods around Cecil Court. Stealing off in those days to the banks of the little stream, I would throw my line, in the water where the shadow of a great elm darkened the limpid surface, stretch myself on the turf, with the leaves whispering over me, and hour after hour of the long summer days would flit by like dreams,—or call them birds, sailing away on silent wings into the past. Then the blue sky was a wonder, with its fleecy cloud-ships; the far coo of the dove came to my ears like dreamy music; the water rippled; the rooks cawed in the tops of the great elms:—I was an English boy in my English home, filled in all my being with the exquisite happiness which comes, to me at least, only amid the dear scenes of Old England.

As I pass away from this tranquil and charming period of my life,—I mean the days of my convalescence, when the old scenes came back so vividly to me, and I was a boy again,—I lean my head upon my hand, muse idly as I remember, and again see the youth lying on the turf beneath the oak, reading Shakspeare's dramas, and thinking of his own life's drama,—brief as yet, and just begun. See, I have written that great name, Shakspeare,—and that, too, arouses many memories. The fame of my father's neighbor and friend has grown quite gigantic now, but at that time he was much less renowned,—indeed, I might say, was little read. 'Tis·so dangerous to one's fame to be its cotemporary and move about in flesh and blood! No man is great to those who talk with him and see him laugh and eat his dinner! " *That* a heaven-born genius?" you say: " absurd! 'tis only a man like myself!" So those who lived near Mr. Shakspeare were not so very enthusiastic about him. He was delightful company, my father said, and of excellent wit and humor; made you laugh very often, and was altogether gay, and healthy, and natural; but he was surprisingly simple, seemed never to have imagined himself of much importance, thought little, it would appear, of his dramas, and preferred Stratford, where life was quite humdrum, to London, where they fêted him and placed crowns upon his forehead. He came often to see my father at Cecil Court; laughed at everything and everybody, with a pleasant wit which did not wound; took an interest in horses, and calves, and the very spring flowers; smoked his tobacco-pipe, and never alluded to *Macbeth* or *Hamlet* in his life.

Such was Will Shakspeare, as old neighbors still called him; and I think my father was one of the few persons who divined the supreme genius of his writings. I was early impressed with their charm, and read him constantly: Titania and Miranda and Ophelia filled my early dreams. Thus the soul of Shakspeare grew as 'twere into my young life; and to-day, reading his

great dramas on the banks of the York, 'tis not so much
Elsinore and Duncan's castle and Bosworth field I see,
as Cecil Court in England, where, stretched on the
turf, I looked upon all these visions !

Need I add that in that spring I saw other heroines
in my dreams than Shakspeare's? Frances Villiers !
—I write that name, and leave the picture of the dis-
consolate lover to be painted by the imagination. I
will not dwell upon that. I grow old, alas ! and romantic writing from an old gentleman would make his
grandchildren laugh. 'Tis the grand privilege of
youth to be absurd gracefully,—to go into raptures
over Dulcinea, and talk nonsense as fresh and charming as the passion it describes. Romance-writers share
that privilege, 'tis true; and were I composing a romance, I might enlarge upon Frances Villiers and my
hero's feelings. If I were only writing the adventures of an imaginary Mr. Edmund Cecil ! Then the
reader should be told everything : my·hero's heart
should be laid bare,—his romantic passion should gush
forth in burning words,—and behold, beloved reader,
you would have a love-romance to amuse you. But
this is my own life, you see. I grow ashamed when I
speak of my own feelings: would you like a third person to be listening, whilst you poured out in some
shady nook the passion of your heart into the ears of
the chosen one? 'Tis thus a sort of shame which seals
my lips : enough that, asleep or awake, Frances was in
my thoughts.

The Cecils are light-hearted, and take trouble easily.
What unhappiness lives forever? what year is all
clouds? The sun *will* shine at length; and 'tis the

happy constitution of my blood to divine it behind the clouds, and think, " 'Tis coming out soon!''

So fled the spring and early summer. I have told you of my occupations and dreams at Cecil Court, and have not said one word of the troubles of the time. They did not find me indifferent; and twice I mounted my horse to rejoin the king in the north, only to faint as often, be borne home, and find my illness renewed. I was thus forced to wait, but with impatience, throughout that fiery summer which burnt into all hearts. My quiet sports had become a weariness then, and more than one event occurred even in our country nook which indicated the tumult surging beyond.

To that I pass now. I have pleased myself by speaking of those spring days at Cecil Court. It was but an eddy in the torrent: the stream soon swept me on again.

II.

A FRIEND OF THE KING.

ALL at once, late in summer, came the intelligence that his majesty had erected his standard at Nottingham, and that his faithful subjects were flocking to him by tens of thousands, to defend him against the " conspirators of the Parliament.''

That version of affairs was somewhat glowing, as events of speedy occurrence sufficiently proved; but everybody placed credence then in the hopeful prospects of the king, and one of our neighbors, Sir Jervas Ireton by name, galloped over to congratulate my father. Sir Jervas was a large florid man, of portly and imposing appearance. He was not very popular, but was prominent in the county.

"Let us rejoice, Mr. Cecil," he cried, shaking my father's hand violently, with an up-and-down pump-handle movement, "that his sacred majesty is about to punish these pestilent knaves of the parliament!"

My father remained unimpressed, and did not seem to share his visitor's enthusiasm.

"Is it so certain?" he said. "And after all, I think, Sir Jervas, there are men in the parliament who are not knaves."

Sir Jervas stared. "You astound me! Then you are one of the 'Godly'!"

My father smiled. "I am for the king," he said, "but without believing him altogether in the right."

Thereat, Sir Jervas exploded, and made an oration of the most violent character. His majesty was a per-secuted saint! the parliament was a gang of mis-creants! every gentleman and honest man should adhere to his majesty, who would soon show the rascals that he had *might* as well as *right* on his side!

Then Sir Jervas puffed and rolled about, so to say, in the excess of his ardor. He remained an hour longer, blazing with loyalty and enthusiasm. Then he mounted his horse and galloped off to congratulate some other friend of the king.

As time wore on,—miserably spent by the reader's humble servant in longing for strength to mount his horse,—the royal prospects appeared day by day less promising. The number of the king's troops was ascertained to be but small, his resources very limited, and the enthusiasm in his cause far from general.

Followed thereupon a second visit from the worthy Sir Jervas, who was much more moderate in his expressions, and less convinced of the justice of the·royal cause. He had been mistaken, he said, in regarding the merits of this unhappy misunderstanding as so wholly on the side of his majesty. The collision between king and parliament was truly unfortunate ; the royal authority should be vindicated *in its just extent,* but he did not hesitate to say that a body of men so virtuous, intelligent, and law-abiding as the great English parliament *could not* be guilty of wrong or injustice. The public troubles were distressing—most distressing—to all good citizens, and it was to be hoped that his majesty *would not persist in armed opposition to the peaceful execution of the laws of the realm.* Thereupon Sir Jervas Ireton bowed to my father, who had listened without a word, and rode away. As he disappeared, my father raised his finger, pointed after him, and said to me,—

"There is a worthy personage who is going to turn his coat."

The reported forces of his majesty continued to dwindle. It began to appear that the parliament was the stronger; and one morning we heard that Sir Jervas Ireton had gone to London on private business.

"He is going to ascertain which side to take," my father said.

But I had no time to think now of Sir Jervas, who, as was shown afterwards, had been to London and returned. At last I was strong enough to mount my horse, and prepared with ardor for my journey to join the Guardsmen again.

I was soon ready. My valise was packed, my sword burnished, my pistols loaded,—for it was said that the country swarmed with friends of the parliament now, prepared to arrest all who attempted to join the royal forces,—and the evening preceding the day fixed on for my departure came.

On this evening Sir Jervas Ireton reappeared at Cecil Court.

III.

A FRIEND OF THE PARLIAMENT.

THE worthy Sir Jervas had evidently imbibed an undue amount of claret. His countenance was rubicund, and his eyes twinkled. Twice he called my father "Cecil," to that gentleman's extreme disgust, and finally spoke of public affairs, up to that moment passed over *sub silentio*, alluding to the king's friends as "malignants," bent on the destruction of "the godly," that is to say, the friends of the parliament.

My father bowed, but only said, with provoking coolness,—

"Well, sir?"

"But the godly are more than a match for you malignants!" cried the inebriated knight.

"You appear to take pleasure in bestowing nicknames on his majesty's friends, sir," said my father, coldly.

"Fight the devil with fire!" cried Sir Jervas, starting up. "When a public ruler disregards all dictates of morality and honor,—when pledge after pledge is violated, and the liberty of the subject is in danger,—when papists and heretics and murderous emissaries are let loose upon an unoffending people,—what, I ask, sir, can be the course of the friends of law and order?"

My father had remained calm until this moment. Now his face flushed; but he controlled himself.

"'Tis distasteful to me to hear his majesty denounced thus, Sir Jervas Ireton," he said; "and you will pardon me for adding that I esteem his supporters to be as little 'malignant' as *your* friends to be 'godly.'"

"A month, or two at most, will decide which is strongest!"

"Ah!" my father said, with some disdain; "then 'tis a question of strength, not right! The strongest side is the right,—that to which all moral and *prudent* gentlemen should adhere!"

Flushed with wine as he was, Sir Jervas understood, and was stung by, the taunt.

"Your meaning, Mr. Cecil!" he said, red and irate.

"I mean," returned my father, "that I had supposed Sir Jervas Ireton to be a friend of his majesty. 'Tis scarce a month since you lauded him as the model of a prince, and no insults were too gross for the parliament people in your estimation, sir. Mr. Hampden was a knave;—I was compelled to defend that high-minded gentleman against your denunciations; Mr. Pym was a wretch; Mr. Cromwell a hypocritical fanatic! Now these are the saints, and we of his majesty's cause are the knaves! Well, beware, Sir Jervas: there are friends of yours who will call you turncoat. I will not, sir, for you are beneath my roof!"

The knight started up at this, and exclaimed,—

" I leave your roof, but give you some counsel first. The eyes of the godly are upon you——"

My father was on his feet too. "In your person, doubtless, sir!" he said, in great wrath. "By heaven, I am not too old, 'malignant' though I be, to defend my honor!"

With three strides he reached an old sword hanging against the wall, and caught it down.

"'This for you, sir, and the rest of the 'godly,'—at all hours, day or night!"

I had risen, half indignant, half laughing at the drunken knight.

"Don't threaten him, sir," I said to my father: "he won't fight."

And the truth of my words was speedily shown. Five minutes had not passed before Sir Jervas was out of the room and on horseback.

"The vulgar turncoat!" growled my father, replacing his old sword on the wall. "A few moments more, and I had spitted his carcase!"

"'''Tis better as it is,' as Will Shakspeare says, sir," I returned, laughing; "and even now this worthy may annoy you in many ways, from his connection with the 'godly' in the neighborhood. I shall not be present to aid you. I leave you at daylight. Now I will go with Cicely to take leave of everything."

I called my little sister, who had been my companion in all my rambles, and she came, with her pretty bright face smiling behind its curls.   In her eyes, however, I could discern the traces of tears, and, as we walked under the great trees towards the stream, she said, in a low voice,—

"Oh, brother, why do you leave us?   Must you go so soon?"

"Yes, Cicely," I said: "this is no time for the Cecils to prove laggards.   I see you have been upstairs crying; but come, smile again.   There is your ardent admirer, Jervas Ireton the younger, coming to meet you through the trees."

Cicely pouted immensely, and said, "He is the most disagreeable little wretch——"

And, as she spoke, the disagreeable little wretch approached, smiling.   It was, however, somewhat of an injustice to characterize the young gentleman thus: he was only weak. About twenty, with flaxen hair, washed-out blue eyes, a feeble smile, Mr. Jervas Ireton the younger was simply insignificant.   He and Cicely were old playmates, as the Ireton estate joined Cecil Court, and the youth had long fancied himself consumed with an ardent passion for the maiden.

"Oh, Cicely, and Mr. Ned," he said, "I am very glad to see you,—that is——"

He stammered, hesitated, and added,—

"That is, I would like to see you alone, Cicely."

The damsel pouted hugely at these words, and said,—

"What do you mean, Mr. Ireton?"

"There it is!" cried the young gentleman, plunged,

it seemed, into despair. "*Mr. Ireton!* The next thing it will be *Captain Ireton!*"

Cicely stared. "*You* a captain!"

"Yes," moaned the youthful warrior, in lugubrious tones, "a real captain. Sir Jervas managed it. A real captain, with a new uniform, and just going away. So I came,—it was the only opportunity I will have,— you will not see me alone. Oh, Miss Cicely! don't let me go without—without—without—one word,— that is——"

Here "Captain" Ireton quite broke down, losing all his self-possession. Cicely's head rose erect, and her eyes were full of fire.

"Which side are you on, sir?" came suddenly from the maiden.

"The—the—that is—I have no opinions myself of any consequence,—of no consequence, I assure you——"

"You are on the parliament's side!"

"Ye—e—s," returned Captain Ireton, hanging his head.

Cicely shot an exterminating glance at her admirer.

"Then you will please never presume to address me again, sir!" she burst forth. "The Cecils are for the king!" And the little maiden's eyes flamed.

"I—wish—I—was," came from her heart-broken admirer, "but,—well—'tis all over, I see, Cicely. I will not say any more.—I wish—but my father will have his way; he's a terrible old screw and tyrant!— I have no opinions of any consequence;—but, well——"

A gleam of intelligence appeared in the youth's eyes.

F   11

"Sir Jervas has the opinions of the family!"

A few minutes afterwards he took a sorrowful fare-well, and went disconsolately away; and I walked with Cicely until nightfall, when, arm in arm, my little sister and myself returned in the grand moonlight which fell upon the old hall in a flood of glory I shall never forget.

IV.

A YOUNG GENTLEMAN WITHOUT OPINIONS OF ANY CONSEQUENCE.

I HAD supposed the adieus of Jervas Ireton the younger to have been final; but on the very next morning, just as I was about to get into the saddle, he re-appeared.

The youth was clad in a superb purple uniform, the colors of Lord Brook, and wore on his shoulder an orange scarf, the badge of Lord Essex, commanding all the parliament forces. He was thus an imposing figure, in his purple and orange adornment, with the huge feather in his hat, and sabre at his side; but more imposing still was his retinue, which consisted of about twenty mounted men, marching martially two abreast. The affair really looked like war! Here was the dis-consolate lover of Cicely coming, it would seem, to have an official interview with Cicely's brother and mildly dissuade him from going to join the king.

My surmise was just.

The martial youth halted his command in a voice of thunder,—an order which they proceeded to obey by huddling together and running against each other in the wildest confusion,—and then, approaching me, he said, in a mournful tone,—

"I hope Cicely's not risen, Mr. Ned; oh, I think there she is, busy with your valise! How I wish I was going with you!"

I could not refrain from laughter.

"Whereas it is I who am going with you,—or at least you think so," I said. "In other words, my good Captain Jervas Ireton, you have brought that fine company of serving-men and cobblers yonder, to arrest me as an adherent of his majesty?"

The warrior hung his head.

"The old man is such a screw!—the greatest tyrant; Mr. Ned, you ever saw! Of course he made me come. Somebody told him you were going away to the king this morning,—so he would not rest till he had me in the saddle, with this tag-rag, on the way to seize you."

I looked at the youth, measuring his stature, then at his company. I could have broken him in two, despite my weakness, with one arm; and the complexion of his followers was far from martial.

"Well," I said, bringing around my rapier and pistol, "what do you propose to do, my good sir?"

"Oh, Mr. Ned! don't speak to me in that way!" remonstrated the young gentleman.

"In what way?"

"So rough! Of course I am going to pretend to arrest you——There is Cicely! Oh! the old man is such a tyrant!"

Cicely came out and stared in amazement. Then her face flushed hot.

"What are you and these people here for, sir?" she exclaimed.

"Nothing—nothing—that is—hem!—it's a mere form, Cicely."

"Please call me Miss Cecil, sir," said the little maiden, turning pale, but speaking with great hauteur.

"There again!—'*Sir!*'" exclaimed the prostrated youth. "Oh, dont call me 'Sir,' Cicely,—that is, Miss Cecil!"

Cicely looked from the speaker to myself in amazement.

"Our young friend is only come to bid me good-by, little sister," I said.

"Yes, yes,—that's it!—and to wish you a happy journey, Mr. Ned!" was the eager response; "in fact, my own opinion is—if I had any—but I have none of any consequence, I do assure you——"

I burst into a laugh, in which my father—who, coming down the steps, had heard the last words, and understood all—nearly joined.

"Come!" I said to the young warrior, "why not choose to have some opinions? Go and fight for his majesty: your bold followers will join you. There's Hob, an old friend of mine, and Tom Diggs and Gregory from Keynton. They don't know in the least what they are going to fight for!"

The youth hung his head, and looked truly disconsolate.

"I don't think we can, Mr. Ned,—the old man is such a screw. I have no opinions myself—but—

confidentially—my sentiments are—'God save the king!'"

He sank his voice as he uttered the words, and added, in the same tone,—

"Could you make it convenient to ride out by the back way, Mr. Ned?"

"No," I said. "I propose riding through Keynton."

The young man started.

"In company with Captain Ireton, at the head of his bold troopers!"

The youth looked quite aghast; but the comedy of the affair had taken possession of me,—I was in the gayest spirits,—and the result was that ten minutes afterwards I had bidden my father and Cicely farewell, and was riding, followed by Dick Hostler, beside Captain Ireton at the head of his company.

The spectacle must have been odd. I wore my rich uniform of queen's guardsman, and my companion the purple coat and orange scarf of the parliament. As we entered Keynton, all eyes were fixed upon us; and I gazed at it as attentively, for the village once so tranquil was almost unrecognizable. The parliament ruled there. The shopkeepers sat on their counters, haranguing crowds; the blacksmith had shut up his forge, and was laying down the law to the wheelwright, who seemed to hold opposing views; the public room at the inn was thronged with idlers, agog for news; and in one end of the long porch, an emissary of the parliament, in full regimentals, was ladling out drink and calling for recruits.

"Oh, Mr. Ned!" exclaimed my companion, "what are you going to do?"

11*

"I? I am going to do nothing," I said, laughing, "since there's nothing to be done!"

"But they see you!—there they come!—and oh, good heavens!—there—there—is——"

Vox faucibus hæsit! The youth, dumb with terror, pointed to the figure of Sir Jervas Ireton, coming rapidly out of the inn, and approaching.

"I see you have him!" exclaimed Sir Jervas; "a pestilent enemy of the good cause! The young bantling now,—the old cock soon to join him!"

The ruddy features of the knight shone, as he drew near. His unfortunate son shrank from him.

"Your servant, my good Mr. Cecil," said the knight, scornfully; "I am very glad to see you."

"'Tis friendly, at least; but the sight of your worship affects me differently," I said, continuing my way.

"Stop!—halt, I say!—seize him!"

And the knight rushed upon me, catching my rein violently.

I did not fancy the movement, and was in a bad humor from the scene at dinner with my father. As Sir Jervas Ireton, therefore, seized my bridle-rein to arrest me, I dealt him a blow with my fist on the side of the head, which caused him to stagger. The act was visible to all, and twenty men darted at my horse.

Had they caught the bridle, I must have been down under their feet the next moment. I guarded against that by striking the spur into my horse's side and whirling my rapier in front.

"Fire! fire on him!" I heard the furious Sir Jervas cry to his son. And the reply of that warrior came as clearly,—

"Oh!—the pistols—they are not loaded!"

The words were followed by an explosion from the porch of the inn; a bullet passed through my hat, and I turned my head in that direction. Through the smoke I caught a glimpse of the parliamentary emissary, who wore a sergeant's badges, and in the close-cropped hair, huge ears, and wide mouth, I recognized my foe the man Hulet, from London.

A longer interview was impossible. I sent a bullet from my pistol at the worthy, which did him no injury.

"Come, Dick, ride!" I then said; "the whole crew are after us!"

And, turning in my saddle, I caught off my hat, waved it around my head, and cried,—

"God save the king!"

That was some satisfaction, at least. Prudence counseled speed now; and Dick and I went on rapidly through the village, pursued by shots and the worshipful Captain Ireton's dragoons. The shots did not strike us, and we were better mounted than the village warriors. A friendly wood presented itself; the shouts behind us died gradually away; and, drawing rein, I went on through the vale of the Red Horse, scarce glancing at the heights of Edgehill, where I was soon to take part in the first battle of the Great Civil War.

V.

I AM CONDUCTED BEFORE PRINCE RUPERT.

THE Almighty, who is also the All-merciful and In-scrutable, sends tears, agony, and utter wretchedness to private individuals; on nations he inflicts at stated periods his great curse of civil war. The human being visited by his displeasure is easily known by the pallor, woe-begone look, and dejected 'havior of the visage; the nation cursed by civil war is marked as clearly by the hand of the Almighty.

In that summer of 1642, England was scarce recognizable. The tranquil and smiling land of the past was dead and gone. You seemed to move on the crust of a volcano, and men's minds had caught the fierce heat and were burnt up by fever. As I rode towards Nottingham, I saw on all sides the traces of the evil spirit of civil contention. In many a field the ripe grain had fallen uncut and neglected. Over others prowled tramps and beggars, firing on the game. The highways were wellnigh deserted; and when you met a chance wayfarer he eyed you sidewise with suspicious glances, and the hand under the cloak, you felt, grasped a concealed weapon. All the face of the land was torn down. The fences were gone in many places, for the war of cavalry-parties had already begun, and the cattle wandered uncared for, trampling down the corn and meadow-lands. The villages were either deserted, or hot-beds of agitation and gossip. In some, the shutters were closed, and women glanced through the cracks fearfully. In others, sullen glances or ardent questions greeted you, as you adhered to one or the other party.

England was thus transformed, in a day, as 'twere, into a war-worn realm. Her people seemed to look forward fearfully to some coming fate. Discussions in parliament had ended; the sword had replaced debate; the harsh thunder of cannon was about to drown the roar of hostile multitudes.

The war, as I have said, had already begun. At Northampton, Lord Essex, general of the parliament forces, lay, I heard, with an army of about six thousand men. And his horse were already scouring the country between that place and Nottingham, where the king had assembled a force scarce half as numerous as his opponent's. Thus the *petite guerre* of cavalry had begun, preluding the greater conflict of foot, and twice I was chased by the enemy's foraging-parties, who very nearly made me a prisoner. I succeeded in evading them, nevertheless, and at near sunset reached the pickets of the royal cavalry towards Nottingham.

My Guardsman's uniform would, I supposed, be sufficient voucher for my loyalty, but the officer of the picket regretted his inability to pass me within the royal lines. He was ordered, he said, to arrest all persons coming northward, and send them to head-quarters. This was reasonable, if not agreeable, and I went on with the escort of two men, to whom I was intrusted. We rode half a league, passed a large camp

F*

of dragoons on the edge of a forest, in which fires had been kindled; then a tent on a grassy hill came in view, and before this tent we halted.

Out of the tent, on the summit of which floated the colors of the king, came a huge personage with a corporal's badges on his arms, a long black beard, and an air of authority.

"Your pisness?" said the new-comer, with a strong German accent.

The guard informed him that I and my servant had been arrested at the outer picket.

"Vait!"

And the giant retired into the tent, from which he soon reappeared, with the guttural announcement,—

"Gome in!"

I entered, and found myself in presence of a young man in a general's uniform, who was lying on a scarlet cloak spread on the grass, and playing with a white spaniel. The appearance of this officer was martial. His boots were covered with dust, his face ruddy from exposure, his eye keen and piercing, his bearing direct, almost abrupt: from head to foot, in every trait of his person, he was a soldier. On a camp couch in one corner of the tent lay a rich belt, containing a fine rapier, and from the holsters of a superb saddle near, protruded the handles of two highly-decorated pistols. The officer was plainly either of high rank, or with a marked fondness for bright colors, or both. I have found eminent soldiers careless of dress often, and prone, indeed, to despise decoration as puerile. The young general before me seemed to delight in such things; to enjoy the bright colors, the pomp and

splendor of war. You could see that he was all im-
pulse, promptness, and impetuosity. His glance was
that of the eagle, and the eyes seemed ready to flame.
It was plain that the first blast of the bugle would pour
fire into this man,—that the hand would dart to the
rapier, the spur clash on the stirrup, the simple soldier
would replace the general, and he would lead the
charge, sword in hand.

All this was plain at a glance. The young officer
responded with a look which took in every trait of my
person.

" Well," he said, with a slight foreign accent, " who
are these ?"

" Brisoners, your highness," returned the heavily-
bearded giant.

" I am not highness ; I am general," said the officer,
briefly.

" Yes, sheneral."

" Prisoners! This gentleman, from his uniform, is
one of the queen's guards."

" Yes, highness,—dat is, sheneral."

The officer had risen abruptly, repulsing his playful
white spaniel, who continued to fawn on him.

" You were arrested at my outer picket, sir?" he
said, looking straight at me.

" Yes, general. May I ask to whom I have the
honor to speak ?"

" To General Rupert, commanding the horse of the
king's army."

I bowed low to his royal highness Prince Rupert,
nephew of his majesty.

" Your arrest, sir," said the prince, " was in obedience to my general order. Your name, if it please you, and whence come you?"

"Edmund Cecil; and I am from near Keynton, where I have lain ill recently, highness."

"Say *sheneral!*" here came from behind the hand of the huge corporal, who had edged towards me, and gave me this intimation in tones of subdued thunder.

"Spare your counsel, Hans," said the prince, briefly, "and go find what horsemen are approaching."

The giant disappeared, and the prince turned again to me.

"What intelligence, Mr. Cecil? You have no doubt looked and listened."

"To little purpose, I fear, your highness. My lord of Essex is at Northampton, with six thousand men, 'tis said."

"Near seven thousand. But the state of the country, sir?"

"'Tis in a fever,—the parliament recruiting everywhere."

"And plundering."

"'Tis so said, my lord."

"I will essay to stop that."

As he spoke, the sound of horses' feet was heard in front of the tent, and an instant afterwards the gigantic corporal ushered in a dignified young gentleman, thin of figure, clad in civil dress, and with something sweet and melancholy in his face.

"My lord Falkland! You are very welcome, my lord," said the prince, cordially pressing his hand. Lord Falkland bowed, and said,—

"A message from his majesty, your highness."

They went to the opposite side of the tent, and conversed for a few moments. The prince nodded.

"Say to his majesty that his order will be promptly obeyed, my lord."

The prince had scarce uttered these words, when a prolonged bellowing was heard without, and this discordant sound was followed by the neigh of horses. The prince glanced at the huge corporal, made a gesture, and the worthy went out. A few moments afterwards he returned.

"Gaptured gattle and horses, highness,—dat is, sheneral!"

"Oh, highness!" said Lord Falkland, in a low, sad voice, "this is very painful!"

Before the prince could reply, a young officer entered the tent, saluted, and said,—

"Your orders have been obeyed, general."

"The house is fired?"

"Yes, general; and you may see it burning."

The prince went to the front of the tent : I followed. A ruddy glare above the southern woods indicated a conflagration.

"It is well," said Rupert: "that will teach them a lesson."

A deep sigh came like an echo to the words. It had issued from Lord Falkland, who was standing behind the prince.

"Terrible! terrible!" murmured Falkland.

Prince Rupert wheeled round, with an angry flush upon his brow.

"I make war!" he said, abruptly; "and war is not rose-water!"

"Pardon me," was Falkland's low, sad response. "I meant not to offend your highness."

"And I am a hot-headed fool," exclaimed Rupert, grasping his visitor's hand; "else I had never taken umbrage at words from the soul of honor—Falkland!"

He paused, and looked towards the conflagration.

"This seems harsh to you, my lord," he said. "Well, 'tis just. The man whose house I have burned over his head has been merciless to the families of my soldiers, pointing them out to the vengeance of the parliamentary troops. That was proved to me. Well, I have punished him, have driven off his cattle and burned his house. History will hate and curse me for these things, if 'tis written by friends of the parliament. So be it; but let me repeat, my lord,—war is not rose-water."

With these words, Prince Rupert re-entered the tent.

An hour afterwards I was in Nottingham, talking of home and home-folks with my dear Harry. When we fell asleep, side by side, we were still murmuring our boyish talk, and Harry's sweet smile went with me like sunshine into the dim and pleasant realm of dreams.

VI.

SWORDS AND PLUMES AT CECIL COURT.

IT was about sunset on a superb evening, late in October, that, looking from an upper window of Cecil Court, beside my father and Cicely, I saw the royal forces move in a long glittering line to the summit of the eminence called Edgehill, near Keynton.

The foes were about to clash together. All attempts to negotiate and compose the differences between king and parliament had failed. Soon after my arrival at Nottingham, the Earl of Southampton and his associate commissioners, sent by King Charles to London, had returned and reported that they had met with scant courtesy, had received a written reply, and had been ordered to depart from London without delay. When the king read the parliament's missive, his face darkened, and his ire was aroused. His antagonists demanded his submission,—that they should control all appointments, occupy all fortresses, and dictate all public measures.

"Should I grant these demands," the king exclaimed, in great indignation, "I should remain but the outside, the picture—but the sign—of a king!"

And I think he was right in that surmise. The parliament distrusted him so, that they demanded extreme concessions. To have yielded then were to have surrendered all.   Instead of doing so, King Charles issued a solemn proclamation to his army, in which he protested the sincerity of his intent to observe the laws, and called on his followers to march with him and put the question to issue on the battle-field.   The proclamation was received by the army — then numbering about ten thousand men — with enthusiasm ; and then the king moved from Nottingham southward to meet Lord Essex, who promptly marched from Worcester to accept battle.

Thus the royal forces came near, and were seen from the windows of Cecil Court.   It was a superb and warlike spectacle.   The ruddy light of sunset fell, in a sort of glory, upon silken banners and bright scarfs, burnished arms and glossy horses.   Foot, horse, and artillery moved slowly to the hill, — a splendid phantom, without noise, save a stifled hum, and now and then a bugle-note from the cavaliers of Rupert.

All at once a noise of hoofs on the avenue came up to the window.   I looked down, and saw the king, Lord Falkland, and a few others spurring towards the house.

" 'Tis his majesty ! He is coming to visit us," I said.

" The king will be most welcome," was the response of my father.

And, descending, he met the king at the great door, and inclined profoundly.

" We have come to take possession of your house, Mr. Cecil," said the king.

" Your majesty does my poor house a very great honor," was my father's response, with a second inclination; and he ushered the king into the main reception-room of the establishment, whither the Viscount Falkland and some other noblemen followed him.

An excellent dinner was speedily served, and the noble guests—kings and noblemen are but men, and grow hungry, reader—evidently derived great satisfaction therefrom. And let me pause here an instant, to notice a peculiarity of my father's ménage. He would always live as well, every day, as his fortunes permitted, not starving his household for a month to give a grand entertainment to invited company.

" 'Tis but a mean manner of living at the best," he would say, "to keep your fine rooms and best food and full dress for state occasions; to live in a cuddy, stint your table, and go slovenly before your family, in order to dress splendidly and make a show when strangers enter your door. My family are as worthy of rich food and the best apartments as any one, and I make my toilette as scrupulously for my daughter Cicely as for my Lady Duchess."

He certainly carried out his philosophy. His dress was ever the same in public and in private; the very best apartments at Cecil Court were used every day, and the table was spread daily with the best food. Then the door was opened; every one was welcome, whether rich or poor, high or low, titled personage or plain countryman, all found a cordial welcome, and were greeted equally by the master of the mansion. I don't think my father was politer to one than to another. He was a very proud and simple gentleman of the old *régime.* On this evening he said to the king, "Enter, your majesty: you are welcome,"

as he would have uttered the same welcome to any
other visitor.

The king retired after dining to the reception-room,
which was thronged with noblemen and officers. Cecil
Court, without and within, had suddenly become a
general's headquarters. Couriers went and came, with
clashing heels and rattling spurs. Officers clad in
superb uniforms stood around the table, beside which
the king sat, writing orders or reading reports. In the
grounds without, horses were tethered, champing their
bits and stamping. In the grass-plat in front of the
hall had been set up the king's banner.

His chief officers had come at his summons. These
were Lord Lindesey, commanding-in-chief; Prince
Rupert, commanding the horse; Sir Jacob Astley, the
foot; Sir Arthur Aston, the dragoons; and Sir John
Heydon, the artillery. I forget the troop of Guards,
whose servants formed a second troop, always marching with their masters. The first were under Lord
Bernard Stuart, the second under Sir William Killigrew.
The wealthiest young noblemen of the kingdom had
flocked to the Guards now: 'twas said, and with truth,
I think, that the estates and revenues of these young
private soldiers exceeded the estates and revenues of
all the members of parliament and the House of Lords,
when the seats of the two houses were full.

Among these gay young volunteers was one whose
name, when I heard it first at Nottingham, had made
me start. Walking arm in arm with Harry, I had
seen him beckon to a youth of about twenty, with
bright blue eyes, chestnut curls, laughing face, and
superbly clad.

"Here's my brother Ned, Frank," Harry said. "Come and shake hands with him."

And as the youth came forward, with an expression of youthful buoyancy and sunshine in his face, Harry added, to me,—

"This is Frank Villiers, brother of our fair friend the maid of honor. We are sworn friends; and you must be his friend too."

The youth squeezed my hand cordially, looking at me with his frank eyes and smile; and in ten minutes we were familiar friends. Three days afterwards, I seemed to have known him from his very childhood; and now he had ridden with me to Cecil Court, and was laughing with Cicely on the portico in the moonlight.

The king was busy until midnight, and then, rising, exchanged a few words with Viscount Falkland, his secretary of state.

"All is ready, you see, my lord," he said, "and 'tis probable we shall fight on the morrow. Come, summon back your smiles: you seem woe-begone to-night."

Lord Falkland sighed. "I know not what oppresses me so, your majesty," he said.

The king looked at him with a glance full of melancholy. "'Tis that woman's heart you possess, my lord. You shrink from battle and blood! See, I utter ungracious words. I seem to impute weakness to Falkland, the bravest of all the brave gentlemen of my kingdom!"

"Your majesty knows——"

"That 'tis kindness, not weakness? Yes! Your heart is bleeding, Falkland, at the blood and agony

which to-morrow will bring. Well, *my* heart too
bleeds; but I am not the author of this conflict. I
shrink from the future; but I go on in my course.
The English monarchy shall not fall, in my person,
without a struggle, Falkland. And now good-night.''

My father, who waited, ushered the king to his apartment, bearing a silver sconce before him. A few moments after their disappearance, my father called me. I
went up rapidly, and the king, who sat beside a table,
upon which lay an open portfolio, said to me,—

"I have a service to ask of you, Mr. Cecil. Are you
well mounted ?''

"Very well, your majesty.''

" I wish you to go to Holland.''

I bowed low, with a beating heart. The king had
turned to my father.

"Two gray-haired gentlemen like ourselves, Mr.
Cecil,'' he said, " can understand each other. I would
write to my wife. To-night my thoughts have never
left her. I shall go into action to-morrow, and, like a
good husband, think of one who is thinking of me.''

Taking a pen as he spoke, the king began to write.
The letter, which filled two sheets, was at last finished
and securely sealed, the king stamping the wax with
a signet-ring which he wore. He then extended the
package towards me, but suddenly drew it back.

"No, I will wait until the event is decided to-
morrow, and add some lines,'' he said. "'Twould be
cruel to write thus on the eve of battle, and leave her
majesty in doubt of everything,—perhaps to torture
herself with fears. Your pardon, Mr. Cecil,'' he added
to my father: "I think aloud, but I take no shame to

myself for my thoughts. To-night I am only a poor husband thinking of his absent wife."

He turned towards me, and added, "'Twould disappoint you too, sir, if I'm not mistaken. Go into action with your friends to-morrow. I shall see and share all. And if you survive, come to me immediately after the battle."

I saluted and retired. Half an hour afterwards I was in camp, and said to Harry, beside whom I lay,—

"I am going to Holland to-morrow, Harry. I shall see her again,—Frances Villiers!"

VII.

BROTHERS.

As I uttered the words, "I shall see her again, —Frances Villiers!" I felt Harry start.

"You say that in an ardent tone, Ned," he replied. "Is the prospect so delightful?"

I was silent, and felt a burning blush rush to my face in the darkness.

"True!" I stammered. "I have never spoken of this even to you, my dearest Harry. But 'tis out now! Yes, I look forward to the moment when I shall see Frances Villiers again with the wildest beating of the heart. When the king said, 'I wish you to go to Holland,' the words were like music. How could I feel aught but joy, or listen calmly, as his majesty spoke thus, Harry? The person I'll see there has long been dearer to me than all else in this world!"

Followed a gushing oration, full of passionate love and general froth and absurdity. What makes young gentlemen when they are in love insist upon bestowing their raptures, with a sort of drunken ardor, on the nearest person? They grow maudlin when the fit is on them, and talk on through the night-watches forever. So I opened my heart to Harry, and told him all, as we lay there on Edgehill,—how I had loved Frances Villiers from our first meeting nearly, had dreamed of her day and night when at Hampton Court, and had sighed bitterly when she went away,—my sun, moon, and starlight all combined! This, and all the rest! I spare the reader, as I did not spare poor Harry. He listened in silence for a long time, and scarce interrupted me to the end. There was something strange in his voice, I thought,—I did not note it then, but remembered it afterwards.

"Well, Ned," he said, at length, forcing a laugh, "I see you are regularly a victim; but I don't wonder, since the enchantress is the fair Miss Villiers, the empress of all hearts!"

He laughed again; but the laugh was discordant.

"What ails you, Harry? Your laugh is strange!" I said.

"Ails me? Nothing, Ned. What *could* ail me? I'm not anxious about the fight to-morrow on Mr. Harry Cecil's score, I swear to you. If I felt solicitude, 'twould be on Ned Cecil's account, brother."

His voice had softened to the sweetest music: there was no longer the tone of frolic laughter in it, but an earnest kindness and goodness that touched me to the heart, as he ended with that word "brother," never employed save in moments of loving regard.

"Then we think of each other," I said; "for I have prayed for you, Harry! You are my only brother, and the very best brother that man ever had!"

Harry's old kind laugh rang out.

"Good! Here we are making protestations," he said. "What's the advantage? Don't I know that you love me, Ned, as I love you? Since we were children we never have quarreled but once, when I beat you and then went and sat on the steps and cried about it! I'll back Ned Cecil for a brother against any man in England! And now let's go to sleep; 'tis near day, and the fight may open at dawn. So you go to Holland?—Well, present my regards to the fair Miss Frances. She's worth loving, Ned,—forward!—I mean to be present at your wedding!"

The words were uttered in a low tone, and Harry turned away, as though going to sleep. Suddenly he wheeled round, and placed his arm around my neck.

"God bless my brother!" he said, in the same strange tone: "that comes straight from my heart, Ned!—and now good-night."

A moment afterwards, a long heavy breathing seemed to indicate that Harry slept. I knew afterwards that, like myself, he lay awake until dawn. Then the bugle sounded, and the camps were astir.

The day of battle had come,—the first battle of the English Civil War.

VIII.

I VISIT THE HAGUE.

THESE memoirs, may it please the reader, are not a history of the reign of his majesty King Charles I., nor even a narrative of the military occurrences of the " Great Rebellion." Guns will roar on the page, bugles sound, and swords clash, sometimes; but 'tis the adventures of Edmund Cecil which will chiefly compose the story.

Therefore of Edgehill I present but a passing sketch; and I think all battles had best be treated in that manner. What are they but a hurly-burly of shouts, explosions, and cheers or groans! The movements of columns or wings are described in a few words; then nothing is left but that confused struggle of the opposing masses. I have been in many battles; and all resemble each other in the one great feature of men in clothes of different colors essaying to tear each other to pieces.

The king's army, of about ten thousand men, was drawn up on the slope of Edgehill. In the vale of the Red Horse, beneath, the ten or fifteen thousand men of Lord Essex confronted them in order of battle. All day the opponents faced each other thus. Towards sunset the battle began. With fluttering banners, blasts of the bugle, and the roar of artillery, the royal forces advanced to charge those of the parliament.

Prince Rupert, on our right, commanding the horse, began the struggle, as was thereafter his wont. He charged the left wing of Lord Essex, consisting of a strong body of cavalry; and, riding with the Guards in front, I witnessed a singular incident. The troop of horse we were charging suddenly fired their pistols into the ground; their commanding officer spurred to meet us, and made a parade-salute with his sabre to Prince Rupert, with whom he exchanged a few words; an instant afterwards the troop had wheeled and ranged themselves on the side of the king. Sir Faithful Fortescue—forced, 'twas said, to march with the parliament's forces against his will—had changed his flag on the day of battle, for which I, a royalist, could never forgive him.

Struck thus by the whole weight of Rupert's horsemen, the enemy's left wing gave way. A wild chaos followed, the pursuers cutting down the fugitives as they fled. They were followed nearly a league thus; and Heaven knows how far the pursuit would have extended, had not a thunder of shouts in the distance recalled the prince to a sense of his indiscretion.

Sir Arthur Aston had broken the right of Lord Essex, as Rupert had broken the left; but the infantry of the king was thus stripped of its supports of horse. Sir William Balfour, commanding the parliament's reserve force, advanced; the lines clashed together furiously. Lord Lindsey, our commander, was mortally wounded and taken prisoner; and Sir Edmund Verney, bearing the king's standard, fell dead,—the standard falling into the enemy's hands.

Such was the state of things when Prince Rupert led

back his horse from the ill-timed pursuit. He came too late to be of much service. The king's standard was recaptured; but the enemy continued to present an unbroken front. Then night descended:—the two armies retained their positions; the watch-fires blazed in long lines within sight of each other in the vale of the Red Horse:—the fight of Edgehill, which left five thousand dead men on the field, had resulted in success to neither side.

The sole ground for claiming a victory over the parliament was the fact that Essex retired, and the king advanced towards London afterwards. But this I did not witness. I was on my way to Holland.

At midnight his majesty had delivered to me his letter to the queen, containing, doubtless, additional matter relating to the battle.

"This with speed to her majesty at the Hague, Mr. Cecil," the king said. "At Yarmouth a vessel awaits you: here is my order to the captain. Travel rapidly; and, if you are in peril, destroy the letter. A good journey, sir! I would fain go in your place."

I took the letter, bowing low, and ten minutes afterwards was in the saddle.

A hand in the darkness was placed on my knee.

"You forget to bid me good-by, Ned!"

The voice was gentle,—almost tender. In my foolish joy at the thought of seeing Frances Villiers, I had quite forgotten my dearest Harry; but he had not forgotten me.

His arm was placed around me: a few words, and we had parted.

Of all persons after my father, I loved this one the

best. 'Tis my pride and joy now to remember that he too loved me.

But I did not think of Harry then; nor did I know the full wealth of that noble heart and the extent of my brother's self-sacrifice.

I passed across the country at full speed, avoiding the enemy's scouting-parties, reached Yarmouth, found the king's vessel—a small sloop—waiting, and gave the captain the order. We put to sea at once, and, after a stormy passage, saw the low shores of Holland appear like a long green line on the water.

In due time I disembarked at the Hague and delivered the king's letter to her majesty.

I X.

A GOOD WIFE.

I WENT to Holland, expecting to return to England at once. I remained there from October until the month of February, 1643.

The queen had said to me, "I wish your assistance here, Mr. Cecil. Remain, therefore; but do not fear: you shall soon see England again."

As her majesty thus spoke, sitting in an apartment of the palace of the Princes of Orange, at the Hague, her face glowed with animation, and her eyes were full of courage.

"You are a friend of the royal cause, sir, and a gentleman of discretion, too," her majesty was pleased to add, smiling. "I shall therefore take you into our confidence and inform you of our good fortune. See this paper: we have the promise of these round sums from the worthy burghers here."

She held out a paper to me, and I perused its contents. Rotterdam engaged to lend forty thousand guilders, and the bank at the same city the sum of twenty-five thousand more. The bank at Amsterdam promised eight hundred and forty-five thousand more. Merchants at the Hague, one hundred and sixty-six thousand more. Another merchant's house offered two hundred and thirteen thousand two hundred, on the security of the queen's pearls. Six rubies were accepted in pawn for forty thousand more. From the paper, in a word, I learned how successful her majesty had been. She had the promise of, and afterwards did actually receive, from these various sources, more than two millions of pounds sterling.

I raised my eyes from the paper, and fixed them upon the animated face of the queen.

"The worthy burgomasters of this good country have not surrendered without a desperate resistance," her majesty added, laughing. "They exhibited at first little favor towards me, and, indeed, scant respect for my person. They entered my presence with their heads covered; threw themselves unbidden into chairs before me; stared at me in the manner of persons viewing some strange wild animal; and, when I spoke of money, more than once turned their backs and marched from the room."

"'Tis not possible!" I said. "And could your majesty endure such treatment?"

"Without a word, Mr. Cecil. The worthy burghers could not repulse me. I responded to all their discourtesy with the sweetest smiles. I would not see the beavers remaining on their heads; I had chairs brought them, and begged they would be seated. Never was bankrupt merchant more polite to those who could assist him. And I have triumphed despite everything; despite Sir Walter Strickland, the parliament's agent here, a brother of Sir William, of the enemy's side in England. I have triumphed, and shall soon set out for England with an armament. His majesty's need is sore there, and my assistance will not arrive too soon. The gentlemen of the parliament seem inspired with a veritable fury against us. I say *us*, since 'tis my pride to have secured at least one-half their enmity! They exhaust every effort, I am told. Plate, jewels, even the thimbles and bodkins of the worthy burghers' wives, pour into the treasury at Guildhall, to support the 'good cause.' Why then should not I, in my turn, give *my* jewels? The good dames of London rush to the assistance of Mr. Pym and Mr. Cromwell and the leaders of the 'godly.' A poor 'malignant' wife, then, may be pardoned for essaying to aid her husband!"

So spoke the queen. Whatever her faults, she was assuredly a brave and devoted wife. Throughout all those stormy times this fealty to her husband shines clearly. At Newark, once, when the ladies petitioned that she would not march till Nottingham was taken, she replied,—

13*

"Ladies, affairs of this nature are not in our sphere. I am commanded by the king to make all the haste to him that I can. You will receive this advantage, at least, by my answer, though I cannot grant your petition: you may learn, by my example, to obey your husbands!"

I see a charming French wit in that reply, and good sense too, I think. I finish the sentence with trepidation, knowing some fair dames who repudiate such humility. 'Tis taught in the holy volume, but is going out of fashion.

So I remained at the Hague until February, 1643, before which time her majesty had not perfected her arrangements for returning to England.

I shall say little of that time: the days followed and resembled each other too. A flat country, and a flat life there; or 'twould have been flat, the life I led, but for the presence of a person who was very dear to me. With one scene, in which this person bore part, I will pass from Holland. I would omit even this, willingly; but 'tis impossible.

X.

MY FATE.

I PAUSE, and lean my forehead on my hand, and laugh. I did not laugh then : the scene I speak of did not arouse my merriment.

It took place at Helvoetsluys, a country palace of the Prince of Orange, whither the queen went on a visit, towards the spring, taking her suite with her.

An old park, beyond which the sluggish waters of a canal were seen,—the country around flat and prosaic; the park bare and dreary with its leafless trees,—amid such a scene I was walking at twilight with Frances Villiers, and had just made a passionate speech, to which the young lady had listened with a burning blush.

Through the mists that have gathered in all the years since that moment, I can see her plainly. She wore a dress of red brocade, and had thrown some furs around her shoulders. From beneath a silken hood her great eyes shone, half covered, as her head sank, by curls; her cheeks were crimson with that sudden blush; and the hand I held in my own was bent upward, with the palm downward, so that the round white wrist was bent.

The hand tried to release itself, and some words came in a sort of murmur from the lips, turned away from me.

" Have pity on me ! You know now that I love you more than my life ! You must have seen it all these days. Now I speak, and await my fate !"

Something like this escaped from the young man holding the hand of the girl; and a long deep breath which she drew, as though to relieve her bosom from a weight upon it, filled the lover with delicious hope.

Alas!——

It came!—that reply which so many a gay gallant has received in this world:

"I cannot!—oh, no! Why force me to this, Mr. Cecil?"

She stopped, and all at once her confusion seemed to disappear. Her head turned towards me; the great eyes were full of calm goodness and sweetness; the blushes had disappeared, and the hand was gently withdrawn.

"There is something terrible in this," she murmured. "Our interview is doubly unfortunate, Mr. Cecil."

"Terrible?—unfortunate?"

"Is it not unfortunate when——"

She paused.

"Speak!—you torture me," I said.

"I would fain speak, Mr. Cecil," she said, with earnest feeling, "but I know not how to tell you all. 'Tis hard for a maiden to say what I desire to utter. And yet—'tis better, is it not, ever to be frank and open?"

"A thousand times better! Speak thus, I pray you!"

She raised her eyes, which had been cast down for an instant, and they beamed with candor and goodness.

"We are friends; I value your friendship: will you then permit me to speak as your friend, with the unreserve even of a sister? Do not woo me, sir:

'twould bring unhappiness: I have read in books that 'tis terrible when two brothers are rival suitors!''

Her face flushed again, and, as she thus spoke, she turned towards the palace.

I followed in a sort of stupor. *'Tis terrible when two brothers are rival suitors!* Those words rang in my brain, and confused me like a blow. Harry was a suitor of Frances Villiers, then! I had never dreamed of that, regarding them as friends only; now the announcement came suddenly that I was my dear brother's rival.

"God help me!" I groaned, at length; "why was this concealed from me? What evil fate has placed me in opposition to my dearest brother?"

"Evil indeed, sir!" murmured the young girl: "were that brothers' love to be broken by me, I should die of grief and shame.''

I walked on in silence beside her, and we drew near the entrance to the palace. Suddenly she turned her head and fixed her eyes upon me. The earnest glance seemed to read all that was passing in my mind.

"There is something I should add," she said, in a low tone; "and I will not shrink now. Yes, your brother is my suitor; but I have no heart for any one, sir. My life—like my character, perhaps—is a strange one, Mr. Cecil. I am an orphan, nearly alone in the world: my life is dedicated to but one great sentiment, —my love for the queen. I shall never marry. Forget me! those are the last words I said to your brother, Mr. Cecil.''

She went up the great staircase slowly, leaving me standing at the foot.

G*

Then Harry loved her,—and he had bid me good-speed in my wooing!

My face must have flushed; a sudden warmth made itself felt in my heart, as I remembered my brother's last greeting when I left him.

"Well, 'tis fortunate," I muttered, "that I have received my *quietus* too! 'Twill make my course easier, my resolution from this moment not to stand in the path of my dear Harry. He abandons the field to me, —I abandon it to him. My heart may break; at least I shall not be dishonored."

Do you smile, reader, and say that all this was romantic and high-flown? Would that to-day my heart were as fresh and true and unselfish as 'twas then, when I gave up the love of a woman for the love I bore my brother!

BOOK III.

I.

THE ADVENTURES OF A QUEEN.

THESE memoirs, fortunately, deal much more in incident than in sentiment. All the love-making they contain was made by my humble self, you see, friend; and, looking back now, those scenes impress me as exquisitely absurd.

Have your laugh, therefore, reader, at that interview in the park at Helvoetsluys; then come with me to some scenes which will possess more interest.

We are going to return to England. The queen had received her two million pounds sterling. With the larger portion she had bought artillery and other munitions; and on a clear day of February, 1643, she sailed from Scheveling, in a first-class ship, the Princess Royal, with eleven transports,—the whole convoyed by a war-fleet under command of Admiral Van Tromp.

The weather had promised to be fine; but the heavens speedily clouded over. Then a violent northeasterly gale began to roar, and the seas to dash. With every moment the wind seemed to become more violent; and I shall never forget the ludicrous scenes which took place on the Princess Royal. There, every one, save the queen, had fallen a prey to sea-sickness. The ladies of her suite were tied in their small beds, I was told, to secure them from the tossing of the ship. All was wailing and moaning, prayers for deliverance, and vows against again tempting the horrors of the great deep. In the general confusion, scarce an attempt was made to preserve etiquette. Those who essayed to serve the queen rolled and fell as they approached her,—thereby causing her to laugh heartily, with her pleasant sense of humor.

The storm grew ever more violent; and now the ship seemed about to founder. Then the ludicrous character of the spectacle presented reached its highest point. The ladies of the suite gave up hope, and began to shout aloud their confessions to the attendant priests. The priests were in wretched plight, as they shared the terrible nausea; and as the strange confessions were cried out at the top of the fair ladies' voices, they vainly strove to pay attention,—pale, woe-begone, and as wretched as their penitents.

In the midst of all sat the queen, looking on and listening. At last the scene overpowered her, and she burst into a hearty laugh.

"For shame, ladies!" she said. "See! there are gentlemen at the door who hear you!"

And indeed several of the queen's gentlemen were looking on, and listening to the strange revelations.

The queen shrugged her fair shoulders after the French fashion, and added,—

"Well, I suppose the extremity of your fears takes away the shame of confessing such misdeeds in public!"

And, rising, she took a step forward to leave the cabin. As she did so, the ship rolled suddenly, and the queen would have fallen had I not hastened to her. I received her in my arms, and she clung to me,—the royal head upon my shoulder! The sea is terribly democratic. The arms of a subject were around his queen!—for a moment only, however: her majesty regained her footing at once, and ascended to the deck.

Here, leaning on the rail, and gazing with perfect calmness upon the wild waters lashed to fury by the storm, the queen uttered these words to the few persons who had followed her:

"Comfort yourselves, *mes chères!*—queens of England are never drowned!"

They were brave words; and 'twas a heart braver than many a man's from which they came.

The tempest continued day and night for many days; and finally the Princess Royal and the whole fleet were beaten back to the coast of Holland,—all but two of the vessels, which foundered in the tempest.

The queen was not discouraged. Her eyes were fixed on England, and again the fleet set sail. This time favoring winds blew, and the vessels ran rapidly before them. At dawn one morning I heard a cry on deck. I hastened up, and saw that the fleet had entered Burlington Bay, on the coast of Yorkshire; and on the hills, now in plain view, a considerable body of the royal cavalry was drawn up in long line, ready to welcome us.

The queen was not to land her stores and regain his majesty, however, without further adventures; and

14

I beg the reader not to suppose from that word "adventures" that I feign these incidents. They are the simple truth.

Her majesty had landed a portion of her stores, and gone on shore with her suite, when an enemy suddenly appeared and roughly saluted her. This enemy was Admiral Batten, in command of a fleet of parliament vessels; and the first intimation we had of his approach was the thunder of guns.

The cannonade began at dawn one morning, before the queen, who slept in a small house on the shore, had risen. She was startled from slumber by the cries of her ladies, and before she was well awake the houses around were battered down, and two cannon-balls struck the roof above her, crashing down through the ceilings. There was thus no time for delay. Van Tromp had engaged the enemy; but a part of their attentions was bestowed upon the house the queen occupied, in ignorance, I hope, of her presence, though Admiral Batten was charged with firing on her majesty.

Scarce stopping to make any portion of her toilette, the queen hastened from the threatened mansion. She had thrown around her shoulders a flowered *robe-de-chambre*, her brown hair fell in masses of curls around her neck, and she had thrust her small white feet into a pair of thin silken slippers, which scarce defended them from the sharp flints of the way. Such was the unceremonious guise in which the queen fled through the street of Burlington. All at once she stopped. I was near her majesty, and cried to her to hasten on.

"No, I cannot leave Mitte behind!" she said.

"Mitte!" I exclaimed.

" My poor lap-dog, Mr. Cecil.''

" I beseech your majesty!—I will return and——''

The queen had scarce listened. She was back again at the house ere I could turn round. I ran after her. The street was raked by cannon-shot, and the hoarse thunder resounded from the sea: with that thunder suddenly mingled the yelp of a dog.

I had reached the door of the house just as the queen, who had run up to her chamber and caught the lap-dog from his place of repose on her own bed, made her reappearance, clasping Mitte in her arms.

" I could not leave him to the mercy of the parliament, Mr. Cecil! They have voted me guilty of high treason, and might condemn him! What a tragedy, to think of his perishing on Tower Hill!''

" Good heavens!'' I exclaimed, " for your majesty to jest at such a moment!''

As I spoke, a cannot-shot passed within a few feet of the queen and entered a house near us.

" Hasten, your majesty!—I beseech you!''

" I am not afraid; but you see I am running, Mr. Cecil!''

The beautiful face, with its flush of excitement, was turned over the shoulder. The rosy lips were parted over the white teeth by a smile; the dark eyes beamed from behind the mass of brown hair—— Pardon my romantic enthusiasm, reader: Queen Mary was very beautiful then, as she ran with her little bare feet and laughed at the bullets.

They pursued her as she fled from the town into the country. Reaching the fields, she crouched down with her attendants in a ditch for protection. As she did

so, a piteous cry resounded a few yards from her.   A
servant of her suite had uttered the cry: he had been
torn in two by a cannon-ball.

All day the roar continued, and all day the queen
crouched down.   As evening came, the parliament
ships sailed away, pursued by Van Tromp.

"And now the rest of my stores may land," said
the queen; "and I'll go dress myself."

II.

A FEMALE GENERAL.

THE queen remained near Burlington for about ten
days, superintending the disembarkation of her arms
and stores.

I say *near* Burlington; not in the town.   Her majesty had removed thence to an old manor-house,
crowning a lofty hill, not far distant; and 'twas surely
a singular freak of fate that this house should be Boynton Hall, the property of Sir William Strickland, the
emissary of parliament who intruded so inopportunely
upon the last meeting of the king and queen at Dover.
Sir William was in London, or with the parliamentary
forces; and her majesty established her headquarters
at Boynton Hall on the military principle, no doubt,
that it is permissible in time of war to live upon the
enemy.

It was a veritable general headquarters,—the old hall
in that spring of '43.   Messengers went and came; the
queen sent off and received dispatches to and from the

king, who faced the enemy near Oxford; a great
company of gentlemen of the region flocked to the
hall; and the result of the queen's courageous energy
was a general movement in favor of the king. The
queen greeted every one with warm cordiality and the
sweetest smiles. Arms were distributed on all sides
from her stores rapidly landing, and from what were
called "the queen's pledges" a very considerable ad-
dition to her treasury resulted. These "pledges,"
which are, no doubt, still retained in many families,
were rings, lockets, and bracelet clasps, with the letters
H. M. R.,—standing for Henrietta Maria Regina,—in
delicate gold filigree-work, entwined in a monogram,
against a background of crimson velvet, covered with
thick crystal. These pledges were offered on all sides,
in return for loans. When the king had his own again,
the loans would be repaid on presentation of the
pledges. In this manner considerable sums were
added to the queen's military chest, and the work of
arming the adherents of the king's cause, and of laying
them under contribution too, went on rapidly.

The enthusiasm of the Yorkshire gentry in the queen's
·behalf soon showed itself. One morning came the intelligence that Sir Hugh Cholmondeley had delivered
Scarborough Castle to the king, and the Hothams, who
had shut the gates of Hull on the king, declared for
him.

The popularity of the queen reached its highest point
a few days afterwards, from the performance of an
action on her part equally generous and judicious.

One of the captains of the parliamentary fleet which
had bombarded the queen in Burlington had ventured

on shore near that place, and been seized by friends of the king. Men's minds were too much inflamed then to pay much regard to law and justice. This officer had simply performed his duty to his flag in firing on the queen; but this construction of his conduct had very few supporters. He was tried hastily, by a military tribunal. The act of intending to fire on the queen was or was not proved against him: the point in controversy was quickly decided by ordering him to be taken out and shot.

The queen, ever on horseback now, going to and fro, met the procession. At the head walked the parliamentary officer, with his hands bound, and an armed escort beside him.

"The meaning of this? Stop!" said the queen. "I command here!"

An officer of the royal force approached, and, doffing his beaver, bowed low.

"'Tis the man who trained the cannon on your majesty whilst in Burlington," he said. "The act is proved upon him; he has been tried and condemned—"

"And you would execute him? No! A thousand times no, sir! He but followed his orders. I was an. enemy, and the king's flag was up."

"But consider that this man very nearly put your majesty to death."

"Ah!" the queen said, "but I have forgiven him all that; and, as he did not kill me, he shall not be put to death on my account."

The officer bowed his head.

"Release him," said the queen.

The prisoner's arms were unbound, and he shook

them to restore the circulation of the blood, interrupted by the cords. Then he turned, and fixed his eyes silently upon the glowing face of the queen.

"Thank her majesty for her royal goodness," said the person who had unbound him.

The officer of parliament turned scornfully towards the speaker, and replied,—

"A truce to your advice, my good sir! 'Tis not you who would have spared me. And I thank no one for not committing murder on my person."

A murmur of indignation was heard; but the adherent of parliament laughed derisively.

The queen approached him, still mounted, and, gazing at him earnestly, said, in her low, soft voice,—

"You are at liberty to go whither you will, sir; and what you say is just. You owe me no thanks. You might justly have died cursing me had I permitted this cruel deed. You are an enemy, and a brave one. Pity you cannot be my friend and the king's. But I will not solicit you, save to entreat you not to persecute one who would not harm you when she could."

As the queen spoke, in her voice full of earnest feeling, a flush came to the face of the officer. He fixed a long, searching look upon the face of the queen, opened his lips to speak, but uttered only some unintelligible words; then he bowed low, doffing his round hat, as the queen, saluting him in turn, rode on.

A week afterwards, this officer, with a number of his men, had deserted to the king's standard. I say deserted: it is always desertion to change your flag in face of the enemy, whatever the merit of the cause profiting by your change.

This act of judicious clemency won all hearts, and made the queen warm friends, even thawing the somewhat frigid faces of the ladies at Boynton Hall, who naturally embraced the parliament cause.

These ladies were now subjected to a somewhat rough test of their equanimity. As the queen rose from dinner, on the last day of her sojourn at Boynton Hall, she paused a moment before leaving the room, looked at the table covered with massive silver plate, and said,—

"I fear, ladies, 'twill be thought I am about to make an ungracious return for the courtesies I have received; but unhappily the king's affairs have come to that pass that he requires pecuniary aid. And this," here her majesty glanced at a portrait of Sir William Strickland on the wall, "through the disaffection and want of duty on the part of some of those who ought to have been among his most loyal supporters."

The preface was ominous: the ladies listened in silence.

"The parliament has refused," continued the queen, "to grant the supplies requisite for maintaining the honor of the crown, and therefore money must be obtained by other means. I am sorry thus to be under the necessity of taking possession of Sir William Strickland's plate. But do not regard this as a confiscation of an enemy's goods, ladies, I pray you. I shall consider it as a loan; and, as I trust the king will very soon compose the disorders in these parts, I will restore the plate, or at any rate its value in money, to Sir William Strickland. Meanwhile, ladies, I will leave at Boynton Hall, as a pledge of my royal intention and a memorial of my visit, my own portrait."

At a sign from the queen, the door opened, and two men brought in a superbly-framed life-size portrait of herself. It represented her majesty clad in white, the open sleeves caught up with broad green ribbon, the bodice laced across with gold chains and ornamented with pendent pearls. The hair was short and in frizzled curls, after the French fashion called *tête de mouton.* The back of the head was decorated with flowers, and the dark eyes looked out from the delicate face with an expression of exquisite candor and sweetness.

"I offer this pledge of my intent to restore what I take, ladies," said the queen. "'Tis hard necessity which impels me: I pray you have charity. I am a poor wife only, striving to aid my husband, and that, you know, ladies, is a duty inculcated by Holy Writ."

The lurking spirit of humor in the queen shone from her eyes as she thus spoke. She saluted with a gracious bend of the head, and left the apartment.

At dawn on the next day she was in the saddle, and, followed by her suite, rode down the hill. Boynton Hall was quiet again : her majesty had taken the field.

On a down a league distant, suddenly appeared, drawn up in battle-array, a body of the king's horse. Their arms flashed, and plumes and banners waved. Then a ringing blast from the bugles saluted the queen, and a fiery cavalier, young, superbly clad, and riding a magnificent charger, came on at full gallop. Fifty paces from the queen he checked his horse, throwing him upon his haunches. Then, doffing his plumed beaver, he saluted profoundly, and said,—

"Welcome to your majesty."

"Thanks, my lord of Montrose," was the queen's

reply, as she saluted the famous Scot. "You are from York?"

"With two thousand horse, your majesty, ready to escort you thither."

"Who commands there?"

"The Earl of Newcastle, your majesty."

"I go to supersede him!" exclaimed the queen, with joyous smiles. "See my reinforcements!"

And she pointed to her train following. It consisted of six cannon, two large mortars, and two hundred and fifty wagons loaded with money, plate, fire-arms, rapiers, and munitions of all descriptions, just disembarked from the fleet.

"With your escort of two thousand gallant cavaliers, my lord, I doubt not I shall safely deliver my stores to his majesty."

"Your majesty will move towards York speedily?"

"I will move to-day,—this moment."

"In that case I beg your majesty will enter the coach I have brought for your use."

"A coach?"

"A very convenient one, your majesty."

The queen shook her head, laughing. "I shall not need your coach, my lord: I have taken the field! I am a soldier of the king's, and soldiers do not ride in coaches. See this spirited little palfrey: I am at ease upon him, and fear no fatigue. Shall I boast too that I am as little afraid of an enemy? Should the forces of the parliament attack you, my lord, I will take command of the baggage. You see I am ready. We go by Malton, do we not? Give the word to advance; and God save the king!"

The queen was now in front of the long-drawn column of horse. They heard her words, and as she rode at full speed to the head of the column, Montrose galloping beside her, a thundering shout and the clash of arms was heard. Two thousand men shouted,—

"God save Queen Mary!"

III.

HARRY AND I.

QUEEN MARY rode across the wolds to Malton, and thence towards York, persisting still in her brave resolution to share the hardships of her soldiers.

She would enter no chariot; paid attention neither to wind nor sun nor storm; ate the rude fare of the men, in bivouac among them,—and they came to adore her almost. This delicate woman, lapped in down from her childhood, and accustomed to all luxuries, cheerfully —even gayly—endured every hardship, and marched, and slept, and ate, and was ready to fight too, like the humblest trooper of her forces.

The queen sat one evening in the doorway of her small tent, which had been pitched beneath a large oak, beside the road, in sight of the great camp. Around her majesty were grouped the ladies and gentlemen of her suite, and a number of officers, including the gallant Montrose.

All at once the queen stopped eating her hard bread, and fixed her eyes on some object in the distance. It was a horseman coming at full speed ; and in five minutes he had approached within a hundred yards of the tent, when he threw himself from the saddle, affixed his bridle to a bough, and, drawing near, doffed his plumed hat, making a profound inclination.

I recognized Harry. He had evidently ridden hard ; and, as he came, he drew from his breast a packet.

"For your majesty," he said, bending his knee, and presenting the packet.

The queen caught it eagerly, and said,—

"You come from his majesty, Mr. Cecil?"

Harry blushed with pleasure at this recognition, and bowed low. ·

"He is well?"

"Quite well, your majesty."

"God be thanked !"

She had torn open the letter, and now read it by the last rays of sunset. As she read, her face flushed. Finishing, she raised her head, and her eyes were full of indignation and martial fire. "Do you know the *ultimatum* of the parliament, my lord?" she said to Montrose.

"Submission, doubtless, your majesty," replied the soldier, coolly.

"You have guessed correctly, my lord. Yes, submission. The Earl of Northumberland, the kinsman of Lady Carlisle, who betrayed me, has had the courage and the want of shame to visit his majesty as the commissioner of parliament; and here is the narrative of his errand !"

She struck the paper with her finger.

"'They demand but little!—they are moderate, these good gentlemen! They simply request that his majesty shall abolish episcopacy and the Church of England, and give up to their tender mercies all who have aided him in his rebellion against them."

A growl from the circle saluted these words. All faces darkened. The queen looked around her.

"You see, gentlemen, there is no retreat now for me or for you. We are to die on Tower Hill, or on the field of battle, fighting bravely. Which do you choose, messieurs?"

The words raised a tumult. The queen listened with glowing eyes to the hoarse noise around her. Suddenly she caught, from the ground near, a small dress-sword, and drew it. She wrapped a scarf around the hilt of the bright steel weapon, and attached it to her slender waist. Then, rising, she threw the scabbard from her violently, and exclaimed,—

"Here is *my* answer!"

Two hours afterwards, I was riding towards Oxford beside Harry, who bore back the queen's reply. I had solicited and obtained this favor: to live beside Frances Villiers had become an agony to me. We had scarce interchanged more than a few words of common politeness since the evening at Helvoetsluys: to be near her, even, was wretchedness to me, and I embraced the first opportunity to leave her.

And this voluntary absence from her side now made it necessary to explain all to Harry. To his laughing demand how it was possible that I had courage to separate from the young lady, I replied,—

"Little courage is requisite, Harry. I live in a dream, yonder, near her,—in alternate torpor and fever."

" You have——"

" Yes, and she has rejected me; but that is the least of it."

" Rejected you? Oh, Ned!—my poor Ned!"

" Don't pity me, Harry. I am a man, and hearts don't break in our family on such occasions. Something more than a love-disappointment fevered me yonder."

" More?"

" The thought that you looked upon me, perchance, as a poor weak creature that loved a woman more than I loved my brother or my honor!"

" Your meaning, Ned! Who dares to say that you love not your honor?"

" None, thank Heaven! You least of all must think that, Harry. But listen! you shall know all. 'Tis but recently that I learned the truth. You sacrificed your love to me,—well, I sacrifice mine to you. She told me all. Shame burned in me like fire, brother, when I thought of your last words after Edgehill. Do you think I'll let my brother break his heart for me? I swear I will not! Go and love Frances Villiers more than ever, and tell your love. Women are weathercocks. For myself, Harry, I'll go no more. My game is played,—I have lost her; but I have your love, Harry, and that's enough!"

I think a groan came as I finished. Harry leaned over and put his arm on my shoulder. His eyes shone through a sort of mist.

" Didn't I say that night that I'd back Ned Cecil for a brother against any man in England? Well, brother, we are left to each other. For myself, I've done with the fair Frances, who'll no more look at me than at you, Ned. What bad taste! Well, court her or not, as you fancy,—but remember one thing, brother, she's not going to have an opportunity again of becoming Mrs. Harry Cecil.''

I knew what the words meant,—that my brother would not stand in my way; and I swore to myself that I would not stand in his. I raised my head, after this resolution, and looked at Harry, smiling.

" Miss Villiers won't be annoyed, it seems, by the importunate Cecil family hereafter,'' I said; and then, by common consent, we spoke of other things, riding on through the night.

Running the gauntlet of my lord Essex's cavalry parties between York and Oxford, we finally reached the latter place, and in one of the grand palaces of the grand city saw his majesty again. He was pleased to give me his hand to kiss, and to ask after the health of my father. My detention in Holland had been explained in the queen's dispatches; and now, losing sight of me and all else, his majesty read the queen's response to his letter.

As he read, the pale and melancholy face flushed red, and the eyes grew soft. I see the king's face now,—long, covered with the pallor of trouble, the lips surmounted by the delicate mustache, the royale long and pointed beneath the chin, and the eyes sometimes cold and austere, but oftener full of brooding sadness. "Doomed" was written on that countenance; 'twas only when he thought of the queen that fire came to the eyes, and they flashed.

"My brave wife!" he murmured, as he refolded the letter: "here at least is one heart that does not despair."

He turned to Harry and myself.

"Thanks, gentlemen," he said; "'tis my happiness to have near me friends so faithful as the Cecils. Faithful hearts are pure gold in my eyes, and I lean upon them. The times are dark, gentlemen, the issue of this struggle doubtful; but, if we fall, let us fall with honor,—as gentlemen should fall. That is my resolve. My enemies are bitter. They hate my brave queen even more than they hate me, and were she to fall into their power their mad passion might lead them to take her life, as they may take my own. Well, so let it be: the more need that we should act like brave men. For myself, I mean not to falter. As king, I defend my crown; as gentleman, I defend my wife."

As the king spoke, the door opened, and Viscount Falkland entered, sad, with his air of gracious dignity mixed with melancholy.

"A last proposition, your majesty," he said. "I have just received this note from Mr. Hampden, and beg to lay it before your majesty."

IV.

I GO WITH LORD FALKLAND TO HIS HOUSE OF GREAT TEW.

As Lord Falkland spoke, he approached the king, and, inclining his head with profound respect, presented a letter.

" From Mr. Hampden ?"

" Yes, your majesty."

The king perused the letter, and then, looking up, said,—

" 'Tis a forlorn hope, Falkland : nevertheless, you must accept Mr. Hampden's proposal. Meet him, therefore, with one attendant, as he requests. 'Twere well to be private ; and as these gentlemen present are in the secret, take one of them."

Lord Falkland, who had already saluted, with his air of sweet courtesy, my brother and myself, turned now, and said to me,—

" You have heard his majesty, Mr. Cecil. If it please you, I should be glad to have you go with me."

I bowed low, no little gratified to have my Lord Falkland recall my face and name so long after our chance meeting in Prince Rupert's tent near Nottingham.

" Your lordship does me very great honor," I said, " and may dispose of me now and always."

" The speech of a gallant young cavalier !" was the reply of the nobleman, with his air of smiling courtesy.

15*

"Be good enough to await me in an hour, sir : we will then report."

A moment afterwards, Harry and myself were in the antechamber ; and an hour afterwards, I was riding beside Lord Falkland, who was attended only by an ordinary groom, towards his palace of Great Tew, not far from Oxford.

I shall always recall that ride with one whose great figure illustrated the epoch. His converse riveted me, and was inexpressibly charming. They say now, in this new age, that all men are equal. Is that true? Were there many human beings the equals of this one? Friend, that doctrine of equality is a chimera. Some men are born to command, as to draw all hearts. This was one such, and the mere rank had naught to do with it at all. Edmund Cecil was not the equal of Lucius Cary ; and a thousand demagogues cannot persuade him to the contrary !

"It is needless to make a mystery of our errand, Mr. Cecil," he said. "The worthy Mr. Hampden, of the parliament cause, requests a private interview with me. He is pleased to say that my well-known moderation, and his own sincere desire for peace, may unite to effect something ; and there is this satisfaction in dealing with Mr. Hampden, that one may be confident throughout all of his irreproachable honor."

"I think of him as you do, my lord ; and I once met and conversed with him upon public affairs," I said.

I narrated then my encounter with Mr. Hampden on the high-road in Buckinghamshire ; and when I had finished, Lord Falkland said,—

"I recognize the worthy gentleman there, sir ; and

would to Heaven we could agree upon some terms, and
so end this terrible war. ' Peace! peace!' is all my
lips seem able to utter in these dark days. Our poor,
bleeding country!''

He uttered the words slowly, his head drooping, and
a deep sigh issuing from his lips; and we rode on in
silence.

At last the magnificent grounds of Lord Falkland's
mansion of Great Tew opened before us; and, riding
through a great park full of deer, and dotted with century oaks, towering above us in the sunset, we drew
near the stately edifice. I have seen in my time the
admired palaces of the noblemen of France, Holland,
and other lands; but sure the houses of the lords of
England surpass those of all other countries. In this
new land I pine sometimes for another sight of those
great old houses,—centuries old, built of massive ma-
terial, adorned with lavish splendor,—the abodes of a
race who have struck their roots deep into the soil of
Old England throughout ages,—who raise their heads
like great oaks in the sunshine and the storm, and who
will stand or fall, I think, with the strength and glory
of England.

The broad front of Great Tew, with its mullions,
armorial devices in stone, and battlements, rose fair in
the sunset; and Lord Falkland ushered me in, with
his smile of gracious courtesy, between a double line
of domestic servants, who seemed to crave some mark
of recognition from their master. It was not withheld.
For each he seemed to have a word; and I think he
addressed almost every one by name. 'Twas plain to
me that the master of the mansion was beloved by all

who served him ; and I can scarce convey an idea of
the atmosphere, so to speak, of kindness and affection,
throughout the stately old house.

An hour afterwards, dinner was served, and I had the
pleasure of being presented to Lady Alice Cary, his
lordship's niece,—a charming maiden of twenty,—
whose sparkling eyes seemed to be seeking on all sides
food for mirth or satire. It was the Beatrice of Will
Shakspeare. After an hour with her, I thought he
must have known her !

The interview with Mr. Hampden was to take place
at sunrise on the next morning, at a point designated,
a league or two distant ; and Lord Falkland had just
summoned his head-groom to give him an order, when
a message from the king was announced, and Harry
entered the great reception-room.

" Welcome, Mr. Cecil," said Lord Falkland,—one
of whose winning traits was to know the name of every
one. He extended his hand as he spoke,—the model
of a gracious host,—and then, turning towards Lady
Alice, presented Harry, who bowed low.

" A note from his majesty, my lord," Harry said,
presenting a package, which Lord Falkland opened
and read. Finishing its perusal, he allowed the hand
holding the royal letter to fall over the red velvet arm
of his chair, and, looking down, murmured,—

" 'Twas unnecessary."

I afterwards ascertained that the king had written
to say that in the interview with Mr. Hampden there
must be no manner of discussion on the subject of sur-
rendering any of his friends to parliament. They had
heretofore demanded that he should give up his aiders

and advisers. He wrote now to say, once for all, that he would die, sword in hand, before adding another name to that of Strafford.

"I will reply at once to his majesty, Mr. Cecil," said the nobleman. And, going to his library, he was absent for half an hour, during which time Lady Alice Cary did the honors with excellent grace and ease. What trait is more rare? With two young gentlemen, strangers but now, she was not stiff, but gracious and even mirthful; and when Lord Falkland returned, he interrupted something resembling a wit-combat between Harry and our fair hostess.

But I linger upon this charming evening, the first and last I ever spent with the great Lord Falkland. 'Tis one of the sweetest and saddest memories I have treasured up. You remember the august orb of the sun, slowly sinking in pensive splendor, when you are never to see him rise more on earth.

Harry returned with Lord Falkland's reply; and by midnight I was asleep in one of the great old chambers, full of antique furniture, rich, massive, and used, perchance, by kings in their day. At sunrise I was in the saddle, and riding beside Lord Falkland. The dewy morning smiled upon us; the air was fresh and bracing; the March winds were chill, but the fields were growing green; the first flowers seemed about to peep out from the budding grass.

"See," Lord Falkland said, "the face of nature wears a peaceful smile! What a pity, Mr. Cecil, that men should frown and cut each other's throats!"

"The most piteous of all piteous things, my dear lord," I replied.

11*

"And yet that is what we are doing in Old England now. Men who but yesterday clasped hands, and sat as brothers around the hearthstone, can find no better means of composing their differences than to blow each other to pieces with musketry and cannon !"

"Yonder is one who deprecates that as much as you do, my lord," I said ; and I pointed to a mounted gentleman who sat his horse motionless at a spot where the road we traveled was crossed by another at right angles. Behind this figure was another,—apparently an attendant.

"'Tis Mr. Hampden," said his lordship: "he awaits us."

V.

THE LAST GREETING.

THE two noblemen—they were such, were they not, reader ?—advanced, and exchanged a warm grasp of the hand.

"I am honored by your prompt compliance with the request conveyed to you, my lord," said Mr. Hampden.

"I esteem it an honor in my turn to meet Mr. Hampden," said Lord Falkland, with his gracious courtesy. "I have come with only a single gentleman, —an acquaintance of yours, I think, sir."

"I know Mr. Cecil very well, and would fain call him my friend," said Mr. Hampden.

And he held out his hand to me, a friendly smile

upon his noble face. That smile was extraordinarily
similar to Lord Falkland's. What was it that made
these two men resemble each other like brothers ? I
think 'twas the great soul in the bosom of Hampden,
as in the bosom of Falkland.

They rode aside, walking their horses slowly over
the deserted road, and, reaching a great tree, dismounted and engaged in earnest converse. The distance was not so great that I could not discern every
detail of their appearance. They faced each other,
holding their bridles, and Mr. Hampden leaning one
hand on the pommel of his saddle. With his dis-
engaged hand, Lord Falkland made grave gestures.
The conversation seemed earnest, but slow and almost
solemn. I did not remove my eyes from them. The
personage attending Mr. Hampden was a taciturn
civilian of middle age, whose name I had not heard
distinctly when Mr. Hampden presented him to me.
Thus we remained silent, gazing at our principals.

In about two hours the interview terminated, and
the two gentlemen came back on foot, and leading the
horses, who hung their heads as though saddened like
their masters.

"Well, well, Mr. Hampden," Lord Falkland said,
as he drew near, " God knoweth if good will come of
this free converse we have held; but may he give us
peace. I am a bad ambassador, I fear, sir. I would
fain, were I asked to draw up articles, take a sheet of
paper and write solely the word 'Peace' upon it. That
would sum up all, in my eyes. ' Do not let us wrangle
about terms,' I would say. Hearts opposed to each
other are bitter, and see things in other lights. But

all may see how blessed peace—only peace!—would prove to England. These terrible opposing flags,—only to furl them, and extend the hands of brethren towards each other! The roar of cannon drowns all. Silence that fearful sound, and let us meet with mutual forbearance. For myself, sir, I would give not only my right hand, but my very heart's bloôd, to see the sun of peace—blessed peace—rise over England again!"

As these noble and earnest words were uttered by Lord Falkland, I saw the face of Mr. Hampden flush, and he bowed low with profound respect.

"I recognize in these words the great soul of your lordship," he murmured. "Would to God we had more such men as yourself in England to-day!"

He was silent for an instant. Then he added,—

"What your lordship has done me the honor to communicate, respecting his majesty's views and wishes, will be repeated to the parliament as you desire, my lord. Would to Heaven I could convey to the gentlemen of that body the manner in which your lordship has spoken! I think hatred and rivalry would shrink away before the very tones! Now I will return."

He paused again, and added, quickly,—

"Do you know, my lord, I have a presentiment?"

"A presentiment, Mr. Hampden?"

"That my days are numbered,—that I shall soon leave this arena of contention. Have you never had similar presentiments, my lord?"

"Last night," was Lord Falkland's calm response, and his eyes were fixed gravely upon the face of his companion. "I know not if 'twere a dream or a waking vision," he said, "but I saw myself lying dead upon the battle-field last night."

"Strange!" Hampden murmured: "*my* presentiment came last night too. And I too saw myself fall. Is not that singular, my lord?"

Lord Falkland shook his head with a sad smile.

"Naught is singular or strange to me in this world," he replied. "I believe in presentiments. I believe I shall die soon; and I am not sorry, Mr. Hampden."

He leaned towards the other, and added, in a low, almost inaudible tone, the words, "We shall meet, I trust."

With a close pressure of the hand, the two men mounted their horses, saluted each other, and rode off in opposite directions.

It was their last greeting on earth; but I think they have clasped hands yonder in heaven, the realm of peace.

VI.

CHALGROVE.

My memory is a gallery of pictures, dark or brilliant, gay or sombre. Here is one of them, which I look at through the mists of many years.

It was a night of June, flooded with moonlight; and under the boughs of a great oak, not far from the village of Chinnor, Prince Rupert stood leaning one gauntleted hand upon the pommel of his saddle, and

bending his head as though he were listening. Within
five paces of him stood Lord Falkland,—a calm, sad
figure in the bright moonlight.   From the wood came
the stamping of cavalry horses, beside which stood or
lay their riders, bridle in hand, and ready to mount.

Prince Rupert had sallied out of Oxford, attacked
an outpost of the parliamentary army, and driven the
enemy; had then pushed on to Chinnor, where he
attacked and routed a second force; and now he was
waiting for a brief space that his men and horses might
rest before resuming their march back to Oxford.

Lord Falkland had ridden with the prince, more, it
would appear, from a desire to divert his mind from its
eternal brooding, than from any wish to take part in
the fighting of the expedition.   Indeed, every one had
recently noted in my lord viscount a weary unrest. He-
was sad unto death, and seemed unable to remain in
one place.   His dress was almost slovenly; his fine
person was utterly neglected.   The roar of guns alone
seemed to arouse in him a temporary sort of excitement; and now in every encounter the men saw his
tall form in the midst of the smoke, an idle spectator
as 'twere, giving no orders, unarmed wholly, and inspired, 'twould seem, by nothing more than a languid
curiosity.

Those who knew this great man best, and talked with
him at that time, explained this indifference to me afterwards, and I no longer wondered.   Falkland was con-
stitutionally fearless, and despaired of his country.   If
he did not seek death, he cared naught for it.

As the prince bent his head, listening, the far sound
of hoofs came from his right.   He turned in that direc-

tion, and a flood of moonlight, passing through the dense June foliage overhead, lit up his proud face and figure. He wore his full-dress uniform, and the golden decorations were dazzling. Around his waist was knotted a red silk sash, rich, heavy, and with superb tassels. His sword-hilt sparkled in the moonbeams. On the heels of his fine cavalry boots glittered golden spurs. Such was this young and headlong soldier. From spurred heel to plumed beaver, in eye and lip and attitude, he was all cavalier.

"They are moving, yonder," he said to Lord Falkland, "and I think your lordship will see some more fighting."

"I am sorry, highness," was Falkland's sad reply.

"Well, we think differently, my lord. I am glad!" was Rupert's impulsive reply.

His eyes sparkled as he spoke, and he turned to summon an attendant. The gigantic Hans, his huge black beard grasped by his huge hand, stood like a Scandinavian statue near.

"Hans!"

"Yes, highness."

"I am general——!"

"Yes, sheneral."

"Order the men to mount; and send me a staff-officer."

Hans disappeared in the darkness, and in five minutes the wood resounded with the noise of spurs, stirrups, and broadswords, clashing together as the troopers got into the saddle. At the same moment a staff-officer hastened up, and the prince gave him an order. I had come to report the result of a reconnoissance I had made beyond Chinnor, and was about to go now, when the prince stopped me with a gesture.

"Remain.   My staff-officers are absent, and I need some one," he said, briefly.

The prince then set out at a rapid gallop in the direction of the sound we had heard, Lord Falkland galloping in silence beside him, I following.

As we went on rapidly through the moonlight, the sound in front grew more distinct.   The distant bark of dogs and crowing of cocks mingled with it.

"A man of brains commands the enemy's front," Rupert said, halting suddenly and listening.   "A force of horse is moving to cut me off at Chiselhampton bridge; and unless I can pass Chalgrove before they reach that point, I must cut my way through."

"Your column is moving, highness."

Falkland pointed over his shoulder, as he spoke, to the long lines of the royal cavalry advancing steadily, with their full forage-wagons—the object of the expedition—in rear.

The prince nodded.

"The race is close, my lord, for all that, and not decided yet."

"For the bridge?"

"Yes.   If I knew the enemy's force, I would not care.   My own is small, and theirs may be great.   I may be cut off from Chiselhampton bridge."

"What will you do then, highness? I ask from idle curiosity, merely: we civilians listen to soldiers with respect."

Prince Rupert turned quickly.

"You are no civilian ! You are a soldier born, from

crown to foot; soldier, *soldier*, my lord,—if soldier means the clear brain, the fearless nerve, and the hero heart! Well, I speak as soldier to soldier,—there is no path to Oxford save over the bridge yonder."

"Then——"

"Yes, my lord,—you will pardon my interruption, —yes, I do not mean to surrender, and one thing is always left to a soldier."

"That is—— ?"

"To die, sword in hand," said Rupert, laughing.

As he spoke, he turned to me.

"Order my column to take this road, inclining more to the right, towards Chalgrove," he said; "the men to advance at a steady trot and prepare for action."

He pointed to a country road coming into the main highway. I saluted, went at full gallop to the head of the column, and delivered the order; then I returned to the prince, who was riding rapidly with Lord Falkland over the road to the right.

The quick smiting of hoofs came more and more clearly on the night breeze. The hostile columns were rapidly converging towards Chiselhampton bridge.

"Here is Chalgrove," said the prince, suddenly, as he emerged upon a large field, bathed in moonlight. "If we can pass ahead of them, then we need give ourselves no further trouble. The bridge is gained."

He was not to pass. As the prince, riding a short distance in advance of his column, entered upon the great field, a dark mass was seen advancing from the left to cut him off. There was no longer any possibility of reaching the bridge without a combat. Shouts from both forces were heard,—line of battle was quickly

16*

formed,—and, sword in hand, at a thundering gallop, the opponents rushed together.

It is hard to describe a fight under the daylight,—a night combat is wholly indescribable. Shouts, cheers, the clash of weapons, the crack of pistol and musquetoon, horses rolling over, with wild shrieks, men dying with curses on their lips, in the darkness,—that is the aspect of a night encounter.

The fight at Chalgrove was such. A painter might delineate the rushing, trampling, gleaming conflict; I cannot. For the rest, a few moments after the collision, I kept my eyes fixed upon one figure.

In front of the enemy, and superbly mounted, I saw Mr.—now Colonel—Hampden. I knew afterwards that the move to cut Prince Rupert off was due to his military energy and brain: Chiselhampton bridge he saw was the point to guard: a mounted force was speedily moving; leaving his own infantry regiment, he took command of the horse, and moved so rapidly as to cut off his able opponent Rupert.

The prince, fighting in front of his men like a common soldier, saw the great figure of Hampden.

"Who is that officer?" he said hurriedly to Lord Falkland, who was calmly riding beside him.

"'Tis Colonel Hampden,—God preserve him!"

As Falkland spoke, I saw the figure of Hampden reel in the saddle. He was within ten paces of us, and the moonlight made everything plain.

As he reeled back, his eyes met those of Falkland.

"See! I am wounded—to the death, I fear, my lord," he cried, in a broken voice. "Remember—we shall meet again!"

As Hampden uttered these words, a sudden rush of his own men carried him away. The parliament horse had broken and were flying in wild disorder. When we saw Hampden last, his head was drooping, and he leaned for support on the neck of his horse, two men assisting him from the field. He had received two bullets, we afterwards heard, in the shoulder, the bone of which was broken; and from these wounds he soon afterwards died.

As his figure disappeared in the moonlight, followed by his men in disordered retreat, I heard Lord Falkland murmur,—

"Farewell, Hampden! Yes, we shall soon meet again, I think."

A bugle-note came like an echo. It was the recall being sounded. Rupert moved on to the bridge, crossed, and proceeded on his way to Oxford, after the successful skirmish of Chalgrove field.

A skirmish;—but in that mean little encounter fell one of the greatest men of England.

VII.

NEWBURY.

SUCH is one of the pictures in that long gallery of memory I spoke of.   Shall I try to describe another? The name of the first picture is " Chalgrove;" the name of the second is " Newbury."

It was the dewy dawn of a September morning, and the forests were burning away, flushed with the fiery hues of autumn.   A dreamy and memorial sadness seemed to fill the air, and not a breath of wind agitated the foliage, as the light in the east deepened.   It was an enchanting landscape of field and forest and hamlet; peace reigned over all, as I think it always seems to reign on the eve of battle.   And this day the semblance was as deceptive as usual, for the royal and parliamentary armies were in face of each other, and about to close in in combat.

The king had prospered of late; but the tide seemed turning.   Rupert had stormed the battlements of Bristol and reduced that city; but the king had been compelled to raise the siege of Gloucester.   My lord Essex entered it, but saw best to retreat soon on London. His majesty thereupon followed quickly.   Suddenly the opponents found themselves in face of each other near Newbury.   'Twas the morning of the great battle there that I have tried to describe,—a dreamy morn of

September, when the coo of the ring-dove seemed an appropriate sound, not the bellowing of cannon.

I emerged at full speed from a copse towards the royal line of battle, having ridden as close as possible to the enemy's front to ascertain their position.

" Good-morrow, Mr. Cecil," said a calm voice near ; and, turning my head, I recognized Lord Falkland sitting his horse motionless on a grassy knoll, from which he looked with sad eyes towards the enemy.

I checked my horse and saluted profoundly.

" Do you know that your lordship flatters me very greatly by recalling my face and name?" I said. "'Tis a way to win hearts, were they not already your lordship's."

The nobleman bowed.

" You do me an honor and a pleasure, Mr. Cecil. But why should I not recall your name, and your face too ?"

" I am obscure, my lord ; the king's secretary of state might well lose sight of me."

He shook his head.

" In this world, Mr. Cecil," he said, " there is neither high nor low. Is the worm on a leaf so much higher than one on the ground ? All are poor and insignificant alike. 'Tis the heart that makes the gentleman, not the star on the breast. And is there anything nobler than to be a true gentleman? I know of nothing. To be a peer of the realm is but little."

He turned his eyes towards the enemy, and was silent for a moment.

" I moralize for your amusement, sir," he said, " but

I am somewhat sad to-day. I have been thinking of
poor Hampden and of *our appointment*."

He uttered the last words in a low tone and with a
singular expression.

" You were present at our interview yonder ;—did
you hear our last greeting, Mr. Cecil?"

" I heard it, my lord," I replied, in a low voice.

" And again on Chalgrove field, last June, when that
great man was wounded to the death ;—did you hear
the words he uttered?—'*Remember, we shall meet again !*'
he said ; and do you know I think that meeting will be
soon ?"

He smiled, as he spoke, with the sweet and noble
composure habitual to him.

" See, this is not a fancy of the moment, my friend,"
he said.

And, holding up his arm, he called my attention to
the extraordinary richness of the silk and velvet composing his dress.

" I donned this fine suit," he added, with the same
sad smile, " that the enemy, when I fall, shall not find
me look slovenly or indecent."

" *When* you fall, my lord ! I pray you choose your
phrases in presence of one who ventures to say that his
love for you is great. Say *if* you fall, not *when*, I
beseech your lordship."

Falkland shook his head.

" Do you know the saying of the Orientals, my
friend,—'*The word uttered is the master*'? I have said
' *when* I fall ;' I add ' when I fall *to-day*.' "

My head drooped. In presence of this profound
composure and hopelessness I was powerless to struggle.

"Your lordship smiles," I murmured, at length. "I know, as all England knows, that you are the bravest of the brave; I did not know that so great an intelligence yielded to fancies and presentiments."

As I spoke thus, Lord Falkland turned his head and looked at me with his extraordinary sweet smile. 'Twas a face exquisitely noble that I looked upon at that moment.

"God is good to his creatures in many ways, my friend," he said. "Shall I speak my whole heart, and explain his goodness to me in forewarning me of my death? The moment will be a happy one to me. I am weary of these times, and foresee much misery to my country; but I shall be spared that. My eyes will not see it. I shall be out of it ere night."

I think I must have sighed grievously, for Lord Falkland added, quickly,—

"Do not lament thus, my friend. What is death? 'Tis a bugbear that frightens children or cowards, not men. I fear it not. And yet 'twould be pardonable were I to regret leaving the world. My station in it is honorable; my taste for the pursuit of learning and mental pleasures—the only true ones—is great; my household I believe love me; and his majesty does me the honor to confide in my faith, though I once strove in parliament to deprive him of some powers deemed by him his just prerogatives. I have loved liberty and struggled to secure it. When its friends went farther and attempted the overthrow of monarchy, I left them. In that decision I have never wavered, and think that falling under the royal flag I fall under the flag of England. But I weary you, Mr. Cecil; and, what is worse, perhaps I detain you. You are a soldier on duty; I only a poor civilian wandering to and fro and musing. Farewell, sir! You are young, and God grant you may see happier days. I am not old, but am rather weary of my life. I shall disappear while the sky is dark still, and not see the sun shine again."

I pointed to the sun, which soared at that moment above the forest.

"See, my lord," I muttered, through tears that seemed choking me, "there he is shining."

"'Tis to set soon; and, short as that time will be, I shall not see it."

He turned his horse as he spoke, made me a salute full of gracious kindness, and disappeared in the wood. As I lost sight of him, a single cannon roared across the fields. Echoing shouts rose from the woods far and near as the grim sound was heard; and suddenly Rupert at the head of his horsemen burst like a thunderbolt upon the enemy.

I have no heart to enter minutely into the details of the battle of Newbury. One picture only stays in my memory, and will stay always. Prince Rupert's charge broke the enemy's horse, but they rallied, and again he made a headlong charge. Before this second charge they fled, hotly pursued by Rupert; but suddenly we came upon the enemy's infantry armed with their long and deadly pikes, which pierced the bodies of the horses or hurled their riders from the saddle.

From this hedge of steel the cavaliers of Rupert recoiled. He was forced to fall back, and, riding beside him, I saw his face flaming hot, his eyes flashing. With hoarse and strident voice he endeavored to rally his men. In this he at length succeeded ; and as he formed a new line I heard loud exclamations near.

I turned my head quickly. At the same moment an officer rode up to Prince Rupert.

"Well!" the prince exclaimed.

"Lord Falkland is shot, my lord!"

Without a word the prince went at full speed towards the group pointed out. Scarce aware of the breach of discipline, I spurred from the ranks of the Guards and followed. At the spectacle which met my eyes a groan forced its way from my bosom. The nobleman lay on the sward, his head supported upon the shoulder of an officer. His face was as pale as death, and his breast was bloody. His eyes were closed, but his lips smiled.

"My lord ! my lord ! Speak, I pray you !" exclaimed Prince Rupert, in a broken voice.

Falkland opened his eyes, and, from the position of his head, saw me first.

"Ah! 'tis you who spoke, my friend," he murmured. "Well, see——my presentiment——!"

He ceased, breathing heavily ; but in a moment he resumed :

"I said—my heart bled—for my country, but I would be out of it ere night."

His eyes were fixed upon the blue sky above him.

"Here I am, friend," he murmured ; "I thought 'twould not be long."

I alone knew to whom he addressed those words. As they left Lord Falkland's lips, his head fell back, and he expired. Even in death the noble face retained its expression of exquisite sweetness, and the lips wore the same sad smile.

I   17

The battle of Newbury, like the combat of Chalgrove, decided little, for Essex fell back in the night.

But Falkland was gone—like Hampden ! Who could take their places ? For me, who knew them and loved them as founts of honor, there were no others like them. When they disappeared, I felt as though England were accursed.

VIII.

I MEET WITH AN OLD ACQUAINTANCE IN DISGUISE.

With a single incident in the autumn of 1643 I pass on.

I was one of a mounted party on a reconnoitring expedition south of Oxford, when we saw approaching our woodland bivouac a party of three persons, consisting of a tall sad-looking man and a very beautiful young girl, with the trooper who had arrested them. It soon appeared upon the highway.

As they drew nearer, I rose quickly from the grass upon which I was lying, and looked at them attentively, certain that the man and girl were old acquaintances. The last rays of sunset illumined their figures as they came,—they had now drawn near,—and I rose to my feet, recognizing Gregory Brandon and his daughter Janet.

The terrible headsman, with whom I had conversed on that night of my adventure in Rosemary Lane, seemed older, more melancholy, and more timid.

Janet was even more beautiful; and there was something saintly in the thin face with the white cheeks and great soft eyes. She was perfectly calm; but her father was trembling,—not so much from fear, I think, as from a chronic disorder of the nerves.

The young girl, who was plainly but neatly clad, looked around calmly. Her eyes fell upon me, and were riveted for an instant to my face; then I saw a slight color rise to her white cheeks.

"I see you recognize us, sir," she said, in her low sweet voice. "Please say that we are not enemies of the king, but do not say aught more."

The latter words were uttered in a whisper almost. Her father evidently heard them, for he clasped his hands and looked at me in a most beseeching manner.

"Who are these people?" said the young officer in command of the reconnoitring party.

"Arrested on the high-road, lieutenant," said the man escorting them, touching his hat; "orders to stop everybody and get information; found this old one and young one out tramping, and brought 'em along."

"Right!" said the young officer; and, turning to the headsman,—

"Your name, and where were you going with this damsel?" he asked.

"My name is Gregory, good sir, and I live with my daughter yonder in the small house in the valley; we were returning from a neighbor's when we were stopped and brought here."

"That account is straightforward, friend; but the times are dangerous. You may belong to the other faction; and I will keep you prisoner."

"Not my daughter too, sir!" exclaimed the heads-man.

"Needs must, friend."

The headsman looked at me with a beseeching expression, and I interposed.

"This old man is known to me, lieutenant," I said; "I vouch for him, and propose that you apply the cavalier test."

"Good!—in case you vouch for him, Mr. Cecil; and your proposal is fair."

A flagon was quickly produced by one of the men and filled with wine. This was handed to the heads-man, and the young lieutenant said,—

"What is the health that all good Englishmen drink first?"

The headsman's face flushed quickly, and, raising the flagon, he exclaimed,—

"God save King Charles!"

He emptied the flagon to the last drop, and the young officer clapped him gayly on the back.

"That satisfies me, old man!" he said. "No one can bring out a round 'God save King Charles!' of that sort, and be disloyal under all. You are free, and your pretty daughter. Return home; and as you know this worthy man, Mr. Cecil, I counsel you to go with him and make him give you a good supper in return for your championship."

I was about to refuse, but the maiden Janet looked at me significantly and made me a slight gesture. I therefore saluted the lieutenant, detached the bridle of my horse from the bough over which it hung, and, walking beside the headsman and his daughter, went towards the small house which they had pointed out as their dwelling.

"I humbly thank you, sir," said the headsman, in his earnest tremulous voice, when we were beyond hearing: "you have been kind in procuring our release."

"I try to repay the debt I owe you and your daughter, sir," I said. "But for her, I had perished one night in London. You no longer live there?"

"I fled thence," was the low reply. "My fearful office of headsman became horrible in my eyes. Things are growing frightful, and no one knows whose head may fall."

He groaned as he spoke.

"I know that that others know not," he muttered, in a terrified whisper. "The new leaders are merciless. They are hungry for blood. Already they have resolved to execute Archbishop Laud; and think! 'twas *I* who must perforce, as headsman of London, sever the gray head of that poor old man from the emaciated body! You start, sir, and refuse to credit that, I see!—but even worse may come."

The speaker's voice was wellnigh inaudible as he uttered the last words.

"You are a friend of the king," he whispered: "when you return, say to him, 'Do not fall into the hands of your enemies, or trust them.' The blood of nobles and bishops is not enough to satisfy them."

He turned fearfully pale.

"They thirst for his!"

It was rather an awe-struck murmur than aught else. The thought seemed to overwhelm the speaker.

"So I fled from them," he added, at length; "pike

or dagger at my throat would force me to my terrible
office. For I am a coward, sir,—a wretched coward!
I should not resist them : so I fled from London. Here,
in the small house you see yonder, once my father's,
I have hid myself with my Janet. God grant that we
may lie here unnoted, and that I may not break my
oath!"

I looked at the speaker, whose brow was bathed in
icy sweat.

"Your oath! What oath?" I asked, struck by his
expression of terror.

"The oath of the headsman to perform his office
whenever an order is brought him," he whispered.
"The oath is a fearful one, and binds soul and body.
From the moment the order comes, the condemned no
longer belongs to the law. The headsman enters his
cell, touches his shoulder, and says, 'You now belong
to me!'"

I could not forbear recoiling from the personage
beside me. *He* had thus spoken often.

"You are right, sir," he groaned. "I am accursed,
and dare not offer my bloody hand to an honest man."

The girl turned her eyes swimming in tears upon
him.

"But you will shed no more blood, father," she
murmured, in a broken voice. "The past is fearful;
but it is past, and will never return ; and you have *me*,
father,—*I* will take your hand."

With a burst of tears she caught one of his hands,
and, throwing her other arm around him, leaned sobbing
upon his bosom.

The headsman raised his eyes to heaven.

"Thank God, this is left me!" he said; "the love of the one I love best."

We had come in front of the small house,—a cottage under a large elm near the roadside.

"I will not ask you to come in and sup with the headsman of London," said the old man, in a low voice; "but one is here now, very sick, and desirous of seeing some one from the king's army."

"A sick man?"

"Or child, sir; I know not which."

"His name?"

"He calls himself Geoffrey Hudson."

IX.

ANGEL AND PIGMY.

IN a few moments I stood beside a bed, in which lay the dwarf, who had disappeared suddenly after his fatal duel with Coftangry in Hampton Court Park.

He was terribly emaciated, and resembled a puny infant. His cheek-bones protruded, his sunken eyes rolled in their cavernous hollows, and the white lips drawn tightly across the teeth distorted the mouth into a species of grin.

"Mr. Cecil!" he exclaimed, in his piping voice, as soon as he saw me. "Is it possible an old friend has discovered and visits me?"

"Yes," I said, "by a singular chance. But how do I find you here?"

His explanation was very simple. After the death of his adversary at Hampton Court, he had fled, fearing punishment, and wandered about England awaiting the moment when the fatal duel would be forgotten. He had finally repaired, when the war broke out, to the army of Prince Charles in the west; had enlisted, as a trooper, acquired the friendship of his commander, and was sent, spite of a wound he had received, to carry a message to the king, then near Reading. On the way his wound had broken out afresh; and he had fallen from his horse at the door of the excellent Mr. Gregory: that good man and his daughter had nursed him with tender care; but his wound had not closed, his life seemed ebbing away; good fortune had sent him at last, however, the sight of a friendly face, and the means of forwarding his message, out of date though it must be.

All this the dwarf communicated in a rapid and feverish voice; he then gave me the message, which was no longer of any importance: thereafter we conversed on all the events which had taken place since our last meeting.

During the conversation the maiden Janet passed in and out, caring tenderly for the invalid; and it was after her disappearance on one of these occasions that the dwarf, who had been silent for some moments, said, in a low voice,—

"I wish to live."

I looked at him. His face had flushed.

"You say that in a singular tone," I said.

He hesitated, and seemed anxious, but afraid, to speak.

"This maiden has made me cling to life," he said, at length, in a low voice.

"This maiden?" •

"Yes; I love her with my whole being! I have only lived since we met. You are a friend, even an old friend; I am here dumb and alone on this bed: I must speak to some one of this. Yes, the wretched, distorted pigmy loves this rose-bud, who is an angel!"

The feverish eyes glowed brilliantly.

"She has watched over me like a sister," he went on; "she has supplied all my wants; her white hand has smoothed my pillow, and I have felt her pitying tears fall upon my face!"

"Well," I said, with deep emotion at this love of a deformed being for the daughter of one who was a social outcast,—"well, your love is not strange. This maiden is heavenly goodness in person."

"And beautiful! very beautiful!"

"Yes," I said.

"While I——"

The poor being stopped suddenly. An acute pang seemed to distort his features.

"While I," he added, in a low voice, "am a deformity, a monster wellnigh,—a poor, wretched pigmy!"

He groaned piteously, and went on in a feverish voice:

"And yet how can I avoid this? I am a man, however small I be in stature, am I not? Has not a dwarf eyes, and a heart, and blood, and loves and hatreds? Does the height make the man?"

His face grew savage.

"I have killed many six-footers in my life!" he

I*

growled. "They despised me, but they fell before me; and yet not one of them, not the meanest full-grown man, but would have been preferred to *me*."

I could find nothing to say, save,—

"Do not yield to these sad thoughts: 'twill retard your recovery."

"I care not whether I live or die," said the poor creature, groaning. "Can she ever love me? No, no, no, no! Oh, thank God that you were not born a deformed pigmy!—thank God for your limbs and stature and *human* appearance! You are a man, not a dwarf,—one a woman may love, not a cur she may tread beneath her heel and despise! To love and be laughed at! it is frightful, and drives me mad! *She* does not laugh at me, but pities me, with the pity of a woman for a pet lap-dog!"

His tones were so passionate and pathetic that I could scarce find words to reply.

"At least," I said, at length, "you have no rival; you are spared that. And your love may melt her."

"No rival? How know I that?" he exclaimed. "Even now some one may be approaching who will snatch her from me!—some *man* who will laugh to scorn my deformed anatomy, and take from me all I live for!"

He had scarce spoken when the young girl hastily entered the apartment. "Save yourself, sir!" she exclaimed, addressing me. "I see a party coming who from their uniform must belong to the parliament!"

I rose and put on my hat.

"Farewell!" I said to the poor dwarf, extending my hand. "And do not despair."

His small hand gripped mine, and he drew me down, whispering,—

"You will say naught of this madness. If I recover, I will return to court. If I die, at least 'twill be here."

"I will say nothing; but you will not die."

"Oh, hasten! hasten!" cried the young girl, looking through the window. "They are almost at the house! And there is that terrible man at their head,— that Hulet, who has persecuted me daily, wellnigh, since he chanced one day to come hither!"

I had not time to question the maiden. The party of mounted parliamentarians were nearly at the door. I had just time to seize the bridle of my horse and throw myself into the saddle, when they charged me, firing, and ordering me to surrender.

My response was to discharge my pistol at Hulet and retreat at full gallop. They pursued me to the edge of the woods, where they drew rein at last, returning towards the house; and, going on at a gallop, I met my friends, who had been alarmed by the shots, coming to meet me. No time was lost in pursuing in our turn. Our force outnumbered that of the enemy, and we chased them for more than a mile. Then, however, encountering at least a regiment coming to their assistance, we were compelled to retreat, hotly pursued; and, finding himself powerless to contend with such a force, the officer commanding our party retired to Oxford.

I had caught a glimpse, and only a glimpse, of a singular drama. Other scenes were to be hidden; but a strange chance was to show me the *dénouement.*

BOOK IV.

I.

BEDFORD HOUSE IN EXETER.

THE winter of 1643–44 dragged its slow steps along,—a dreary time to us in camp, for the Guards were now part of the regular army; and the coming of spring was hailed by all with rapture. Regard it in what light you may, war is disgusting when it means "winter-quarters." You mope in your tent, with the rain dripping, dripping; no movement, sunshine, or adventure cheers you; and the jests and old stories become so wearisome at last! Even Harry's charming good humor failed to cheer me.

For a long time now we had not uttered the name of Frances Villiers, nor had we even seen her. Harry never went near her, and I remained as faithful to my resolution. Such was the singular result of the love of two men for a woman. Neither would speak to her,— poor damsel!

So the winter passed away. The king and queen held their court at Oxford, undisturbed by hostilities. Protracted negotiations filled up the time; but these came to nothing: arms, and arms alone, it was seen,

(204)

could decide the great issue. And with the coming of spring both sides prepared to renew the struggle.

The queen's condition forbade her to remain near her husband in the exciting time which approached. She was near that period when the holy claims of maternity render serenity, absence of anxiety, and physical quiescence necessary. It was a long time, I heard afterwards, before the king could persuade the queen that a journey to the west was essential. She consented to this with sobs and tears, and it was the saddest of faces that was seen through the window of the royal coach as it set forward, escorted by his majesty, one April day; towards Abingdon.

I was one of the small troop of Guardsmen detailed to accompany the king and queen. Half of the troop preceded and half followed the three carriages which held their majesties and the ladies of the queen's suite. And among these ladies was Frances Villiers, —calm, earnest, beautiful, devoted, as I had always seen her.

More than once on the journey my eyes encountered her own, but, after the first quiet and gracious salute which the young lady bestowed upon me in response to my own, no evidence of recognition was given on either side. The fair one cared naught for me, or that passionate love of hers for the queen dwarfed every other sentiment.

At Abingdon their majesties parted,—the queen's face streaming with tears, and the king's voice. trembling. For the last time I witnessed that profound and almost passionate devotion of these two human beings. They clung to each other for a moment ; the wet faces

18

touched: a heart-broken sob came from the lips of the queen, and she leaned her head, like a suffering child, on the bosom of Frances Villiers, watching through tears the retreating figure of her husband.

I did not return with the king, but remained with her majesty, in obedience to her commands to that effect. The queen was pleased to say to his majesty, in my presence, that I had proved myself one of the most faithful and devoted of her servants; and I was commissioned by the king to bear a letter from him immediately to Sir Theodore Mayherne, formerly court physician, returning with the great doctor to the queen at Exeter.

On the next morning, accordingly, I set out for the residence of the physician, a country-house in the neighborhood of Salisbury, and, having the good fortune to evade the enemy's horse, found him, and delivered the king's note.

Sir Theodore Mayherne was more like a thunder-gust than before; scowled terribly at me as I stretched my weary limbs in an arm-chair; and his long gray hair was tossed about his leonine head in a more eccentric manner than ever.

"Here's a pretty kettle of fish!" he roared. "A pretty pother her majesty is raising! This is no time to be bearing children! Children! To be plagued with them, when cutting throats is the fashion!"

I knew my host by this time, and only laughed.

"So the note I bring you, Sir Theodore, is a summons to attend the queen?"

"A summons? Yes, it amounts to that. Read!"

I took the paper, and read these words:—

" MAYHERNE :—

" For the love of *me*, go to my wife.

                                        " C. R."

" There it is !" thundered the leonine personage, as I gave him back the king's letter. " ' C. R.,'—*Carolus Rex !* The time comes when men are stripped of their trappings: here is a plain *man* who wants a doctor for his *wife !*"

" So the worthy Sir Theodore Mayherne is one of the godly?" I said, laughing. " I did not know that."

" One of the devilish—if I belonged to the party of such rogues !" growled the physician. " Curse every one ! If there's anything I despise more than a stuck-up, ruffling, dice-rattling court popinjay, it is a psalm-singing, puritanical, hypocritical rascal. Now I'll go."

This eloquent speech seemed to relieve Sir Theodore amazingly. He ordered his carriage, put a change of linen in a portmanteau, swallowed a hasty meal, and— his groom riding my horse—we set out for Exeter. I will not stop to repeat the eccentric physician's talk on the way; and yet it was admirably entertaining. Never have I seen so queer a mixture of traits. In the midst of a tirade of withering scorn and denunciation of something or somebody, he would burst out with a roar of laughter, go on in a strain of the richest and broadest humor, snatch a bottle of wine from the pocket of the coach, thrust the neck into my very mouth, and, slapping me on the back, salute me with,. " Ho, my learned Theban ! drink ! drink !" then take a sip himself, thrust the bottle back, and begin denouncing, storming, growling, laughing again. Never was such a strange mixture; never had profound science and great faculties of head and heart been hidden beneath so strange an outside.

Thus the journey passed, and we reached Exeter, where the queen was to await Sir Theodore. We found that she had just arrived, and had taken up her residence in Bedford House, a large and commodious edifice, where there was ample room for herself and her suite.

What was my astonishment, as the coach of Sir Theodore Mayherne drove into the court-yard, to see Sir Geoffrey Hudson, the dwarf, whom I had last encountered near Oxford, come walking forth gravely from the royal apartments! I afterwards learned that he had been ill throughout the winter, had finally recovered and left the house of the headsman, and on the very day of the queen's departure from Abingdon had presented himself before her, and been received as if naught had happened; and here the pigmy was ushering the great physician and myself into the queen's presence.

Her majesty was seated in a large apartment, attended by only one or two ladies. Her appearance was feverish and excited.

"Ah, here you are, Mayherne!" she exclaimed. "Welcome! you come promptly."

"It is the duty of a physician, madam. What's the matter now?"

The growl had lost none of its force. The physician scowled at her majesty Queen Mary as he would have done at the wife of his groom.

For response the queen blushed, and said,—

"I have a fever. Parting with his majesty was a terrible trial at such a time as this."

"Well, why did you part?"

"He required me to do so; and you know, Mayherne, a wife must obey her husband."

She smiled sweetly as she spoke: the feverish face, with the sparkling eyes and the red cheeks and lips, was very beautiful.

"*Required* her!" growled the physician. "As if with that face a woman doesn't rule!"

"What do you say, Mayherne?" asked the queen, feverishly.

"I say your majesty is sick."

"That is great intelligence, truly!. Oh, I am very sick indeed,—sick in mind and body. I am afraid I shall go mad some day."

"Your majesty need not fear that," growled the cynical personage. "You have been so for some time."

"Out on your abuse of me!" exclaimed the queen. "You are as fierce as a wolf, Mayherne. Feel my pulse."

She extended her hand to the physician, who gazed at her with a singular mixture of satire and tenderness.

"I'll go through no such farce as feeling your pulse," he said. "To what advantage? You are a woman, and your ailment is one that most women have at one time or another,—fever, fits of depression, nervousness, hysterics, fear of mice and spiders. Send away these handsome young maidens around you, madam! Lady Morton can stay, if she chooses: if *she* doesn't object, *I* don't. This is a simple ailment, in which

18*

your majesty is going to be worse before you are better. Send off the maidens !''

The maidens had already scattered in dismay from the apartment. They had an awful dread of the sardonic Sir Theodore, who always managed to say what shocked them. I had witnessed this interview from the doorway, through which the young ladies now vanished. I closed the door, and know nothing further of the interview.

Early in June was born, at Bedford House, the Princess Henrietta Anne.

A fortnight afterwards, her majesty, in her weak and prostrate condition, was informed that the Earl of Essex, in command of the parliament forces, was rapidly approaching Exeter with a view to capture mother and babe,—the queen to be escorted to London to be tried for treason.

Strange and tragic drama! One would think that Fate might have spared the pale young mother clasping the few-days-old babe to her bosom and fondling it. The poorest rests there, and is surrounded by care and tenderness. This mother—so much poorer in another sense of the word—was to hear the tramp of soldiery growling curses and threats against her; was to narrowly evade death; and, more than all, was to be parted in those first sacred moments from her babe!

Make me a tragedy, O poet! I make none: I record simply the memory of what I've seen.

II.

I AM SENT WITH A FLAG TO LORD ESSEX.

THE rumor of Lord Essex's approach was speedily followed by the appearance of his cavalry vanguard on the high hills northeast of Exeter.

I was looking from an upper window of Bedford House, when I saw clear cut against the sky the figures of armed men, on spirited horses ; and these descended, followed by others. In a few minutes a column of light dragoons was defiling into the plain.

I went at once to give information of the enemy's approach to her majesty, and she commanded that I should be introduced into her sitting-room, where she lay upon a couch, holding her babe resting upon her right arm, passed beneath the little one's neck. The attitude of the queen was exquisite, and her pale face was quite illuminated by the charming smile of the mother who looks at her babe.

"You have something to communicate, Mr. Cecil?" she said.

"Yes, your majesty ; 'tis my duty ; and yet I shrink from performing that duty."

The queen smiled.

"I am brave, I think, sir ; not happy in my fortunes, it may be, but not unnerved yet. Speak, Mr. Cecil."

"The enemy are in sight, your majesty, approaching Exeter."

She closed her eyes, and her lips moved. I think it
was in prayer.

"God's will be done!" she said, a moment afterwards; "and I expected this intelligence. Oh that I
had some of the brave friends of the king to go and
meet them!"

Her face flushed, and from the beautiful eyes darted
a sort of fire. It quickly died away.

"I must banish these feelings," she murmured; "I
am no longer anything but a poor mother trying to
escape with my child."

Some moments passed in silence. The queen was
evidently reflecting.

"I must send and parley with Lord Essex," she said,
at length; "the woeful days have come upon me, and I
must act as I best may."

I advanced a step and bowed low.

"If your majesty will permit me to be so bold as to
offer myself——"

"Yes, yes! This is not the time for ceremony."

And, rising to a sitting position, the queen clasped
her babe to her bosom, and said,—

"Yes,—go to my lord Essex; I will give you a line
as your credentials. Inform him of my condition; say
that I am very ill, and that I crave his permission—
hateful, odious term!—Oh, it is too much!"

Her eyes flashed, and her voice shook.

"This is folly," she murmured: "yes, yes,—ask his
august permission that I may retire with my child from
Exeter before the place is invested. I will go to Bristol
or Bath. I cannot bear, in my present condition, the
alarms of a siege."

With a feverish hand she wrote a line on a portfolio which Frances Villiers, at a sign from her, brought and held before her. This she gave me hastily. Half an hour afterwards I was spurring at full speed out of the city, waving a white scarf upon my sword's point, to indicate my errand.

III.

LORD ESSEX.

A MILE from the city I nearly ran into the column of dragoons, whose commander, seeing me approach, ordered a halt. He was an officer in the uniform of a colonel, and said, coolly,—

"You bring a flag of truce, sir. Is it for the surrender of the city?"

I shook my head. "A missive for Lord Essex."

"From whom?"

"From her majesty the queen."

The officer reflected a moment. "Give me the missive."

"I am ordered to deliver it into the hands of Lord Essex."

"Lord Essex is not here present."

"Doubtless, sir, he can be found nevertheless."

"You refuse to deliver your credentials to myself?"

"I obey my orders."

"Right, sir. You are a soldier. Two troopers to

escort this officer to his lordship,'' he added, to a staff-officer.

Five minutes afterwards, I was again on my way,—passing a long column of cavalry. Behind these appeared foot-soldiers. The force was heavy.

At last the men drew rein at the foot of an eminence, upon which I saw a group of mounted officers, and the tall figure of Lord Essex, whom I knew by sight, was seen in the centre of the group. I rode up to him and saluted. He gazed at me with attention, evidently recognized my Guardsman's uniform, and said,—

"You are from her majesty, sir?"

"Yes, my lord."

"I am sorry to hear it," he said, gravely.

"I have a missive from her majesty for the hands of your lordship."

"Give it to me."

He extended his hand, and I presented the queen's letter, at sight of which I saw a cloud pass over his brow.

"This is a wretched business!" he muttered. "I know the contents of that paper, and I do not wish to read it."

His chin sunk upon his breast, and his brows were knit together.

"Her majesty has given birth to a daughter, has she not, sir?" he said, in a low tone.

"Yes, my lord."

"A handsome child?"

"Yes, my lord."

"What name does she propose to give the princess, sir?"

"Henrietta Anne, if I do not mistake, my lord."

Lord Essex uttered a deep sigh, and slowly opened the letter, which he perused thoughtfully, folded up, and placed in his breast.

"I was mistaken: this paper is merely your credentials, sir, and her majesty asks simply a verbal response."

I bowed, and waited.

"I am loath to give it."

He spoke in tones of deep depression, and I gazed at him attentively. The nobleman and the soldier were contending in him, fiercely.

"It is not possible," I said, "that your lordship can refuse the request I come to make,—namely, that her majesty may be permitted to retire with her child from Exeter before the place is invested? She is extremely feeble, since the princess is but a few days old, and the privation and excitement of a siege might be fatal to both mother and babe."

As I spoke, an expression of great pain came to the face of the general.

"Cursed war!" he muttered; "why did I ever embark in it?"

"Your lordship said——"

"That I am powerless,—utterly powerless! I can do nothing! But now came my orders from the people in London! The crop-eared—bah! whose fault is it that I'm here but my own?"

His teeth were set together as he spoke.

"Return to her majesty, and say," he added, "that *Lord* Essex, if he were untrammeled, would send her a guard of honor and his own coach to convey her whither she would go,—that *General* Essex, of the parliamentary forces, cannot grant her request to leave Exeter."

"Your lordship cannot possibly——"

"Act like a ruffian? Yes, sir! I am not Lord Essex; I am a servant of these people, and these are the orders from my masters!"

He flirted at me, rather than presented me with, an official-looking document which he drew from his pocket. I glanced at it, and saw that it was an order to seize the queen and escort her to London, where she was to be tried by parliament for treason in levying war upon England.

The sight of the paper filled me with indignation.

"And your lordship will not disregard this outrageous order?"

"I cannot."

"And yet your lordship commands here: the civilians yonder are a poor set!"

"Sir, I am a soldier: I obey orders!" he growled.

"And her majesty will be tried for treason?"

"You see," he said, coldly, pointing to the paper.

"And his majesty, if he be captured, will he too be tried for the same offense,—the penalty of which is the axe of the headsman?"

Lord Essex turned pale. "Let us terminate this interview, sir!" he said, almost hoarsely.

"As your lordship will!" I said, unable to control my indignation. "For my part, I know the side that, as an English gentleman, I'll adhere to!"

A fiery glance replied to this covert insult; but Lord Essex immediately made me a ceremonious salute.

"Each gentleman decides for himself, right or wrong, sir," he said, austerely. "Say to her majesty the queen that I am pained to refuse her request, in consequence of orders which I am not at liberty to disobey. I am ordered to convey her to London to be tried for treason, to which is attached the death-penalty; and I shall probably invest Exeter before midnight."

I looked keenly at Lord Essex. Was this a notice to the queen to escape? I could not determine, and, bowing, turned my horse's head to ride back.

"A moment, sir," said Lord Essex, approaching me. "Is her majesty in bed?"

"On her couch, my lord."

He hesitated.

"In a condition to be moved?"

"Scarcely," I said, guardedly.

"Because——"

And Lord Essex looked at me, leaving the sentence unfinished. Then he saluted, turned away, and with my escort I rode back, soon entering Exeter again.

IV.

THE FATE OF A QUEEN.

THE result of my mission showed that her majesty could expect no favor from Lord Essex; and preparations were begun with a view to her escape.

There was no choice but to leave the babe behind; and it was long before her majesty could be brought to this cruel resolution.

"My poor child!" she sobbed, with tears streaming from her eyes, "how can I leave you,—perhaps for months,—perhaps for years? Oh, I cannot, cannot!"

She hugged the baby to her bosom, with passionate sobs, and covered its small face with kisses.

"It breaks my heart to leave you!" she sobbed; and then she began to prattle baby-talk to it, holding it tightly to her bosom, and looking at the little round face through her tears.

There was no alternative, however. The child could not possibly accompany her on the arduous journey she must make. And that attempt to escape was a dire necessity. Once captured and taken to London, her fate would decide the fate of the whole conflict. With his queen in the hands of her relentless enemies, the king would yield his crown rather than see her blood flow. She must escape,—leaving her child, against whom no order of seizure had been issued. Perhaps a kind Providence would soon enable her to secure possession again of the infant; and meanwhile the ladies of her suite left with the princess would tenderly care for her.

Night came, and the queen had formed her resolution. She would take one cavalier, one lady of her suite, and her confessor, and steal forth on foot. All her preparations were rapidly made. Her money and jewels were placed in a casket; the whole party were disguised in plain clothes; and, remembering Lord Essex's intimation that the place would be invested before midnight, I hurried the arrangements for the escape. In spite of everything, however, it was nearly daylight before the party left Bedford House. I was witness of the parting between her majesty and her child. I cannot dwell upon it!—'twas agonizing. With a burst of tears, she at length tore herself away, leaving the baby in charge of Lady Morton and Frances Villiers, and, leaning upon my arm, for I had been selected to accompany her majesty, went forth, a lonely fugitive, —worse still, a poor mother without her babe.

We passed the city gates, which were guarded by a sentinel. He permitted us to pass, regarding us, in our plain clothes, as country-people. Already in the east a faint streak of dawn was seen; and at every moment, as we hurried on, I expected to encounter some part of the hostile force. As yet none appeared. Had Lord Essex delayed his advance for many hours after the time announced by him,—" before midnight"? I like to think so.

We pressed on. The light in the east grew brighter. All at once a dull sound issued from beyond a clump of woods which we were traversing, and I said, quickly,—

"That is the enemy, your majesty! We must seek some place of concealment."

"Oh, very gladly!" the queen murmured; "my strength is wellnigh exhausted."

I saw a hut in the wood, not far from the road. The windows had been torn from their hinges, and the desolate appearance of the place indicated that it was uninhabited.

"Here is a hiding-place, your majesty," I said; "lean your full weight upon my arm, and endeavor to hasten."

The queen panted, and I could feel her leaning heavily upon my arm. She clung to me, almost exhausted, and her head half fell upon my shoulder.

"Oh, I cannot go farther!" she murmured; "my strength is quite exhausted. Save yourself!—go, leave me! I will die here."

I drew her on rapidly.

"Come, your majesty!" I said; "here is the hut."

"I can go no farther."

"Then I at least will die with you."

"No, no! I will try——"

And she tottered on. The gleam of arms was already visible through the woods, and I heard the close tramp of the soldiery.

"A few more steps, and we are saved!" I said.

The queen went on with faltering steps, leaning heavily upon me, and we all reached the hut. As we entered it, the head of the enemy's column emerged from a bend in the woods. Had they discovered us? I knew not; but there was the chance of having eluded their observation. The hut was empty, save that a pile of straw lay in one corner. In this I speedily made an opening, begged her majesty to lie down, and covered her with the straw. The maid of honor and father confessor rapidly concealed themselves in the same manner; and, lastly, I made myself a burrow beside her majesty, and hastily covered my person, leaving only a loophole to look through: then we lay still.

I had scarce concealed myself, when the enemy's column began to pass within a few yards of the hut. They were burly, begrimed, close-cropped pikemen, who uttered rough jests to each other as they tramped on by the hut; and many of them turned their heads and looked in, as they passed.

Suddenly the talk of some of the men attracted my attention; and I listened with a sinking heart.

"We are going to catch the Canaanitess at last!" said one, with a laugh.

"The Jezebel!" said another. "It was she who brought arms and money from over seas to help the malignants!"

"We will have her before night," said a third. "Parliament has offered fifty thousand crowns for her head. She'll be in London soon, to be tried for treason; and then hey for the fine sight on Tower Hill! The axe is sharpened already, and Gregory Brandon will make short work of her, the painted French ——!"

Oaths, imprecations, and ribald jests finished the sentence, which was only a specimen of their talk. The queen lay perfectly still. The column tramped on. The day broadened; the hours passed on. Still the army continued to defile by, no doubt slowly in-

vesting the city, in order to shut in the hoped-for
prey.

It was not until night that the troops ceased to pass.
I then cautiously emerged from my place of concealment, and, in a low voice, inquired of her majesty how
she felt.

"Oh, so weary!" she murmured; "but, thank God,
we have not been discovered."

"The enemy have passed on, your majesty."

"Doubtless Exeter is invested."

"Yes, madam."

I could hear the queen weeping quietly; then there
came in a murmur, interrupted by a sob, "My poor
babe!"

"Do not grieve for the princess, your majesty," I
said: "she is quite safe, and will not be molested.
And now I will go reconnoitre."

The result was discouraging. The vicinity was filled
with rabble followers of the army, whose bivouac-fires
sparkled in wood and field. More than once dusky
figures passed near the hut; and finally I was compelled to hastily re-enter my place of concealment.
There, in the pile of straw, the queen and all of us lay
until the next evening,—without food, surrounded by
the enemy,—not daring to move. I have often thought
since of that terrible time, vainly asking myself how
this poor mother, just risen from her sick-bed, sustained
that ordeal of fasting. It remains incomprehensible.
Was it the fever of excitement which bore her up?

At length the welcome shades of night came, and the
vicinity of the hut seemed free at last of enemies. I
assisted the queen from her place of concealment, and

summoned the rest of the party. Their appearance was almost comic. The worthy priest was covered with straw, and the fair maid of honor looked utterly woe-begone.

There was no time now to lose. The queen's destination was Plymouth, where she hoped to find a harbor of refuge; and, tottering on, she managed to proceed, with the support of my arm, over the road trampled to a quagmire by the horses of the army-wagons. At an humble house I managed to secure some food for the party; we then hastened on as rapidly as the queen's exhausted condition would permit; and thus passed the long hours of the night. Towards morning we found ourselves in Dartmoor Forest; here another deserted hut gave us shelter, and, to our great satisfaction, several ladies and gentlemen of the queen's suite, who had escaped in disguise by different gates of Exeter, joined her, and cheered her by intelligence of her babe's well-doing.

Towards evening we ventured forth again, determining to run the risk of encountering scouting-parties. We had scarce started, however, when the tramp of hoofs was heard behind us, and through the twilight a horseman was seen coming on at full gallop.

I drew my rapier, and turned to meet the newcomer, resolved to supply her majesty with a horse.

"Halt!" I ordered, as he drew near; but the rider came on at full speed. I presented my weapon at the animal's throat and prepared to seize the bridle, when suddenly I recognized the dwarf Geoffrey Hudson.

"Ho! ho!" I said; "'tis you, then!"

"With a horse for her majesty," said the pigmy,

leaping to the ground. "I dismounted a six-footer
with a bullet to procure it."   •

And, walking gravely with the bridle of the tall ani-
mal.thrown over his arm, the pigmy approached the
queen, made her a formal salute, and said,—

"I beg your majesty to accept my horse: my cloak
will serve your majesty for a cushion."

He threw the right-hand stirrup over the saddle,
spread his velvet cloak—a mere baby garment—over
all, and, holding the bridle for the queen to mount,
made another low salute.

"You are a faithful friend, Geoffrey," said the
queen, smiling sadly; "and indeed I am exhausted."

I hastened to assist her majesty to mount, and she
uttered a sigh of relief. The poor weary foot in its
half-worn slipper was thrust into the stirrup, I took
my place beside her majesty's rein, and then the whole
party advanced rapidly through the gloomy Dartmoor
Forest towards Plymouth.

It was a strange and silent march, and a strange
party. A queen and a bevy of noble young ladies, in
rough clothing, worn and dusty; gentlemen, once
ornaments of the court, in the garb of plowmen;
and in front of all, striding on with grave dignity, a
pigmy being,—the dwarf,—whose appearance was that
of a babe, save that at his side he wore a good sharp
sword.

We reached the vicinity of Plymouth, but there discovered that the place was dangerously favorable to
parliament. It was necessary to proceed still farther,
in the direction of Falmouth; and, emerging from a
wood, we perceived a large castle crowning a promon-

tory. A countryman passed at the moment, gazing curiously at our party.

"What castle is that?" I said.

"Pendennis," was the brief response. A second question drew forth the information that a gentleman of the royal party commanded at the castle. We hastened on joyfully, were received with enthusiasm upon announcing ourselves, and at last her majesty was in a place of refuge.

"The news from Exeter, sir?" she said hastily to the officer commanding.

"It is regularly invested by Lord Essex, your majesty; but his majesty the king is said to be advancing by forced marches to relieve the place."

As he spoke, the officer looked curiously forth.

"What is the matter?" the queen inquired, with sudden agitation.

"A courier, your majesty, from the way he rides."

And, soliciting permission to leave the apartment, the officer went to meet the man. In fifteen minutes he returned, bearing a dispatch.

"For your majesty," he said, presenting it with a bow.

"Is it possible? How was my presence here discovered?"

"The courier entered Exeter just as the enemy approached the place, and, discovering from some one of your majesty's suite that you had left the city to go westward, followed you, heard of you by the way, and has reached you with his majesty's missive."

"His majesty!" cried the queen; and she hastened to open the letter.

K*

As she read it, her pale face flushed with happiness; then she turned pale, and let the letter fall in her lap.

"Oh, I cannot! I cannot!" she exclaimed.

As she uttered these words, her eyes encountered my own.

"He commands me to sail for France!—to leave England!—him!—my babe! Oh, no! no! I cannot! I will not!"

And the queen began to tremble, her eyes filling with tears. Brushing them away with one of her thin hands, she rose and went to the chamber prepared for her. An hour afterwards she summoned me to her presence, and said, in a broken voice,—

"I sail for France to-morrow,—there is a ship in Falmouth harbor, sent by my son, the Prince of Orange.—His majesty orders me to go,—mark me, *orders* me to go! I dare not disobey him!—My heart is breaking!—Oh, my child! my child! my poor, poor little deserted babe! I will not! Oh, no! no! I cannot! Who would ever think me aught but a wretched, heartless mother! But my husband—he commands me, saying in that letter there that my capture loses him his crown."

The poor queen rose, wildly clasping her hands.

"But to leave my child! my little one but a few days old!—my little babe that looks at me already laughing from her eyes, as though she loved me even now! Oh, what can I do?—My heart is broken!—I can never leave her;—but the king,—his crown—I will—obey my husband!"

The queen tottered, and I caught her in my arms as she was falling.

V.

THE COURAGE OF A WOMAN.

TWENTY-four hours after this scene, the queen, accompanied by her suite, had embarked for France.

A leaden torpor seemed to weigh her down. She no longer sobbed, cried, or exhibited indeed any emotion whatever. Seated upon the deck of the vessel, she looked back towards the English coast, in the direction of Exeter; and we who stood around her dared not intrude upon that august despair.

Others less ceremonious, however, were speedily to appear upon the scene.

The vessel containing her majesty was making straight for the port of Dieppe, on the French coast, and had long left the English headlands behind, when through a slight mist there appeared indistinctly the outlines of several sail,—cruisers, it was feared, under the flag of the parliament.

The commander of the queen's vessel carefully reconnoitred through his glass, and then, closing it, announced that this fear was correct. His only hope now was to pass them unseen, or uncared for, and he crowded on all sail for that purpose.

Suddenly an ominous "boom" echoed from the fog, and a cannon-shot passed in front of the vessel, dipping and disappearing.

It was the signal to stop. The commander looked at the queen.

"That is an order to heave to, your majesty," he said.

"Well, sir?" said the queen, in a low, monotonous, apathetic voice.

"I await your majesty's orders."

"My orders?"

"Shall I proceed, or obey the signal, your majesty?"

"Proceed."

The vessel continued its way, dancing upon the waves, now rising before a fresh gale, and dashing the foam from her cutwater.

Suddenly a second shot came, and this time it passed over the deck of the vessel.

"This is becoming somewhat dangerous for your majesty," said the captain. "What shall I do?"

"I am ordered by my husband," said the queen, in the same low, monotonous voice, "to leave England to avoid capture, and sail for France."

The officer bowed low.

"Your majesty's order agrees with my own wish. I will then continue my way."

"Do so, sir."

A third cannon-ball passed like a sea-gull at the instant, and one of the sailors who was leaning over the gunwale was hurled, a mangled corpse, into the sea. The captain looked at the queen.

"Go on, sir," she said, coldly.

The pursuers now commenced a rapid and continuous cannonade. The balls passed to the right, left, and through the rigging of the ship. At every instant those on board expected her hull or masts to be struck ; and the chasing vessels seemed to gain on her moment by moment. Ever nearer and nearer came the now frightful roar of the big guns ; the cannon-balls of the enemy skimmed the deck, or tore their way into the hull.

The captain hastened to the spot where the queen sat beside the helmsman. His face was flushed now, and he had evidently had aroused in him the ire of the sailor who sees his craft in danger of destruction.

" Shall I return the fire, your majesty?" he asked. "I hate to see my ship cut in two by these people, and I have a gun that will send back a good ball and make them keep a little farther off, perchance."

The queen raised her dull eyes.

" You wish to fire?"

" Yes, your majesty."

" I forbid it. Time would be lost. I wish to escape."

The captain saluted.

" Your majesty's order will be obeyed, and any others she may give."

He waited.

"You desire my orders, sir?" the queen said, still in the same apathetic voice.

"Yes, your majesty."

" Set every sail."

" It will be dangerous, your majesty. Look! yonder comes a storm. "

He pointed to an inky cloud, heralded by gusts which struck the vessel, almost drowning the roar of the cannon.

" Set every sail, in spite of the storm," the queen replied. " I am ordered to escape."

"And if the enemy come up with us, or disable my vessel,—what orders then, your majesty?"

"Fire the powder-magazine and blow up the ship," said the queen. "I do not mean to be taken."

And she sank again into apathy; but the expression of her countenance indicated clearly that she was profoundly in earnest in giving the order.

The captain saluted and turned from the queen. At the same instant a cannon-ball cut the mainmast in two, and it fell over the side, with sails and rigging. The ship shuddered through every timber, and the huge mast, held by the rigging, became an enormous battering-ram, hurled at every instant against the vessel's side by the waves now lashed to storm.

"I think the time has come, your majesty," said the captain. "We shall be captured in thirty minutes, if we do not sink."

"My order remains unchanged," the queen replied, coldly.

"Your order—— ?"

"To blow up the ship."

Suddenly a cheer from the crew was heard. The captain turned quickly. A mile to windward, three or four vessels were rapidly bearing down, and the French flag was plainly made out. They quickly approached, and the crew uttered a second cheer. The parliamentary ships had drawn off, and a gun only at long intervals now indicated that they had given up the pursuit.

The queen had not moved or spoken. As the storm drove the disabled ship towards the French coast, now in sight, she continued to gaze out upon the waters towards England with the same despairing apathy. It was only by the happiest chance at last that the vessel reached a cove in the rocky coast. There the queen entered one of the boats, and was tossed on the summit of the great waves towards the shore. All at once the boat grounded, and I leaped into the sea. The queen rose at my signal, I took her in my arms, after the sailor fashion, bore her to shore, and deposited her upon the rocks wet with spray and sea-weed. The rest landed, and, with the members of her suite, the queen wandered along the shore, seeking shelter from the storm. This we found in an assemblage of fishermen's huts; and a messenger was sent thence to the château of a gentleman in the vicinity to announce the presence of the daughter of Henry IV. on French soil.

The intelligence spread like magic, and the rude fishermen's village was soon crowded with the coaches of the neighboring nobility, eager to succor the English queen thus thrown upon French hospitality. She left the village in one of these chariots, and was graciously pleased to signify her wish that I should occupy a seat in the same vehicle.

"Well, Mr. Cecil," she said, as the coach rolled on, "God has mercifully preserved us."

She spoke in the same sombre voice; but I could see tears in her eyes now.

"From the storm, your majesty, and the enemy: that is doubtless your meaning?"

"Yes, and from my wicked self too. I have been thinking of my child, and of my sinful order to blow you all up in the ship. I had no right to give such an order; and yet I gave it calmly and meaning it. I can now accuse myself of want of moral courage to master my pride; and I give thanks to God for having preserved me at the same time from my enemies and from myself."*

Her head sank as she spoke, and gradually tears gathered in her eyes and rolled slowly down her cheeks.

"My poor husband!—my poor, poor little babe!" she sobbed. "Oh, when, when shall I ever see them again?"

VI.

MY PROMISE.

THESE events took place in the month of July, 1644.

In the autumn of the same year I was back in England, bearer of a private dispatch from her majesty, then at the baths of Bourbon, to his majesty the king, then in the neighborhood of Oxford.

I need not speak in these memoirs of my brief stay in France at that time, any more than I did of my sojourn in the Low Countries. This volume strives to depict incidents occurring on English ground; and accordingly I pass to the moment when I again trod the beloved soil of my home-land.

The times I found more than ever "out of joint." The struggle between king and parliament had steadily become more bitter and envenomed. It was now a

---

* Her majesty afterwards used nearly these same expressions in speaking to her friend Madame de Motteville, as may be seen in that lady's Memoirs. " I did not feel any extraordinary effort," she said, " when I gave the order to blow up the vessel."

conflict of life and death ; and during my absence at
Exeter with her majesty, disastrous events had taken
place for the royal cause. Early in July was fought the
great battle of Marston-Moor, where, against the protest of my lord Newcastle, his highness Prince Rupert
attacked the enemy and was badly beaten. Later in the
same month, York surrendered to the parliament. In
October the king sustained a second defeat on the old
ground of Newbury, and, save that Lórd Essex was
defeated in turn with the force he commanded in
Cornwall, no gleam of light came from any quarter
to cheer the adherents of his majesty. Shut up in the
city of Oxford, deprived of the consolation of the
queen's presence, seeing all around him evidences of
failing fortunes, the king had little to cheer him, and,
when I saw him first after my return, seemed plunged
in melancholy.

He received me in private audience, and questioned
me minutely as to the health, spirits, and surroundings
of the queen. I informed him upon all points, and
gave his majesty a detailed account of her strange
adventures at Exeter and on the sea. As I spoke, his
pale cheeks filled with blood, his eyes flashed, and he
exclaimed,—

"''Twas like her ! Brave and true ! brave and true !''

His majesty was pleased then to express his satisfaction with the humble part I had borne in the escape of
the queen, to declare his confidence in me, and to dismiss me with expressions of his royal regard.

As I issued from the royal presence, Harry met me,
arm in arm with the gay young Frank Villiers, whose
blue eyes gave me friendly welcome. We all went to

the quarters of the Guards, now on duty at Oxford. My old friends received me with an ovation, and during the winter I remained at Oxford, dreaming of Frances Villiers and wondering where she then was. The victim still of my old passion, I could not banish her from my mind. But I never spoke of her to Harry, fearing to arouse old memories. He was equally reticent: her name was never uttered by either of us. I knew not whether he still pined for her, and could only resolve to adhere to my resolution not further to prosecute my suit.

Spring came, and both sides assembled all their forces. Fairfax was appointed general-in-chief of the parliamentary troops. Under General Fairfax nominally, but in reality over him, was the cold, resolute, ardent, explosive General Cromwell. He it was who now came to put the *coup de grâce* to his majesty's fortunes. Intellect governs the world; and 'twas the brain of that single man that shaped the history of England. Of the loose and disjointed armies of parliament he made one great engine: the troops became inspired with his own indomitable will to conquer: his pikemen marched to battle chanting uncouth psalms, despising death and wounds, raised by that afflatus above care for life. In the person of the plain countryman whom I had met at Mr. Hampden's in Buckinghamshire, now become the supreme ruler of the minds and hearts of his men, the troops had found their master and the name that led them to victory.

'Twas a strange fanaticism, that of the puritan soldiery then,—those "Independents" advancing re-

morselessly over church and king. I will not laugh at
it: 'twas grotesque, but terrible too. I pass on to events.

June of the dark year 1645 arrived, and the flags of
king and parliament fronted each other on the soon-to-
be-famous ground of Naseby.

Harry and I were lying in our tent on the night
before the battle, and, as the long hours went on, we
remained awake, talking of a thousand things. At last
our talk came to concern one subject alone,—Frances
Villiers and the love we bore her. Harry laughed
rather than replied to me, and I loved him more than
ever for that. Convinced that his passion was unchanged, and penetrated to the heart by that great
wealth of brotherly love which thus surrendered the
dear object to his rival, I saw in his laughter but a
new evidence of his noble delicacy, but proof of the
fact that he wished to make light of his great sacrifice.
The thought brought tears to my eyes.

"You shall not find me less magnanimous than
yourself, brother," I said.

"Pooh, Ned!" was his gay reply, "go on and court
the fair one. Why not?"

I rose on my elbow from the camp-couch, and, with
flushed cheeks, said, in a low tone,—

"I will not! Never will I utter word of love whilst
I am my brother's rival!"

Harry laughed aloud thereat, and said,—

"Suppose I go under to-morrow, old fellow?"

"No matter!" I cried: "I have promised! Whether
you pass unharmed or fall, my word is given: until I
obtain my Harry's permission I swear I will never utter
love-word to Frances Villiers!"

As I spoke, the sudden sound of a trumpet was heard without, and footsteps hastening to and fro, mingled with the neighing of horses. A sergeant put in his head.

"To horse, gentlemen!" he cried; for it was the fashion in the aristocratic corps of the Guards to observe this courtly and very unmilitary mode of address.

Harry sprang up. "What's the matter?" he cried.

"The enemy's horse threaten the train," was the reply.

The trumpet sounded more shrilly the call "Boots and saddles!"

In ten minutes we were mounted, and, commanded by Prince Rupert in person, were moving rapidly to the point of danger.

The parliament horse had indeed advanced to attack the king's trains, but at our appearance they gave up the design, and retreated, skirmishing, to their main body again.

The day dawned as we fell back; and soon the sound of martial music indicated that the camps were astir.

The king was forming his line of battle. As the sun rose he was ready.

The disastrous day of Naseby had come.

VII.

THE LAST HOPE OF THE KING AND OF THE CECILS.

I SHALL speak but briefly of the tragic combat of Naseby. For long a curse seemed to weigh on the very name, to me; even now, I wellnigh shudder when 'tis pronounced.

The king commanded his army in person,—Prince Rupert leading the right, Sir Marmaduke Langdale the left. On the enemy's side, Fairfax was the general-in-chief; and his right was led by General Cromwell, his left by Ireton.

Rupert opened the battle, as was habitual with him, by a cavalry charge. He rushed upon Ireton, and to that resolute officer I found myself personally opposed. A brief sword-encounter followed, and I was near disarming him.

"Surrender!" I cried.

"Never!" was his gallant reply.

With a sweep of his broadsword he cut the feather clean from my hat, and it is probable that I would have fared badly in the encounter, when a trooper ran his weapon through his thigh, and he was taken prisoner, still fighting and refusing to surrender, like the brave man he was.

Rupert had meanwhile pushed on, driving the enemy's left before him. It was the strange fate of this head-long cavalier to defeat the enemy always at the outset, but ever by some blunder to lose all the fruits of his victory. Such was the event now at Naseby. The enemy's left was routed and driven. The prince could fight, but could not command : he stopped to summon the enemy's artillery to surrender before charging it ; thus precious time was lost, and the golden moment passed. A deafening shout from our left and rear attracted all eyes to that quarter.

The spectacle was terrible.

As Rupert charged, the king had advanced his whole line, leading it in person. Mounted upon a superb charger, his head bare, and waving his hat, his majesty rode in front of his line, exposing himself to the heaviest fire, and calling upon his troops to follow him. They responded with cheers, and in a moment the opposing lines clashed together. Before the royal charge the parliament forces gave back, as before Rupert ; but suddenly there appeared upon the scene that terrible new element, the "Independent" pikemen of Cromwell. These now advanced, slow and stern as an incarnate Fate. Nothing stood before the surging hedge of steel ; the triumphant royalists were first checked, then forced back, then broken wellnigh to pieces : the whole left wing of the king was crushed by this irresistible weight of pikes.

We saw this, we of the Guards, from a distance, and heard the fierce shouts. Prince Rupert understood all, and his eyes blazed as they witnessed the spectacle. I was near him, and our eyes met.

"Go to the king ! go to the king !" he cried, "and say I will be with him instantly !"

I saluted, and wheeled my horse.

"Stay! Take Hans with you. You may be shot. Say I will come instantly."

And, turning to the gigantic corporal who always rode near him, the prince exclaimed,—

"Go with him."

At the word, the huge black-bearded Hans thundered to my side.

"I gome mit you," he said, drawing his sword, and putting spur to his horse. Without a word, I went back at full speed, and we were near the king, when I saw my companion reel.

"You are shot!" I cried.

"*Hilf Himmel!*" escaped from the giant's lips. Then he raised his huge hand to his breast, threw back his head, and, falling from his horse, was trampled under the iron hoofs.

I had no time to aid him, even had not a glance told me that he was dead. I spurred straight to the king, who was fighting in the midst of his men. He saw me coming, and exclaimed,—

"Where is the prince?"

"He bids me say he will be with your majesty instantly."

"I fear 'tis too late; the left wing is broken."

The tumult drowned his voice, and the king continued to fight personally, like a private soldier, careless of all peril. I was near him, and now witnessed a still more tragic event. The hedge of steel slowly moved, as on a pivot, and enveloped the king's left. Stern and menacing swept round the immense wall of pikes, and through the smoke I saw their commander, the thenceforward terrible General Cromwell. He sat his horse perfectly motionless, in front of his left. No statue could be stiller, and he resembled rather a bronze or stone figure than a man. From time to time his lips moved, and a brief command seemed to issue from them. Otherwise the man was even fearfully cold and immovable,—a Fate incarnate.

Suddenly Rupert appeared, and I wheeled my horse and joined my comrades. Without a word, and seeing all at a glance, the prince charged straight on the hedge of steel. It did not move: the horses impaled their chests on the sharp steel points, but made no opening. Then I knew that all was over: the terrible wall was closing around us; nothing was left for the followers of the king but to die, sword in hand.

I had faced that conviction, and set my teeth close for the event, when Harry, covered with dust and blood, rushed past me on his superb courser.

"Come on, Ned!" he shouted, waving his sword, and laughing; "there's time yet ere sunset to drive these carles back!"

I spurred to his side.

"The day is lost, brother, but we can die here," I said; and we charged side by side.

A moment, and all was over. A pike pierced the chest of Harry's horse, and the animal reared and fell backward. At the same instant my own horse was wounded and recoiled. Harry's sword cut the air; I heard him utter a defiant shout; then he was hurled to the ground, and a pike was driven into his breast.

The awful sight unmanned me, almost. A second cry—of agony this time—burst from my lips. I seemed to see for an instant, through the cloud of smoke, the dying face of my brother; his eyes turned upon me for the last time. Then a hot iron seemed to pass through my breast,—a bullet had struck me,—and I reeled in the saddle. My bridle was violently grasped by the pike-man in front of me; I could make no resistance; but suddenly my horse tore away from his assailant, turned, and lashed out with his heels; the man was hurled back by the iron feet, and I found myself—faint, reeling, senseless almost—borne, at a swift gallop, back to the king's line.

I ran almost against his majesty. He was bareheaded; his eyes flamed. With clothes covered with dust and grimed with smoke, and cheeks which seemed on fire, he drove into the midst of the combatants, waved his sword above his head, and shouted, in hoarse tones, which echo still in my memory,—

"One charge more, and we recover the day!"

A roar drowned his voice, and there was scarce more than a feeble cheer in response to his shout. The day was decided: all felt that Cromwell's terrible pikemen, advancing resistless as fate, would bear down all before them. No further stand was made; and the royal forces were seen on all sides retreating in disorder from the field.

I was tottering in the saddle, and through the mist before my eyes I could see but little. I made out, however, in that cloud, one face, over which was spread the pallor of despair. It was the face of the king, who had checked his horse and sat looking with a sort of stupor upon the scene before him. He sat thus for a moment only. Two noblemen seized his bridle and bore him from the field at a gallop.

L   21

Unconsciously I followed ; leaning upon my horse's neck, faint and dying almost, I went on at full speed. After that I remember only confused cries, the clash of arms, the roar of guns in pursuit. Then green woods were around me, the noises died away, darkness seemed to descend upon me, and I lost consciousness.

VIII.

BACK TO CECIL COURT.

WHEN I fully regained my senses, and realized my actual whereabouts, I found myself lying in my bed at Cecil Court, with the eyes of my father and Cicely fixed upon me.

"Thank God!" exclaimed my father, drawing a long breath, "the fever has taken a turn at last."

Tears came to his eyes, and Cicely threw herself, sobbing for joy, upon her knees, and pressed my thin hand to her lips.

From that moment I began to convalesce, and was soon informed of my own adventures after the battle. Frank Villiers had come up just as I was falling from my horse, and had managed to secure a hospital-wagon flying wildly from the field. In this I was placed. A considerable sum in gold had bribed the driver to convey me to Cecil Court. I had arrived raging with fever. For months my life had been despaired of, for a bullet had passed through my chest ; but finally youth and health had conquered, and I rallied from the very brink of the grave.

It was to find the arms of my father and sister around me, but to realize that the royal cause was lost, and that our brave, our dear Harry was forever taken from us. His last charge and his fall had become known at Cecil Court, and the woeful duty devolved upon me now to relate the particulars. I did so, in the midst of sobs, and with a great gush of tears from my own eyes. Father and sister wept in silence. Cicely drew close to me, kissed me, and murmured,—

"You alone are left us."

Months passed on, and I grew stronger. Finally I left my sick-bed and began to totter about the house. A hopeless sadness had taken possession of me. I scarce gave a thought to the fate of the cause I had fought for, thinking only of my brother and his dying face.

A languid interest in public affairs came finally to dispute this possessing thought. Naseby had ended the struggle. Soon thereafter Prince Rupert surrendered Bristol, for which, 'twas said, the king had disgraced and banished him. Then his majesty took refuge with a remnant of force at Oxford. Then he fled to Newark, delivering himself up to the Scottish army.

It was not until late summer that I was able to leave the house and move slowly about the grounds at Cecil Court. No one molested me. Sir Jervas Ireton's flaming loyalty to the parliament had secured him an official appointment in London; and no one in the vicinity seemed disposed to harass the poor wounded officer. Still, there was no certainty that, at any moment, I would not be arrested. I was therefore anxious to leave Cecil Court and not compromise my father. Whither I should go was a difficult question. But I could find a refuge somewhere. And it was just at the moment when I heard that Sir Jervas Ireton was coming down from London that an unforeseen incident occurred which was to send me forth again upon the stormy waters of that troubled epoch.

IX.

I GO TO CHARLECOTE AND MEET WITH AN ADVENTURE.

THE incident which I shall now relate leads me to speak of a spot connected with a very great writer. I mean Charlecote, the residence of the Lucy family, near Cecil Court,—Charlecote, where Will Shakspeare was seized by Sir Thomas Lucy for trespassing on his park and shooting deer.

As this adventure has been discredited of late days by some persons, I will stop here in my narrative to briefly record the actual truth. 'Twas vouched for to my father by no less a personage than Will Shakspeare himself. And this is the story told by the great play-writer, laughing over his wine at Cecil Court. The knight's gamekeeper, a huge, black-bearded individual, had really seized him, he said, whilst trespassing one moonlight night on Charlecote Park to shoot the deer.

'Twas in company with some roystering young blades of Stratford, and the affair was a mad frolic; but it speedily became serious. Shakspeare shot and killed a stag with his old matchlock, and alarmed the game-keeper. At his approach the party fled; but Shak-speare's foot caught in a root, and he fell. Thereupon the gamekeeper darted upon him, pinioned his arms without difficulty, as he was a mere boy and powerless in his opponent's hands; and, after a night's imprison-ment in the gamekeeper's lodge, he was conducted before Sir Thomas Lucy, who had been notified of the fearful outrage upon nis rights of landed proprietor. My father described the account given him by Shak-speare as excellently entertaining. The irate knight, Sir Thomas Lucy, he said, sat in awful state in his great hall at Charlecote, and listened in stern silence to the animated harangue of his gamekeeper. There was no doubt of the youth's guilt: he had been caught in the act, and the dead deer lay on the floor. The knight gazed on the beardless culprit, burst forth at length into an address full of rage, and swore that but for the respectability of his father, John Shakspeare, he would put him in the stocks. He was finally discharged, the knight declaring his intention of proceeding regularly against him for trespass. And, not liking the aspect of affairs, Shakspeare determined to go with one of his wild companions to London. He did so, began writing for the stage, acquired great fame, and when afterwards he met Sir Thomas, now a gray-haired man, said, laughing,—

"See, Sir Thomas! 'tis your fault that an excellent poacher has become but a poor writer of plays!"

21*

Such had been the incident which attached an historic interest to a plain old manor-house. 'Tis the fate of places and personages connected with great men to become famous. .Doubtless, outside of Warwickshire no one had ever heard of Charlecote had not a scapegrace shot deer there and afterwards written *King Lear* and *Hamlet*.

Well, to come back now to myself and my own adventure at Charlecote.

Lady Lucy, the wife of Sir Thomas, son of the old knight, was my firm friend; and one of the first houses I visited, as soon as I rode out for exercise, was Charlecote. It was a beautiful day of summer when I entered the great park and walked my horse slowly up the long avenue of century elms and oaks. The old park was exquisite, and quite charmed the eye. The Avon makes a bend there, and runs through the grounds, sweeping around the base of a grassy hill. Some stately swans were sailing majestically upon the surface of the stream, deer were seen stealing away through the vistas in the trees, and the rooks were cawing dreamily in the summits of some great elms, where they had built their nests, year after year, for more than a century, 'twas said.

I approached the old mansion,—which was of the Elizabethan style, with stone groins and shafts, lofty casements, and armorial bearings cut over the gate,— entered the little court-yard, where beds of brilliant flowers delighted the eye, and, giving my horse to a groom, entered the great hall, with its rows of family portraits in stiff ruffs and powder, and thence to Lady Lucy's drawing-room, where I was received most graciously.

Sure, naught on earth is more charming than the sympathy of woman. Lady Lucy smiled with an exquisite sweetness as she greeted the poor pale soldier, pressed my hand with affectionate warmth, and an hour passed, full of sunshine and sympathy.

At last I rose to go, and had taken my hat and gloves, when the door, which stood ajar, was thrust open by some one, and I saw a child standing on the threshold and looking in furtively. It was a little beauty,— a girl with rosy cheeks, bright eyes, and profuse brown curls, about two years of age, and full of health and joy.

I was about to ask the name of this child, for Lady Lucy had none, when her ladyship rose hastily, exclaiming,—

"Run away, my child! You must not——"

The caution came too late. The little girl ran to the lady, caught a fold of her dress, looked furtively at me for a moment, then gradually approached me, grasped with her tiny hand the feather trailing from my hat, and, raising her brilliant brown eyes to my face, said, in baby patois,—

"What dat is?"

"It is a feather, my child," I said, smiling. "And now, can you tell me your name?"

Instead of doing so, the little one continued to regard with the deepest interest the plume depending from my beaver.

"Your ladyship has a charming little relative there," I said, smiling; "but do you know I have not yet had the honor of an introduction? A sweeter face I never saw, I think, with its bright eyes and curls."

Before Lady Lucy could reply, the little maiden

wheeled, and ran to and fro, singing. The song seemed suggested by the word "curls," which I had used: it was a baby lyric, delivered with baby pronunciation, and was word for word what follows:

> "There was a little *durl* [girl],
> And she had a little *turl* [curl]
>   Wight in de middle of her *for'wid;*
> When she was good,
> She was *vewy, vewy* good,
>   And when she was bad she was *ho'wid!*"

"There, there, my child! the servants have taught you these foolish songs," said Lady Lucy; "that is enough! Run away now!"

"Not before I know the name of my little friend," I said, puzzled by Lady Lucy's persistent avoidance of that point; and, smoothing the child's curls, I asked, smiling,—

"What is your name, little one?"

"Henwietta Anne."

The name struck me suddenly. It was that of the queen's child born at Exeter. I looked quickly at Lady Lucy.

"Do not ask me anything!" she exclaimed. "You are a friend of the good cause—I rely upon you; but this is not my secret: not even to you may I——"

"You may venture to tell Mr. Cecil our secret, Lady Lucy," came in low tones from without the door: "he has seen the princess before,—soon after her birth, at Exeter."

And Frances Villiers, mild, calm, queenly, with her air of unmoved sweetness, glided into the room and saluted me.

X.

THE FLIGHT FROM CHARLECOTE.

THIS unexpected encounter with Frances Villiers astonished me beyond words; but the young lady soon explained all, and I shall sum up her explanation in a few sentences.

The king, when informed of Lord Essex's advance upon Exeter to seize the queen, had hastened by forced marches to relieve the place. This he had effected. Essex retired before him, and the king, entering the city, embraced at Bedford House the poor child, to whom he gave the name Henrietta Anne, as the queen desired. Compelled then to take the field again, he left the babe at Exeter, in charge of Lady Morton and Frances Villiers; and there the child remained until the decisive battle of Naseby. Thereafter she was not safe; and, as Lady Morton was very ill, Frances Villiers took entire charge of the child, flying first to the house of one friend of the royal cause, then to another. Thus, in course of time, she took refuge at Charlecote,—the Lucy family being relatives of the Villiers and warm friends of the king. Here the young lady and child had now been for many months; but the time had come when they would be compelled to seek a more secure hiding-place. All this Frances Villiers related in her calm, composed voice, which made the strange romance of the whole

L*

affair seem the most commonplace series of events in the world.

"And what, if I may ask, is your intention now, Miss Villiers?" I said.

"To leave Charlecote, and, if possible, England, sir. This neighborhood is not safe. There is a Sir Jervas Ireton in the vicinity, who has gained information, 'tis said, of the presence of the princess. He will aim therefore, as he is a flaming zealot, to seize the child and deliver her up to parliament; and to avoid this we must resume our wanderings."

She spoke in her sweet, calm accents, looking tenderly at the child. Something exquisite appeared in her eyes :—was it the sacred maternal instinct? I think that is in all women.

"But whither will you go?" I said.

"I have nearly resolved—I may say quite resolved—to try to take the princess from the country," she replied.

"But you will be arrested on the way."

"Not if a good disguise be assumed, sir. I think I might elude the king's enemies."

"A disguise ! what?"

"That of a beggar-woman and child."

The plan seemed wild and impracticable. How could this delicate young lady trudge through half England on foot, with a child nearly two years old toddling on beside her or borne on her back? But as Miss Villiers spoke further, and developed her scheme,—as, with cheeks glowing now with love and devotion, she unfolded her resolve,—it began to assume a new shape; I gradually passed to her side; and, despite the opposition of Lady Lucy, it was decided, before our interview terminated, that the romantic attempt should be made, and that *I should accompany Miss Villiers.*

Against that, I must do her the justice to say, the young lady fought hard. Wholly destitute of primness and prudery, she was yet a person who never forgot the strictest rules of propriety; and it was long before I could prevail upon her to consent to my companion-ship. At last, however, she yielded,—Lady Lucy in-sisting that if the attempt was made I *must* accompany them; and it was determined that we should set out, as soon as night had fallen, on the next evening.

I returned to Cecil Court to arrange my disguise and prepare for my journey. I was all excitement and agitation. Thus fate had once more thrown me with the woman whom I loved more than I loved my own life. I was to accompany her as companion, friend, and defender, if necessary, on a long and perilous journey, which would throw me into hourly contact with her. I was to look into her eyes, hear the accents of her voice, feel the pressure of her hand, and through-out all I was to conduct myself as a friend, and only as a friend. For I recalled my promise to poor Harry, that I would never without his permission utter a word of love to Frances Villiers. He was dead: that per-mission could never be accorded: my best course, therefore, was to remain away from temptation;— and here I was to be thrown, every hour, day and night, for days, weeks, it might be months, with the woman whom I loved with my whole soul, between whom and myself rose nevertheless that impassable barrier, my solemn promise given to the dead!

Returning to Cecil Court, in a mood of greater agitation than I had believed possible, I set about procuring my disguise for the journey. This was easily effected: the cast-off livery of a serving-man supplied me with just what I required; and then, shutting myself up with my father in the library, I revealed my intent.

He warmly commended the design,—instead of opposing it, as I had feared. Miss Villiers, he said, was a true heroine, and the project was not so wild as it seemed. He would provide me with gold for the journey, and pray for my welfare. But we must hurry: that man Ireton was coming, and would nose out something.

All things having thus been arranged, I retired, not to sleep, however, but to lie awake and think of Frances Villiers. The morning came, and the day dragged on. The sun slowly declined, and, retiring to my chamber, I assumed my disguise. I descended then, embraced Cicely, who started back in affright as I entered, pressed my father's hand, and was just issuing forth, when Sir Jervas Ireton was seen galloping rapidly up the avenue.

No time was to be lost; and I ignominiously fled out of the back door. My horse had just been saddled, and was about to be brought. I leaped upon him, put spur to his side, and went at full speed across the fields, leaping fences and ditches, towards Charlecote.

Had I been seen? I could not answer that question. I either saw or fancied that I saw some troopers who rode in the suite of Sir Jervas Ireton hastily separate, gesticulating and pointing me out. This might have been fancy, however. Under any circumstances, no time was to be lost. I went on at full speed, stopped for nothing in the way, and, reaching the grounds around Charlecote, galloped up the long avenue to the house.

Lady Lucy met me at the door, and I hastily informed her of the danger. I had probably been perceived. If Ireton had knowledge of the presence of the princess at Charlecote, he would have intelligence enough to suspect that I had gone to give warning of the danger. He would thus press forward at once. No time was to be lost. Where was Miss Villiers?

The young lady replied to the question in person. I could scarce realize that it was the elegant and highborn maid of honor who now stood before me in the dingy and tattered garb of a beggar-woman. The disguise was perfect. The slender figure of the young girl was a shapeless bundle of rags; her beautiful hair had been remorselessly shorn; a huge hood covered her head and scarce allowed her face to be seen; and the fair skin had been pitilessly stained with some dye which brought it to resemble the weather-beaten complexion of a beggar-woman.

The princess had been metamorphosed in a manner equally perfect. The little figure was bundled up in an old gown and tattered cloak. On the delicate feet were coarse shoes. It was not an aristocratic young dame and the daughter of a king I saw before me, but a mendicant and child in the last stage of poverty.

"Your disguise is excellent, Miss Villiers," I said, hurriedly; " but we have no time now for compliments. Sir Jervas Ireton is coming!"

And I related, in brief words, my escape from Cecil Court. I was still speaking, when Lady Lucy uttered an exclamation. I looked through the window, and saw the burly personage thundering straight up the avenue, followed by his men.

"We must separate," I said, "and endeavor to leave the house instantly."

Miss Villiers inclined her head. Save a slight color in her proud cheeks, there was no indication of emotion.

"Endeavor to leave by the side court," I said, hastily. "I will go out by the rear gate and join you on the road to Stafford, where the three elms crown the hill."

The rendezvous was a well-known spot, and I knew Miss Villiers could not mistake it. She disappeared, with the princess, towards a side door; and, running to the rear of the house, I reached my horse, which stood there, just as a trooper galloped around and approached.

The incident was far from unacceptable. It was gall and wormwood to me to skulk away thus before the enemy of my family. I went up to the trooper, who was an open-mouthed clodhopper, seized his bridle, and, before he could realize my design, caught him by the throat and dragged him from the saddle.

As I did so, he woke as it were from his astonishment, and uttered a loud shout. I picked up his musquetoon, which had fallen near him, dealt him a blow on the head, which silenced him, and, leaping on my horse, gained the dense foliage of the wood.

Sir Jervas Ireton appeared suddenly, spurring furiously towards the fallen trooper. As he passed around the house, another spectacle made my heart beat fast. I saw Frances Villiers, in her disguise of a beggar-woman, with the princess bundled up in a ragged cloak on her back, quietly pass out of the house by the side door, take a path which led to the wood, and gain its shelter entirely unmolested.

Her enemies had either not seen her, or did not suspect for an instant that their prey was thus escaping them. Whatever the explanation may have been, the young girl with her precious burden had passed safely through the very midst of her enemies. Without further apprehension, I leaped a low place in the park wall, turned my horse loose, knowing that the intelligent animal would find his way back to Cecil Court, and rapidly ran in the direction taken by Miss Villiers.

In ten minutes I had joined her. I assisted her over the wall; we hastened on by a path which I knew perfectly well. Darkness quickly descended, and, taking the young lady's hand, I led her on until we gained a country road.

"Yonder is the north star, Miss Villiers," I said, "and this is the road to Campden. Give me the princess."

I took the child in my arms and walked on steadily.

"Every step we take now brings us nearer to France!"

XI.

ON THE HIGHWAY.

I look back on that journey with Frances Villiers and the little princess to the sea-coast as the most remarkable passage in a life filled with singular adventures.

Trudging along on foot, or securing places in some chance conveyance,—the cart of a countryman going to market, or other humble vehicle,—we went upon our way, the young lady, the princess, and myself, and thus passed safely through the torn and distracted realm until we were in the southern shires and neared the Channel. The land was all laid waste, and an inexpressible disquiet and unrest filled the face of every one. War had come to overthrow the old peace and happiness of merry England. On all sides dismantled houses, torn-down fences, and deserted villages marked the presence of that cruelest of all demons, the demon of Civil War.

The war was virtually over; but the land had not settled to rest again, for the triumphant side had divided into two factions, the Presbyterians and the stern Independents, the latter led by Cromwell now; and 'twas a question whether a new struggle, more violent than the first, would not ensue. From this general sketch, however, which might lead me into political and historical disquisitions, for which I have no fancy, I pass to my personal adventures.

I have said 'twas a strange passage in my life, that journey; and my relations with Frances Villiers made it stranger still. A lover who had sworn to utter no word of love, but whose passion was no secret from its object, was journeying with the one dearest to him; and the singular character of that journey threw him incessantly with his companion. Over long miles of heath, through great woods, across desolate moors, by day and by night, we traveled in company; and all this time it was only as friend to friend that we addressed each other. The child walked sometimes, but was generally carried upon my back or in my arms. This I insisted upon; though more than once Frances Villiers compelled me to yield her charge to her, and the delicate and aristocratic girl would, for hours, against my protest, bear the child in a bundle upon her own shoulders.

More than once we were suspiciously gazed at by chance wayfarers wearing the colors of the parliament; and twice roving parties peered into wagons wherein we rode, but without finding good reason to stop us. 'Twas in this latter manner that much of the way was traversed. The poor and humble proved themselves our best friends; and often, as we went on slowly, we heard, from some yeoman in a smock-frock, earnest wishes expressed for the happiness of the king, now routed and a fugitive. The only danger was from the princess, who had been dressed as a boy and in rags,—to her huge disgust,—and called Pierre. When asked her name by these poor people, she babbled the word *princess*, however, and we were often in great trepidation.

22*

"That is the manner in which he pronounces his name,—Pierre," the young lady would say; and an opportune diversion of the conversation would do away with further danger.

At last we reached the sea-coast, and, leaving the young lady and child in a fisherman's hut, I went to reconnoitre, and discover, if possible, the means of crossing the Channel. The result was extremely discouraging. The coast was thoroughly guarded, and no vessel of any description could pass to France without being stopped. I returned with this discouraging information to Miss Villiers: we took counsel together, and finally came to the resolution of boldly proceeding to Dover and taking the packet which ran at stated periods across the Channel.

We proceeded, therefore, along the coast, reached Dover, and luckily found the packet just about to set sail.

"Come," I said, in a low tone, as we mingled in the crowd, "we will go boldly on board, and I will undertake to answer all questions."

We had just reached the deck, when the commander gave the order to take in the plank leading to the jetty.

"Have all the passports been examined?"

I shrank back with the young lady and child into a corner.

"Ay, ay, sir," was the reply of the person addressed, a rough-looking personage in a broad hat.

The next moment the plank was drawn on board, the cable was unslung from the wharf, and the packet moved under full sail out into the Channel, heading towards France.

I was still shrinking low, with my companion, in my corner, when the man in the broad hat passed near me, and said, without turning his head,—

"I was groom in the Guards once, sir. I know you, but am not the . man to betray you. Many a friend of the good cause is leaving the country. Go down in the aft cabin, and mix with the crowd."

I hastened to follow this friendly advice, and we were soon lost in the mass. On the same evening we were on French soil, and set forward, without stopping, for Paris.

Three days afterwards, Queen Henrietta Maria, in an apartment of the Louvre, was holding in her arms the poor child whom she had last seen at Exeter, sobbing, and covering her with kisses.

Such was that singular adventure. I look back to it now, when my hair grows gray, with more pleasure and satisfaction than to all else I had part in during the great English civil war.

XII.

MY PARTING WITH FRANCES VILLIERS.

I REMAINED in France until the ensuing spring, performing the duties of private secretary to her majesty.

Then there came to me a great longing to return to England. I was ill at ease in the Louvre. The splendid French court jarred a discord upon my feelings.

I longed to go back to my home-land, and to leave Frances Villiers.

Does that last statement appear strange? 'Tis true, nevertheless. To be near her was torture; alternate torpor and fever possessed me. Loving a woman with my whole soul, and yet bound to the dead by a solemn promise never to speak, I found my heart agitated and torn, my very health giving way.

The queen came to my relief. She summoned me to her private apartments one morning, and, extending towards me a packet, said, with deep sadness,—

"I wish you to convey this to his majesty, Mr. Cecil."

I bowed low and took the letter.

"He is at Holmby House, in Northamptonshire," said the queen. "Escaping from Oxford, to take refuge with those people at Newcastle, he has been sold by them,—sold, for the sum of four hundred thousand pounds! And—oh!—it is infamous!—it is infamous!"

And the queen burst into a passion of tears.

"Bear with me," she faltered, at length, through tears and sobs. "I am only a poor woman! I will try to be calm."

And, passing a handkerchief across her eyes, she added, more composedly,—

"The parliament people hold him a prisoner, not knowing what to do with him. The Presbyterians and odious Independents differ. I would have him decide the matter by leaving the country and taking refuge in France. Bear him this letter, Mr. Cecil: it contains my prayer that he will make the attempt. Do not let it fall into the enemy's hands; and may Heaven prosper you in your journey!"

She covered her face with her hand, and attempted to speak again, but no words came; and I retired respectfully from the apartment, leaving her majesty bending over the little princess Henrietta and weeping.

On the same night I had assumed my disguise and was on the road to England. A last interview with Frances Villiers had gone near to unman me. At the moment of parting, when 'twas doubtful if we should ever meet again, she permitted her feelings to show themselves; and 'twas this which made my heart sink. Let me pass briefly over this, and say simply that something had at last touched her. Was it that long journey we had made together, sharing a common danger, and ever beside each other? Was it the womanly heart yearning at last, now when the queen was in safety, for some refuge for itself? I know not: I can only say that, as I held her hand at parting, the beautiful eyes dwelt upon my face for an instant with an expression which I could not misunderstand, and her voice died away in a sob.

"Good-by," she murmured, smiling through her tears, and gazing at me with blushes in her cheeks. "We may never meet again; but I pray God to bless you and watch over you!"

A strange, delicious thrill passed through my heart; my face flushed. I bent down and pressed my burning lips to her hand. Before I could speak,—Heaven be thanked!—she had left the apartment; and as she disappeared I heard a low sob.

BOOK V.

I.

ON THE BRIDGE NEAR HOLMBY HOUSE.

I MADE my way in safety across the Channel, and reached the vicinity of Holmby House in Northamptonshire, where the king was kept close prisoner by the parliament.

I could see him only by stratagem; and to effect my errand I saw no means but to watch for the king when he was out on one of his riding-excursions. An honest woodman, a friend of the royal cause, who had given me refuge in his hut not far from Holmby House, informed me of the king's habit; and for some days I watched for the opportunity of delivering the queen's missive.

At last it came. My friend the woodman went to Holmby House one morning,—the great edifice was visible through the forest,—and returned with the information, derived from the retainers of the palace, that his majesty would ride out that morning and pass over the road near the hut.

"Take your stand at the little bridge yonder, master," said the woodman, "and when his majesty passes, go up to him as if you wished to be touched for the king's evil."

"Excellent!" I exclaimed. And in truth the advice was admirable. The belief that the royal touch cured scrofula was then widely prevalent : numbers flocked to be cured wherever his majesty passed ; and I could thus approach the king, 'twas to be hoped, without exciting suspicion.

I hastened to take my stand on the rustic bridge over which the high-road passed ; and I had not waited ten minutes when the king appeared on horseback, escorted by half a dozen troopers. His face was pale, and he had changed greatly. All the harsh and corroding emotions which try the human soul seemed to have shaken his strength : the plowshare had furrowed his brow deeply.

As he reached the bridge, his eye fell upon my face, and I saw that he recognized me under my disguise. He checked his horse.

"You wish to speak to me, I think, my good man," he said.

"Yes, your majesty,—to pray that you will touch me for the king's evil."

I approached, and, concealing the queen's letter in my sleeve, extended my hand, as though to invite the royal touch. The king did likewise ; but suddenly a loud voice cried,—

"Hold ! What is that?"

I turned and saw the fierce eyes of the leader of the troop fixed upon the letter. He was already spurring forward ; but in another moment it was torn into a hundred pieces, and the fragments floating on the stream beneath.

I was seized, and violently hustled by the troopers.

"What letter was that?" cried the commander of the squad.

"A trifle," I replied, calmly. "Beyond that I shall say nothing."

"We shall see!" was the threatening response; and, ordering one of the troopers to take me behind him, the officer forced the king to turn back. Half an hour afterwards the whole party were back at Holmby House.

I was a prisoner, and under circumstances which rendered my fate rather menacing; but a new incident speedily diverted attention from my humble self. The king had scarcely entered Holmby House, and had not taken off his gloves, when the clatter of hoofs was heard in the park; a heavy detachment of dragoons approached at a gallop, and in the commander of the new-comers, who wore the distinctive uniform of the Cromwellian Independents, I recognized no less a personage than the tailor Joyce, who had measured me for my Guardsman's coat in Rosemary Lane when I first went up from Cecil Court to London.

II.

TAILOR TURNED SOLDIER.

THERE was no mistaking the face or figure of this singular person who thus came at a critical moment to decide the fate of the king. I recognized at a glance the important look, the nose in the air, the short figure, and the free-and-easy air of the ex-tailor of London, who had dropped his civil garb for the uniform of a cornet in the Cromwellian Independents.

Joyce rode straight up to the great portal, dismounted, and, walking on the points of his feet to increase his stature, head raised and nose elevated as before, gave a thundering knock.

"Your pleasure?" said the leader of the troop which had escorted the king, appearing at the door and confronting Joyce.

"To see Charles Stuart, formerly King of England," was the reply, in a consequential voice.

"From whom do you come?"

"Where is Charles Stuart?"

"He is not at leisure to see you."

Joyce turned to his men.

"Attention!" he said. "Get ready to fire through this door!"

"Are you mad?" cried the officer.

Joyce quietly gave an order to his men, and they leveled their musquetoons at the door.

"Hold!" said the officer. "His majesty shall himself decide whether he will grant you an interview."

The officer closed the door as he spoke, and ascended to the apartment occupied by the king. Joyce had quietly walked up behind him, and entered the room at the same moment. In his hand was a cocked pistol.

"It is hard to obtain audience, it seems, in this house," he said, consequentially.

The king was half indignant, half amused, at sight of this unceremonious personage.

"Who are you?" he said.

"It is enough, sir, that you must come with me," was the reply.

"Whither?"

"To the army."

"The army! By what warrant?"

Joyce pointed through the window to his men, drawn up, armed, and ready.

"There is my warrant," he said.

The king smiled, and seemed to yield to the comedy of the occasion.

"Your warrant is writ in fair characters, and legible without spelling," he said. "But here are the worshipful commissioners of parliament, sir. Be pleased, gentlemen, to decide this affair, as I am not in a condition to make my authority respected."

The grave commissioners entered as the king spoke, and the foremost said to Joyce, coldly,—

"Have you orders from parliament to carry away the king?"

"No," said Joyce.

"From the general?"

" No."

" By what authority, then, do you come ?"

" By my own authority."

The commissioners frowned.

" We will write to the parliament to know their pleasure," said the leading commissioner.

Joyce turned to the king.

" You will prepare to go with me immediately, sir," he said.

" We protest against this outrage !" came from the commissioner.

" So be it ; and you can write to parliament. Meanwhile, the king must go with me."

And, turning to the officer, he said,—

" If the king has a coach, order it. I will set out in half an hour."

Turning his back, the important functionary thereupon went out of the room and down-stairs, where he mounted again and drew up his men in order of battle.

A stormy discussion followed ; but there was no means of resisting. The guard stationed at Holmby House to watch the king were seen laughing and talking with Joyce's men, their army comrades. The commissioners yielded, the king entered his coach, and the vehicle, followed by the troop led by Joyce, rapidly rolled away. I had been made prisoner anew by the redoubtable ex-tailor. Mounted on horseback, I trotted along scarcely observed in the party. Two days' journey brought us to Cambridge, and thence— the people crowding along the route to be touched by his majesty for the king's evil—the captive was conducted to Hampton Court.

Strange fate of the fallen monarch, to return thus to
the scene of his happiness and power! At Hampton
Court he had spent the serenest hours of his life. Here
he had basked in the smiles of his beautiful queen and
shared the gambols of his innocent children ; here he
had reigned a king, only to return to the place a poor
prisoner, disarmed and doomed to destruction!

III.

THE ESCAPE FROM HAMPTON COURT.

In narrating the adventures of his majesty from this
time to the end of his career,—adventures with which
I was more or less connected, and in which I may be
said to have borne a not unimportant part,—I shall
occupy as little space as possible, indulge in few notices
of public events, and mention only the salient incidents
leading by a sort of fatality as 'twere to the window at
Whitehall. I would fain pass over all. But that is
impossible. At least I shall narrate rapidly.

Joyce, the ex-tailor, was thus far friendly to the king,
that, without asking any one's authority, he permitted
me to remain at Hampton Court and share his majesty's imprisonment, under the guise of private attendant or secretary.

From that moment I resolved to effect the king's
escape, if possible. I ventured upon every opportunity
to urge his majesty to attempt it, declaring to him my

conviction that otherwise his life was in danger. His choice lay between flying to France, where he would regain his beloved queen and find a place of safety, or remaining to undergo all that the malice of his bitter enemies might devise.

For months he resisted my appeals, which I scrupled not to make in season and out of season. Finally, one day, after a stormy and exciting interview with a commission from parliament, he said to me,—

"Your advice is good, Mr. Cecil. This day's scene has decided me to leave Hampton Court, if possible. Now let us try and devise some means."

These words filled me with joy. I believed—with what truth let events which followed determine—that the king's life was in danger. I said, therefore, with animation,—

"Your majesty shall have it in your power to leave Hampton Court secretly,—to-morrow night, if you desire. Leave the arrangement of all to me."

"You have a plan?"

"I have had it for months, your majesty."

"And afterwards?"

"France," I said.

The king knit his brows.

"The King of England a wretched fugitive!" he muttered.

"Or his queen a widow and his children fatherless," I said, briefly.

He looked at me with deep sadness, and said,—

"Would that be so great a calamity to them, friend? All connected with me is unfortunate. But go: do what you will."

This was all I wanted. I saluted profoundly, left
the apartment, sauntered past the guard out into the
park, where the gentlemen of the king's suite were
permitted to walk, and, finding myself out of sight of
the sentry, hastened down to the bank of the river.
Here I stopped and waved my hat. Ten minutes
afterwards a boat detached itself from the opposite
bank, and lazily crossed, propelled by the paddle of a
waterman. The boat reached me. I entered, and was
paddled across. Five minutes after reaching the opposite bank I was mounted upon a superb horse, which
had stood bridled and saddled in a shed attached to
the waterman's hut, and was going at full speed towards
the south.

Half an hour's ride brought me to the manor-house
of Colonel Edward Cooke,—the gentleman with the
fine stud of horses, to whom the queen had written
when her children were threatened at Oatlands.

Colonel Cooke was a warm loyalist, and his swift
horses were needed then to bear the royal children, in
the event of danger, from the country. They were
now to be put in requisition to effect the escape of the
king.

I had long before arranged everything with Colonel
Cooke. It was his horse I bestrode. And I now saw
him advance quickly as I galloped up the avenue leading to his mansion.

"What intelligence, Mr. Cecil?" exclaimed Colonel Cooke, who was a tall and stately old cavalier,
with a heavy mustache and royale, shaggy eyebrows
half concealing a pair of dark piercing eyes, and the
erect bearing of the thorough *militaire*. "What intel-

ligence, I pray you? Has his majesty consented to go with us?"

"He has consented," I replied, with ardent feeling. And, leaping from my horse, I entered, and informed Colonel Cooke of my interview with the king.

"Faith! his majesty decides in time, and just in time," was the colonel's comment. In his glowing cheeks I read a satisfaction which, cool and reserved as he was, the old soldier could not conceal. He went and poured out two flagons of wine.

"To our success!" he said. "And now for our arrangements, Mr. Cecil. I and my friends are ready. His majesty shall bestride an animal fit for a king. The jades they ride yonder at Hampton Court will have no showing! Come! Now for every arrangement!"

The plan was speedily agreed upon. Colonel Cooke, with a party of friends, was to be at the waterman's hut the next evening at sunset, with horses saddled and ready, and two led horses for the king and myself. His majesty would then steal forth to enjoy the evening air. The guard over him had been relaxed recently, and this would not be hazardous. The river's bank would be reached, the stream crossed in the boat, then to horse, and, encircled by friends, he would fly to France.

I left Colonel Cooke with a close grasp of the hand, reached the river, was paddled over, and regained Hampton Court without having excited the least suspicion. Ten minutes afterwards I was alone with his majesty, and told him of the plan for his escape.

"So be it," he said, calmly. "Whither I will bend

my course afterwards may be left to the future to decide."

I saw that the king could not yet bring himself to the resolution to take refuge in France; but to this I thought he must surely be driven. I therefore lost no time in combating his indecision, proceeded to prepare for the flight, and finally lay down with a beating heart, impatient for the morrow.

That morrow dawned, dragged on,—never was day so sluggish!—but finally evening came, and the king descended to the hall of the palace, I following him.

As he attempted to issue forth, the man on guard held his musquetoon across the doorway.

"You cannot pass," he said, roughly,—for he was one of the Independents.

"You will surely suffer me to walk in the park for the benefit of my health?"

"No!"

The sound of feet tramping towards us was heard, and the guard saluted. It was a sergeant, with a new sentinel.

"Sergeant," I said, "this man on guard here bars the way against his majesty, who wishes to walk for exercise in the park."

"He obeys his orders," was the consequential reply of the sergeant, who was about five feet in height.

"He was right, then, sergeant," I said, saluting; "but you, a superior officer, are fortunately here now. Has his majesty your permission to walk for half an hour beneath the trees?"

I had conquered my man. "Superior officer" and "permission" effected the victory.

" Hum ! Well," said the highly-flattered small personage, " if only for half an hour. Orders are strict;
but I will send an escort to keep you in sight. Pass!"

A moment afterwards the king and myself were on
the lawn, the man just relieved from guard following
us at a distance and lowering at us.

All depended now upon giving the signal without
being discovered. I succeeded in doing so by gliding
behind a clump of bushes on the bank of the stream.
I saw the boat put off at the signal and slowly paddle
across, and the king sauntered, at a sign from me,
towards a spot agreed upon. Behind came the guard :
it was impossible to escape him.

" Enter the boat, your majesty," I said, hurriedly,
" and leave me to deal with this man."

The king shook his head. " I will not desert you,
friend. Come ! He can fire but once upon us, and I
fear not bullets."

Naught I could say moved the king. Thus no course
remained but to risk everything. We were now at the
bank; the boat touched it. The king leaped on board,
dragging me after him, and the boat darted into the
stream again.

The sentinel uttered a tremendous imprecation, and,
taking deliberate aim, fired at the king. The ball only
clipped a feather from his hat, and there was no more
danger now,—from the sentinel at least. The shot
would give the alarm, however,—the troops would soon
hasten towards the bank.

We were not mistaken. The boat had not reached
the opposite shore when the grassy banks in Hampton Court suddenly swarmed with soldiers. Loud cries

M*

to halt rose from the crowd, and a volley from their musquetoons whistled around us as the boat ran aground. The king's friends, headed by Colonel Cooke, hurried down the bank and bore the king to shore.

"There is no time to lose now, your majesty," said the colonel. "Your horse is ready. I beseech you hasten!"

The horse, a superb hunter, was led up quickly, and the colonel held the king's stirrup. His majesty mounted, and all did likewise. As we did so, half a dozen boats put off from the opposite shore.

Colonel Cooke caught the king's bridle, exclaiming,—

"Come, your majesty!"

"In an instant, sir," was the calm reply. "I would take a last farewell of my palace."

And, reining in his horse, he sat quietly for some moments, gazing at Hampton Court.

"'Tis very beautiful; and I was once very happy there!" I heard him murmur.

He remained for some moments gazing towards the stately edifice with the same sad expression; then he turned his horse slowly, just as the boats full of soldiery touched the bank.

"Come, gentlemen!" he said.

And, striking the spurs into his horse, he set out for the southern coast. Behind him thundered the rest. The spirited horses swiftly bore their riders beyond danger. King Charles I. had effected his escape from Hampton Court.

IV.

CARISBROOKE CASTLE.

THE pages of my memoirs I am now about to trace will contain a brief narrative of some of the saddest and most terrible events in English history. Looking back now in my calm old age upon those days, I seem to see a huge black cloud drooping low and full of mutterings; and truly the storm was about to burst on the head of the unfortunate king.

Of the events which followed the escape of his majesty from Hampton Court, I shall present only a rapid narrative. I have not the heart to dwell upon all the details. Again my pulse throbs, and the long shadows of memory fall like a pall.

The king and his party of cavaliers traveled at full speed all night, and at daybreak were received into the house of a lady passionately attached to the royal cause. It was necessary, however, to put more distance between him and his enemies: the king and his attendants set out again at dawn. At last the frowning battlements of Carisbrooke Castle, on the Isle of Wight, rose before us, and the murmur of the sea indicated that the Channel was not far distant.

Now arose the question what the king's next course should be. Should he leave England and escape to France? He was obdurately opposed to that. The armies under General Cromwell and the parliament were wéllnigh at loggerheads at last; each was manœuvring, it seemed, to compose matters first with his majesty; and the English people had of late exhibited unmistakable indications of a desire to throw overboard both army and parliament, and restore the king, taught now, it was supposed, discretion by his sufferings and misfortunes.

"I will not go to France," the king said, reining in his horse, which seemed intent on bearing him towards the coast. "That is Carisbrooke Castle, is it not?"

"It is, your majesty," returned Colonel Cooke.

"The name of the commandant?"

"Hammond, sire."

"Hammond? Ah, yes! a relative of my chaplain. Go to him, colonel, take Mr. Cecil with you, and demand whether he is ready to receive me as a guest, not a prisoner."

"But, your majesty——"

"Go, colonel."

"It will endanger your majesty's·safety."

"You need not tell him where I am. I will await your return in this wood."

There was nothing to do but to obey; and I went with Colonel Cooke. A short ride brought us to the gateway of the great fortress, as I may call it, rather than castle, and Colonel Hammond speedily made his appearance. He was a tall and very stern man, with one of those secretive faces which express nothing.

"Your pleasure, gentlemen?" he said.

Colonel Cooke gave him the king's message. I saw him start imperceptibly almost, but in an instant this emotion disappeared.

"Where is his majesty?" he said, coolly.

"That is beside the question, sir. Will you receive and protect him ?"

A brief pause ensued.

"I will go with you,—alone. I must see his majesty before I reply."

"Content, sir," said Colonel Cooke, after a moment's reflection. "You have only to come with us, and you will be conducted to the king."

Ten minutes afterwards, Colonel Hammond was riding with us towards the wood in which the king was concealed. I went before my two companions. As I approached the king, he said,—

"That is Colonel Hammond, is it not ?"

"Yes, your majesty."

"Has he given his written promise to receive me as his guest ?"

My head sank. These simple words indicated the extent of the imprudence of which we had been guilty.

"I think your majesty may depend upon him as a man of honor," I said.

The king shook his head. "I have lost my faith in men," he said, sadly. "I am Colonel Hammond's prisoner."

The words drove my hand to my sword-hilt.

"It is my fault,—in part at least! I will kill him!" I exclaimed.

The king raised his hand with a gesture of royal dignity. "No: I am weary of seeing blood shed in my behalf. Let there be surcease of this. Rather than leave my kingdom, or be hunted like a wild beast all along the coast here, I will put myself under charge of this officer, trusting that he will prove a friend."

Colonel Hammond had now reached the spot, and made the king a low salute.

"You are Colonel Hammond?" said the king.

"I am, your majesty."

"You command at Carisbrooke Castle?"

"Yes, your majesty."

"I will go thither with you, sir."

And the king advanced on horseback towards the castle, whose ponderous gates soon closed behind the whole party. They were not guests, but prisoners.

On the same evening, Colonel Hammond dispatched a fast-riding courier to London, to announce to parliament that King Charles I. was a prisoner at Carisbrooke Castle.

V.

EIKON BASILIKE.

So woefully had ended the hopeful design of bearing his majesty beyond the reach of danger. Once beyond the walls of Hampton Court, he had been free. He might have taken refuge in the western shires, still faithful to him, and perchance have once more found an army flock to his standard; or he might have embarked for France, escaped the hostile cruisers, and rejoined his beloved queen. All this was possible on the day of his departure from Hampton Court. Now it was a dream: the prey was in the clutch of the furious huntsmen.

The outward signs of respect from Colonel Hammond

and the garrison only added to the bitterness of the king's imprisonment. A cautious game was evidently going on. This human being might some day be the master again. He never appeared, accordingly, upon the battlements but the sentinel saluted; Colonel Hammond ever doffed his hat and inclined profoundly upon entering his majesty's presence. I, in common with the other members of the king's party, was treated as a guest rather than a prisoner. The future was too doubtful to render harshness prudent.

Nevertheless, the king's health and spirits rapidly failed him. Day by day life seemed dying out from the worn frame, as hope disappeared. He grew thin and gray. His face was covered with an unsightly beard. He neglected his dress, grew older and sadder hour by hour, and would wander to and fro with his eyes fixed upon the ground, or, sighing, would gaze towards France.

One day I saw him standing on the battlements, looking in the direction of the French coast, and holding in his hand a half-folded paper. He turned his head, and, seeing me, motioned to me to approach.

"Would I had followed your advice, my friend," he said, "and sought refuge in France. I could have done so, perchance. 'Tis impossible now."

His head sank, and he remained silent for a moment.

"This letter is from——"

His voice died away, and his lips trembled.

"She has begged the people in London, she writes me, to accord her permission to come to me. She went only at my bidding; she would return now, like a good wife, when the dark hour has come upon her husband."

"And they have refused, your majesty?"

"They have refused!"

A deep groan issued from the king's lips. He turned his face towards France again; his thin hands were clasped for a moment; and then, turning away, he slowly went to his chamber.

When I attended him there, an hour afterwards,—for I shared with his grace the Duke of Richmond the duties of groom of the chamber,—I found him writing.

"See," he said, raising the sheet, "I am writing my last will and testament, friend. I strive herein to show my subjects my inmost heart. In this 'Eikon Basilike,' as I call it, naught is concealed."

He sighed, and added,—

"Shall I read you the words I have just written? 'I am content to be tossed, weather-beaten, and ship-wrecked, so that she be safe in harbor. I enjoy this comfort in her safety, in the midst of my personal dangers. I can perish but half if *she* be preserved. In her memory, and in her children, I may yet survive the malice of my enemies, although they should at last be satiate with my blood.'"

The king replaced the paper upon the table, clasped his hands and leaned them upon it; and upon the hands thus clasped his forehead drooped slowly, his long gray hair falling around the emaciated cheeks and concealing them.

In presence of this immense sorrow I could say nothing and offer no condolence. There was something terrible as well as heart-rending in this royal despair; and, without speaking, I turned to leave the apartment.

As I approached the door, I saw a man standing without and gazing at the king. This was one Osborne, appointed by Colonel Hammond to attend the king.

As I came out, he made me a sign that I should follow him; and I did so.

VI.

THE PLAN OF ESCAPE.

OSBORNE went on until he reached a retired nook, and then, stopping suddenly, said, in a low tone,—

"You are the king's friend, I think, Mr. Cecil?"

"His faithful friend, I hope, sir, as I trust you are."

"I am," was his reply. "I was not, a month ago; but his majesty's looks haunt my sleep. They are going to try and murder him. He must escape."

I looked at the speaker keenly.

"I know what you mean," he said. "You distrust me—well. But I am the king's friend. I slipped a note into his glove two days since, offering to risk my life to secure his escape; but he has not spoken to me. I know not if he received it."

"Your plan?" I said.

"Listen, sir. There is a certain Major Rolfe in the garrison here,—a wretch bent on earning blood-money. He proposed to me to entice the king to attempt an escape from this place. Files and a rope-ladder were to be supplied. The king was to descend from his window and escape from the castle. Then Rolfe, with others, lying in wait, was to assassinate him."

24*

I listened with attention.

"And your plan, Mr. Osborne?"

"To conspire against the conspirators, to get the king out of the castle, and cut the throats, if necessary, of Rolfe and his gang."

I reflected for a moment with all the power of my brain. Had Osborne the design which he attributed to Rolfe, or was this man a true friend of the king?

"You would be ready to receive his majesty when he descended by the ladder?" I said.

"Yes."

"I will be at liberty to take part?"

"Assuredly."

"To stand beside you?"

He looked at me with firm eyes.

"I understand. Yes. Stay! you are unarmed. Here is a dagger which you may plunge into my heart, if you have reason to believe in my treachery."

I took the weapon and placed it in my breast, looking fixedly at the speaker.

"I accept your offer," I said, "and will go immediately and apprise his majesty."

I left Osborne, went to the king's chamber, and informed him of the plot. He shook his head.

"It will fail," he said, "or I will end my life in a midnight brawl in this corner of my kingdom. I do not wish to die thus. I would perish in public, before the eyes of the whole world."

I combated this resolution with all my powers, and the king, enfeebled by sickness and sorrow, began to waver.

"The one your majesty loves best in all the world

awaits you yonder," I added, extending my hand towards France.

His face flushed. "Enough! you have conquered me," he murmured. "Go. I will do as you wish."

I hastened from the apartment; and obtained a second private interview with Osborne.

"The king consents," I said. "And now to arrange all!"

The arrangements were speedily made. Files were to be supplied me, with which I would file through the iron bars of the king's window; a rope-ladder was ready, procured by Osborne for the purpose. Once the obstructions were removed, his majesty could descend by it, the key of a postern in the outer wall had been obtained, and Charles I. would be free.

"Rolfe will know of but a part of the plan," Osborne said; "and we are playing a dangerous game. But it must be risked. Now I will go and gain over some men whom I think we may count upon. If all is ready, the attempt will be made at midnight, two nights from this time."

With these words we parted.

On the second night thereafter, all was ready for the hazardous undertaking. I had passed the preceding night in hard work on the iron bars, which I attacked with a file dipped from time to time in grease to dull the grating sound. This occupation lasted for eight hours. At the end of that time the bars hung by a thread. I announced the fact to his majesty, who had fallen into a feverish sleep on his couch; and, as I had managed to convey the rope-ladder of fine twisted hemp to his chamber unperceived, all was ready.

Midnight came at last. The night was dark; and this favored the dangerous scheme. A chill wind whistled drearily around the battlements of the great castle, and from beneath came the long dash of the waves against the base of the cliffs.

"The moment has come, sire," I said, in a low voice. "Be firm and fearless."

The king smiled sadly. "Feel my pulse, friend," he said, extending his hand. "The Stuarts are unfortunate, but they are at least brave. This will fail; but I fear nothing. Is all ready?"

"Yes, your majesty."

"Osborne and his friends are beneath?"

"As well as Rolfe and his party; but ours outnumber them greatly."

"Then all, I see, is ready. You will descend after me——"

"A moment, your majesty. I will remove the bars and attach the ladder; then I will simply go out of that door yonder and join the party below."

"Join the party?"

"Yes, your majesty."

"You cannot: the sentinel."

"I am allowed to pass about: it is only your majesty that is guarded."

"But why not descend by the ladder?"

"I have an arrangement with Osborne, and will see that Rolfe is a party to it."

"What arrangement?"

"To bury this dagger in his heart,—in the hearts of both,—if they have betrayed you!"

The king extended his hand, as a man does to grasp

that of a friend. I took the hand and kissed it. Then I rapidly drew out the bars, saw that a confused group awaited below, affixed the ladder, and turned for the last time to the king.

"Your majesty is not fearful of growing dizzy?"

"No: my nerves are perfectly firm."

"The descent is considerable."

"It is nothing,—since France and my wife are at the foot of the ladder."

"Then may God guard your majesty!"

As I spoke, I opened the door; but suddenly I recoiled. The corridor was full of armed men, at the head of whom advanced Colonel Hammond.

"I have come to save your majesty a dangerous essay," he said, coldly. "Your plan of escape has been discovered, and Osborne is already under arrest. To-morrow he will be hanged and quartered."

The speaker inclined stiffly.

"Place two men beneath the window there," he added, to a sergeant, "and a regular guard, to be relieved every two hours, in this corridor. The parliament will decide the rest."

VII.

THE HOUR AT LAST.

THREE days afterwards,—days passed by myself as a captive in the same room with the king,—Colonel Hammond made his reappearance.

"Your majesty will be released from further imprisonment in this apartment," he said, stiffly. "I am directed to announce so much by the parliament, who will send further orders. If agreeable to your majesty, you may now descend to dinner, which is prepared in the great hall."

The king inclined coldly, and was about to decline.

"I pray your majesty to descend," I said. "Your health fails from confinement."

The sad smile, now habitual with him, came to his lips.

"Content," he said; "but you use but feeble reasoning, friend."

I assisted him to make his toilet, and he descended to the great banqueting-hall of the castle, where a crowd of persons had assembled, as was customary then, to see the king dine.

The king had no sooner taken his seat than the company were startled by a sudden apparition. . This was a solemn, funereal, and cadaverous personage, clad in black, but wearing a military belt and scarf, who stalked into the hall, posted himself opposite the king, and fixed his eyes upon him in sombre silence. The king gazed at this strange person with undisguised surprise, but, finding that he was apparently dumb and might be deaf, did not address him: the whole meal passing in silence.

As the king rose, I approached the funereal personage.

"Your name, if I may ask, sir?" I said.

"Isaac Ewer, an unworthy follower of the godly cause."

"Colonel Ewer, I think."

"I am so called."

"Your object?"

"I am come to fetch away Hammond to-night."

These words dissipated all doubt. This singular personage, representing the "Independents" of the army, had come to order away Hammond, who represented the parliament. From this moment it was obvious that Charles I. had ceased to be the prisoner of the civil power, and had become the prize of the military. The full significance of the change may be stated in a few words: the name of Isaac Ewer appears among the regicides.

This man had just uttered the words I have recorded, and Colonel Hammond had started up, as though determined to resist this summary order from the military authorities, when I heard a familiar voice near me, and, turning my head, saw Colonel Cooke. How this faithful friend of the king gained access to the castle I never discovered. He had been released months before, and had passed from my mind; but I afterwards knew that he had kept watch over the king and laid many plans to effect his escape.

Colonel Cooke now approached the king hurriedly, and said to him, in the midst of the confusion,—

"Your majesty must attempt to escape."

"To escape?"

"At once," he replied, quickly. "The army has a plan for seizing you immediately. This must be prevented. All the preparations are made. We have horses all ready here, concealed, in a pent-house. A vessel is at the Cowes waiting for us. We are prepared to attend you."

The king turned pale.

"No," he said. "I have given my word to Hammond and the House that I would make no further such attempts. They have promised me, and I have promised them ; and I will not be the first to break promise."

"Your majesty means by *they* and *them* the parliament ?"

"Yes."

"They have no power to protect you! You are a dead man if——For God's sake, your majesty, consent !"

The face of the speaker flushed.

"For the queen and your children's sake !"

The king shook.

"No, I cannot : do not tempt me !" he murmured. "My honor of gentleman alone is left to me !"

A thundering knock was heard at the door as the king uttered these words, and a file of soldiers entered, in front of whom advanced, with heavy tramp, two or three sombre-visaged officers.

They went straight to the king.

"You must come with us," said one of them.

"Who may you be ?" the king asked.

"Officers from the army. Come !"

"Whither ?"

"To the castle."

" 'The Castle' is no castle ! I am prepared for any castle, but tell me the name."

"Hurst Castle."

"Indeed !" the king said, calmly. "You could not have named a worse."

In truth, the selection of that gloomy fortress, a

species of dungeon, fitted for murder, seemed an ominous indication of the designs of the king's captors. It stood on a desolate promontory, approached from the Isle of Wight by a narrow causeway; and an hour afterwards the king was conducted thither.

In this sombre keep he was immured now, and I confess my heart sank. I had remained with his majesty, along with others, and experienced very great solicitude for his safety. Everything now seemed to depend upon the result of the struggle between the army and parliament. The latter was known to embrace a number of prominent persons who favored the king's release: if the army were overthrown, the king, thus, would be saved.

One morning came intelligence that the army under General Cromwell had crushed the parliament. Soon afterwards the rattling chains of the drawbridge were heard as the ponderous mass fell. The emissary of the army had come to conduct Charles I. to Windsor Castle.

He was conducted thither. A month passed: I had begun to dream of happier times for this poor husband and father, so long the sport of his enemies, when, on the 15th of January, 1648, a squadron of horse appeared and escorted the king to London.

The hour had come.

VIII.

THE SCENE AT WESTMINSTER HALL.

I HAVE shrunk from dwelling at length upon the days passed by the king at Carisbrooke and Hurst Castles; for a stronger reason still, I shall pass hastily over the last scenes of the tragedy, the memory of which still affects me profoundly.

This human being, now approaching death, had his weaknesses, his prejudices,—committed crimes more than once,—claimed prerogatives inconsistent with the liberties of England; but he had suffered, had grown gray in prison, and all the glory of royalty had been stripped from him, and now his enemies, in an evil hour for them, were going to commit the blunder of making a martyr of him by putting him to death.

The forms were speedily gone through with. From Windsor Castle, where he had enjoyed a brief season of tranquillity, not divested of hope, he was taken in his coach, under an escort of troopers with drawn pistols, to St. James's Palace in London, where his treatment at once indicated that his fate was sealed.

I had remained with him, as had his grace the Duke of Richmond, his faithful Herbert, and other friends. We were mercifully permitted to share his last hours; and the terrible details of these hours are here recorded briefly.

It soon became known to us that the military power

was completely in the ascendency. General Cromwell, its head, proceeded to turn out of parliament all opposed to the fatal resolution at last reached. The king was transferred to a wing of Edward the Conqueror's Palace; and speedily came the order that he should be brought to Westminster Hall for trial.

It was a dark and chill morning in January when the order came. The king rose calmly, put on his hat, took his cane and gloves, and bowed to the officer bearing the order.

"I am ready, sir," he said.

The officer did not return the salute. The days of royalty, and the respect due it, had passed away now. The officer simply pointed to the door.

The king went out, and found himself in face of a body of armed men, who gazed at him, some with lowering faces, others with undisguised pity and compassion.

"Forward, to Westminster Hall!" the officer commanded; and the troop moved, escorting the king, who walked in the midst. I was near him, and went on in a dream, as 'twere. The fatal pageant affected me as men are affected by things seen in sleep.

All at once, as the procession moved along, I heard, from a window above, the hoarse words,—

"Here he is! here he is!"

I looked up. The king was passing the "Painted Chamber;" and the hoarse speaker was General Cromwell. For the third time in my life I saw this terrible man:—first in Buckinghamshire, at Mr. Hampden's, a shuffling, absent-looking countryman; again at Naseby, a cold and immovable statue on horseback;

now a judge, pale and purple by turns, looking upon his victim.

I heard afterwards that he and others had met here to see the king pass, and that General Cromwell, after uttering the words above recorded, added to Marten, one of his associates,—

"The hour of the great affair approaches. Decide speedily what answer you will give him; for he will immediately ask by what authority you pretend to judge him."

"In the name of the Commons assembled in parliament," Marten replied, ironically, "and of all the good people of England."

The purlieus of Westminster Hall were nearly choked with troops. These, too, seemed divided between bitter enmity and compassion. Many of the citizens had mingled with the soldiery, and cried aloud, as the king came,—

"God save your majesty!"

The soldiers did not suppress this cry; and the fact seemed to enrage their commander, Colonel Axtel. Suddenly the tall form of that officer advanced, the dark face full of anger. This sentiment became fury when some of the soldiers, whose backs were turned to him, shouted, compassionately,—

"Justice! justice!"

With a cane which he held in his hand, Colonel Axtel struck them vigorously over the shoulders; and the men who had just clamored for justice to the captive now shouted as loudly,—

"Execution! execution!"

The king entered Westminster Hall in the midst of

his guard. Behind came the procession of his judges, with the sword and mace borne before them.

The king sat down, keeping his hat upon his head, and looked around him with calm and even curious eyes. His bearing was composed, and his eyes seemed to express a grave wonder at the scene. He was yet thin and pale, and the curls beneath his beaver were silvered with gray.

The judges took their seats above him, and the ceremony began. An advocate rose, and began to read from a paper which he held in his hand that the king was "indicted in the name of the Commons assembled, and the people of England."

The king interrupted him here with some words which I did not hear. The advocate scowled at him, but continued to read; whereupon the king extended his slight cane, and touched him with the gold head upon the shoulder. The head detached itself from the cane, rolled on the floor, distinctly heard in the profound silence; and the whole assembly, wound to the highest pitch of nervous excitement, rose in mass.

"God save your majesty! God save the king!" rose from the crowd of people in the hall.

Scuffling succeeded: the troops, under direction of their officers, were buffeting and hustling the malcontents. The advocate's voice, loud and monotonous, resumed the indictment. It was finished; and Mr. Bradshaw, who presided, demanded of the king what his plea was,—guilty or not guilty of the crimes laid to his charge.

"I make no plea. I deny the authority of this

25*

court, though not the power," the king replied.
"There are many illegal powers, as those of high-
waymen and bandits. The Commons agreed to a
treaty of peace with me when at Carisbrooke, and
since that time I have been hurried from place to place.
Where are the just privileges of the House of Commons? Where are the Lords? I see none present.
And where is the king? Call you this bringing a king
to his parliament?"

Bradshaw scowled, retorting in some violent words,
and a discussion ensued. The court promised to break
up in the midst of a brawl,—perhaps a conflict between army and citizens. It was hastily adjourned,
therefore; and the king was reconducted to his prison,
the people shouting, as he passed,—

"God bless your majesty! God save you from
your enemies!"

The first scene of the first act had thus been played.
The rest followed rapidly, and the catastrophe was
at hand.

The king was again and again brought before his
judges. He resolutely refused, however, to acknowl-
edge the competency of the tribunal; and it was plain
that violent measures would be called for. These
were adopted. The king's enemies had gone too far
to recede: their own safety absolutely required that
his blood should be shed.

All was resolved upon at last; and for the fourth
time his majesty was conducted to Westminster Hall.

Bradshaw had already taken his seat, and wore a red
dress. The fact was ominous, and the proceedings
were brief.

"Read the list of members of the court," growled the president, Bradshaw.

The clerk began to read. At the name of "Fairfax," a voice from the gallery cried,—

"Fairfax has too much wit to be here to-day !"

All eyes were raised. The voice was seen to have issued from a group of ladies who attended as spectators.

Colonel Axtel, commanding the soldiery, shouted, with fury,—

"Present pieces !—fire !—fire into the box where she sits !"

As he spoke, one of the ladies rose, in the centre of the group. For a moment she remained motionless, looking down with great scorn upon the rough faces of the troops, who were confusedly raising their musquetoons. She then slowly went out of the gallery ; and I heard from the crowd around me,—

"'Tis Lady Fairfax ! They dare not harm her !"

The reading of the list proceeded. At the name of Cromwell a new tumult rose.

"Oliver Cromwell is a rogue and a traitor !" cried a second voice from the gallery.

Axtel raged ; but the president made a gesture, and the reading proceeded. The clerk concluded by declaring that the king was "called to answer by the people before the Commons of England assembled in parliament."

"'Tis false !" shouted the voice in the gallery ; "not one half-quarter of them !"

At this renewed interruption and open defiance, Colonel Axtel seemed ready to lose his head. He

foamed with rage, and shook his clenched hand towards
the spot from which the voice had issued, shouting,
" Fire ! fire on them !"

Bradshaw again interposed.   Silence was obtained ;
but a more important interruption was to come.

The president began to pass sentence.

" I demand," said the king, " that the whole of the
members of the House of Commons, and such lords
as are in England, shall assemble to hear the sentence
about to be pronounced upon me."

Bradshaw frowned angrily, and was about to proceed
without noticing this protest, when one of the court
started to his feet in great agitation and with tears on
his cheeks.

" Have we hearts of stone ?" he exclaimed.   " Are
we men ?"

" You will ruin us, and yourself too !" came in a
hoarse undertone from those near the speaker, whom
they violently attempted to hold in his seat. .

" If I were to die for it !" was the renewed protest.

·Cromwell, who sat just beneath, turned and looked
at the speaker with lowering eyes.

" Colonel Downes," he said, sternly, in his deep
voice, " are you mad ?"

" No !"

" Can't you sit still ?"

" No !   I cannot and I will not sit still !"

He broke from those attempting to hold him down.

" I move," he exclaimed, " that we adjourn to deliberate !"

Cromwell rose in a rage, and his eyes seemed to dart
lightning as he looked at Downes.

"You wish to save your old master!" he said, in a storm of wrath; "but make an end of this, and return to your duty!"

Cries and confused voices were heard, however, throughout the great hall; and, doubtless reflecting that nothing would be lost thereby, the court determined to retire to deliberate. They went out at a side door, and remained absent for about half an hour; then they reappeared, defiling in, stern, silent, and ominous.

Bradshaw took his seat in the midst of cries of wrath, pity, and horror from the crowd, where Axtel exerted himself to obtain silence.

In the midst of this silence, sentence was passed upon the king.

He listened without a word, and, at the termination of the sentence, rose and put on his gloves. Axtel advanced and motioned to him. He obeyed the order of the man who now stood in the place of the headsman, passed through the crowd of furious soldiery, who puffed the smoke of their pipes in his face, spat upon him, and yelled, "Justice! execution!" in his ears, and, entering his sedan-chair,—a luxury still permitted him,—was borne back to his place of imprisonment, a man condemned to die.

As he disappeared, a great cry rose above the crowd, struck with awe and horror.

This cry was,—

"God help and save your majesty! God keep you from your enemies!"

One of the soldiers, even, joined in this cry, and was seen to do so by an officer, who felled him with one ·

N*

blow. This took place as the king passed. He looked
at the unfortunate man with a smile of sad pity.

"Poor fellow !" he murmured, sighing: "'tis a heavy
blow for so small an offense !"

———

I X.

THE HAMMERING.

THE terrible comedy of the king's trial had been
played at Westminster : the tragedy in front of Whitehall was to follow. it speedily.

Of those days which passed between the king's sentence and execution I have no strength to speak. I
was near him, with other friends, and was witness to a
calmness and dignity worthy of a brave man and a
monarch. The king's nerves were unshaken : he prepared for his end with august composure ; and when
he was informed that the people in power had consented to permit him to see his two children before his
death, a smile of joy lit up the pale and emaciated face.

This intelligence was brought to him on the night
before his execution. He was writing at the instant,
and laid down his pen to clasp his hands in deep grati-
tude, raising his eyes, as he did so, to heaven.

As the messenger disappeared, he turned to the
friends around him, and said, with a smile,—

"'Tis not forbidden a poor king in captivity to
make verses, my friends : I have thus employed myself

after writing my last adieus to one from whom I am severed,—one very dear to me."

He took up the sheet upon which he had been writing. As he did so, a sudden hammering began in front of Whitehall. I shuddered; for I knew that 'twas the workmen erecting the scaffold.

"What is that?" the king asked, turning his head, and listening.

No one replied. The sound of hammers continued. Suddenly the king's cheeks filled with blood.

"I understand now. God's will be done!" he murmured. "But this shall not fright me!"

The smile came back to his face, and he said,—

"Will you hear one or two of my poor verses?"

In the midst of sobs, he then read these verses:—

> " The fiercest furies which do daily tread
>   Upon my grief—my gray discrowned head—
>   Are those who to my bounty owe their bread.
>
> " Yet, sacred Saviour, with thy words I woo
>   Thee to forgive, and not be bitter to
>   Such (as thou knowest) know not what they do.
>
> " Augment my patience, nullify my hate,
>   Preserve my children, and inspire my mate,
>   Yet, though we perish, bless this Church and State!"

As he finished reading these words, the door opened, and Bishop Juxon appeared, his face pale, his bosom heaving. As he approached, the old prelate's equanimity gave way, and he began to sob violently.

The king raised his hand calmly, with a gesture of kindness.

"Compose yourself, my lord," he said to the bishop.

"We have no time to waste on grief: let us rather think of the great matter. I must prepare to appear before God, to whom in a few hours I have to render my account. I hope to meet death with calmness, and that you will have the goodness to render me your assistance. Do not let us speak of the men into whose hands I have fallen. They thirst for my blood: they shall have it. God's will be done! I give him thanks. I forgive them all sincerely; but let us say no more about them."

A harsh growl at the door was heard. The sentinels, guarding the king night and day now, had opened the door, and expressed by the growl their disgust at the supposed hypocrisy of the king.

The weeping bishop motioned them away.

"Suffer us, my friends," he said.

And, as though these mild and faltering words had affected even the rough natures of the sentinels, they closed the door with a crash.

The king then knelt and prayed long and devoutly. As he rose from his knees, he turned his head quickly. His face beamed with joy.

"What has your majesty heard?" the bishop said.

"I know not if I have heard them, but 'tis the feet of my children!"

Footsteps approached along the corridor, and reached the door: it was opened, and the little Princess Elizabeth, a girl of about twelve, and the Duke of Gloucester, still younger, ran forward into their father's arms.

The children had burst into passionate tears; but there were no tears in the eyes of the king. A delight beyond words shone in his pale face.

"My little ones!" he murmured, covering their faces with kisses. "Thank God, they have permitted you to come to me! Oh, yes, yes! now I forgive them from my heart!"

Some moments passed in those half-inarticulate exclamations, mingled with caresses, which are so touching,—above all in a father embracing his children for the last time on earth. The children sobbed and held him closely. He never seemed weary of caressing and kissing them.

At last he grew more composed, and his countenance assumed an expression of solemn gravity.

"Sweet-heart," he said, to the little princess, "do not forget what I tell thee. I wish you not to grieve and torment yourself for me; for it is a glorious death I shall die, for the laws and religion of the land. I have forgiven all my enemies, and I hope God will forgive them; and you and your brothers and sisters must forgive them also."

He paused, and I saw an expression of deep tenderness come to his eyes.

"You will see your mother, sweet-heart," he said. "Tell her that my thoughts have never strayed from her,—that my love for her remains the same to the last. Love her, be obedient to her, and do not grieve for me: I die a martyr."

Nothing was heard in the deep silence which followed these words but the sobs and broken words of the little princess promising to obey these last commands of her father.

The king raised his hand and passed it across his eyes. He then turned to the little Duke of Gloucester, and, placing his arm around him, drew him upon his knee.

26

"My child," he said, "I wish you to heed what your father now says to you. They will cut off my head, and perhaps make thee a king; but you must not be a king so long as your brothers Charles and James live. I therefore charge you, do not be made a king by them."

The child's face flushed suddenly, and he looked at the king with a flash of the eyes shining through his tears.

"I will be torn in pieces first!" he exclaimed.

The king's face glowed.

"That is spoken like my son!" he said. "You rejoice me exceedingly!"

He bestowed a warm embrace upon the child, then, drawing the princess towards him, clasped both to his bosom.

As he did so, the ominous sound of the hammers in front of Whitehall broke in. The king sobbed, nearly unmanned, and covered the children's faces with kisses. As he did so, the guard advanced to remove them, and Bishop Juxon groaned.

The king raised his head. "Oh, 'tis pitiful! Do not take them from me!" he exclaimed.

The guard drew nearer, stern and unmoved. The hammering was heard through the open door.

The king saw that the hour had come. With heaving bosom, he placed his hands on the heads of the children and blessed them. They sobbed passionately as the guard took them away; and the king rose to his feet and turned aside to hide his tears. A window looked upon the court. He went to it, to see the last of them, if possible, and, leaning his face against the frame-work, sobbed aloud.

The children were passing through the door now, in charge of the guard, when all at once the king turned and hastened to them in an agony of weeping. Clasping them for the last time in his arms, he covered them with kisses and caresses, called upon God to bless them, and, releasing them, staggered rather than walked back to his seat, into which he fell, concealing his face in his hands.

The hammering from the front of Whitehall had never ceased.

X.

THE WALK TO WHITEHALL.

At midnight the king, after performing his devotions, lay down, and was soon asleep. All had retired but his attendant Herbert and myself, who had been commanded to remain.

The king had given me both a letter and messages for the queen. I was to convey these to her majesty after witnessing the king's last hours, of which I was to give her a detailed account.

I lay down on a pallet,—Herbert occupying another, —but could not sleep. The terrible events occurring around me excited my nerves and drove away my slumbers. Providence had decreed that I should thus witness the last moments of a condemned king, should be beside him and lose no detail of the tragedy. All had passed before me; I was to be present to the end; and the thought of what would take place on the morrow banished sleep.

The night thus passed, the chamber lit only by a large taper which burned in the centre of a silver basin. Long shadows, funereal and ominous, fell upon the walls: nothing was heard but the quiet breathing of the king, who had for the time lost all consciousness of his misfortunes.

About daybreak I was startled, however, by a deep groan from the pallet occupied by Herbert, the king's attendant. I looked in the direction of the sound, and saw that the sleeper was tossing to and fro, the victim, it seemed, of some painful dream. Suddenly I saw the king rise on his elbow.

"Herbert!" he called; and the faithful attendant at once awoke.

"What is the matter?" said the king. "You groan fearfully in your sleep!"

Herbert passed his hand across his brow, as though he were confused.

"I have been dreaming, your majesty," he stammered.

"Tell me your dream," came from the king.

Herbert sighed, and said,—

"I dreamed, your majesty, that Archbishop Laud, in his pontifical robes, entered this apartment and knelt before your majesty, who looked at him with a pensive expression of countenance. Conversation then took place between the archbishop and your majesty; he sighed deeply, seemed in pain; then the talk ended; he inclined before your majesty, and was going towards the door again, when suddenly he fell prostrate on the floor."

The king had listened without interrupting the speaker. He now remained an instant buried in reflection.

"Your dream is remarkable, Herbert," he said, at length, in a pensive tone. "But the archbishop is dead."

He paused again for a moment.

"Had I conferred with the archbishop," he added, "it is possible, albeit I loved him well, that I might have said somewhat which would have caused his sigh."

As he spoke, the king threw aside the coverlet.

"I will now rise," he said. "I have a great work to do this day."

He seated himself, and motioned to Herbert to dress his hair. The attendant obeyed, but his hand trembled, as though from cold,—the fire in the apartment having died out.

"Nay," the king said, calmly, "though my head be not to stand long on my shoulders, take the same pains with it that you were wont to do. This is my second marriage-day, Herbert."

Herbert obeyed with trembling hands, and I observed the king shiver.

"'Tis very cold," he said. "Give me an additional shirt. The weather may make me shake; and I would have no imputation of fear. Death is not terrible to me. I bless my God I am prepared."

As he spoke, Bishop Juxon entered, his face pale and woe-begone.

"Welcome, my lord," the king said. "Will you pray with me?"

The bishop knelt down, and in a faltering voice uttered a fervent prayer, which the king listened to, kneeling also devoutly. He then resumed his seat; and the bishop read from the Gospel of St. Matthew.

"Did you choose this chapter, my lord, as applicable to my situation?" asked the king, when he had ended.

"It is the gospel of the day, as the calendar indicates, your majesty," replied the bishop.

The king's face exhibited great emotion. The chapter read by the bishop was that which gives an account of the trial, condemnation, and execution of our Saviour. A strange chance—if there be any chance—had made it the regular gospel of the day, in accordance with the calendar. The king resumed a moment afterwards his kneeling position. I could see his lips moving. A deep silence—the silence of prayer and pity—reigned in the apartment.

The king had just risen, when the door opened, and the guard appeared.

"I am ready," he said, calmly.

And, placing his hat upon his head, he descended the staircase into St. James's Park. The path to Whitehall was lined with ten companies of infantry. In front of the king moved a detachment of halberdiers, with drums beating and colors flying.

The king walked on slowly, exhibiting no emotion of any description,—on his right the good bishop, on his left Colonel Tomlinson, of the army, and myself. The king was absolutely composed, the soldier full of compassion for him. This sentiment was so plain that his majesty observed it, and, taking a gold *etui* which he wore, said,—

" I beg you will accept this, sir, as a token of remembrance, and that you will not leave me until all is over.''

The soldier bowed his head, and took the gift with deep emotion.

"I will observe your majesty's command," he said. " Dare I ask your majesty if there be any truth in what I conceive to be a terrible slander concerning you ?''

"Ask your question, my friend."

" Did your majesty concur with the Duke of Buckingham in causing your late father's death ?''

The king's face assumed a smile of pity.

" My friend," he said, " if I had no other sin than that, God knows I should have little need to beg his forgiveness at this hour.''

" Then——''

The reply was not finished. A sudden roar from the drums interrupted it. They were near Whitehall, and the king said to the guard,—

"Come on, my good fellows : step apace."

And, pointing to a tree, he added, to Bishop Juxon,—

" That tree was planted by my brother Henry."

These trifles all engraved themselves indelibly upon my memory. If they are otherwise unimportant, they still indicate the king's calmness.

He had now reached the flight of stairs which leads from the park into Whitehall. As he entered the palace, Colonel Tomlinson said,—

" Here are two Independent ministers, your majesty, who offer their spiritual aid and prayers."

The king paused, but replied, almost immediately,—

" Say to them frankly that they have so often prayed against me that they shall not pray with me in my agony; but if they will pray *for* me now, tell them that I shall be thankful."

As he spoke, the king turned to me, and held out his hand.

"I must leave you now, friend," he said. "You must not go with me to the scaffold. You have my last request. Convey the letter you wot of; tell her to whom 'tis addressed that she was in my heart to the last; and may God bless and keep *you,* as my faithful friend, always!"

I could make no reply, but, falling upon my knees, pressed the king's hand to my lips, with sobs.

A moment afterwards he had disappeared within the palace.

XI.

THE EXECUTION.

I HASTENED to the front of the palace, where rose, grim and threatening, the scaffold with its block, upon which the execution was to take place.

A frightful dream, rather than a series of real events, seemed playing before me, and I could scarce collect my thoughts or reason upon the situation. A great crowd blocked up the street, of mingled soldiery and civilians. Round hats and gleaming arms were mixed together in enormous confusion; and through the mighty multitude awaiting the terrible scene ran a low, vague murmur, like the sound of waves before they are lashed to fury in a tempest.

I staggered on, rather than walked, and almost by main force made a path through the mass towards the scaffold. More than once I came near becoming engaged in a personal collision from my urgency. A soldier whom I had thrust aside aimed a savage blow at me with his halberd, and a burly ruffian into whose ribs I struck my elbow overwhelmed me with blasphemous curses. I disregarded all, however, and, thanks to my persistence, reached a position near the scaffold.

The crowd was agitated, and many faces were pale.

"Poor king!" said a woman,—for there were many in the mass;—"see! they have driven iron staples in the scaffold, to chain him down if he resists!"

"Poor heart!" came in response; but with these pitying exclamations mingled hoarse shouts of "Execution! execution!"

I was now in the immediate vicinity of the scaffold. My head was turning, wellnigh, at thought of the coming spectacle; but in the midst of this confused dream, as 'twere, rose clear and vivid the thought, "Who will act as executioner?" Gregory Brandon, the official headsman, had fled from London, and would not strike off the king's head if they found him. Who would? To volunteer was too infamous for the most infamous. It might be that no Englishman could be found who would act as headsman!

A fearful commentary upon this desperate hope was speedily presented. The crowd surged to and fro; a path was made through the compact mass; and through this opening advanced two figures, from whom the most brutal shrank back.

The figures were clad in a close woolen garb, then

peculiar to butchers. One wore a long gray peruke, beard, and black mask; the other a black peruke and mask, and a black hat whose heavy flap was caught up in front. Something peculiar in the walk of this latter proved that it was Gregory Brandon. But who was the personage in the gray beard?

The men mounted the scaffold in the midst of loud cries. Then all became silent. Through a window in front of the palace, the king walked straight to the scaffold, accompanied only by Bishop Juxon and Herbert. As he reached it, I saw the figure taken for that of Gregory Brandon kneel to him. I pushed nearer, and came within hearing just as the king turned quickly, seeing some one touch the headman's axe, exclaiming,—

"Have a care of the axe! If the edge is spoiled, 'twill be the worse for me!"

Meanwhile the headsman had remained upon his knees. He now said, in a muffled, voice,—the voice of Gregory Brandon,—

"I entreat your majesty's forgiveness for performing this terrible duty."

The king shook his head.

"No," he said: "I forgive no subject of mine who comes deliberately to shed my blood!"

The headsman groaned, and I saw a shudder pass through his frame.* He rose, and, with head bowed upon his breast, awaited.

---

* Sir Henry Ellis records that Gregory Brandon, dragged unwillingly to execute the king, pined away for want of the forgiveness refused him, and died less than two years afterwards, declaring that "he always saw the king as he appeared on the scaffold, and that, withal, devils did tear him on his death-bed."—EDITOR.

The king had turned away, and uttered a few words to Bishop Juxon. He then raised the long locks of gray hair flowing upon his neck, and said to the headsman,—

"Is any of my hair in the way?"

"I beg your majesty to push it more under your cap," came in muffled tones from the black mask, whose wearer bowed low.

In observing this ceremony, Bishop Juxon assisted his majesty.

"There is but one stage more, your majesty," faltered the good bishop, "which, though turbulent and troublesome, is yet a short one. Consider: it will carry you a great way,—even from earth to heaven."

The king inclined his head.

"I go from a corruptible to an incorruptible crown," he said, "where no disturbance can take place."

As he uttered these calm words, the king threw off his cloak, and gave his George to the bishop, with the single word, "Remember!" He then removed his coat, resumed the cloak, and, pointing to the block, said to the headsman,—

"Place it so that it will not shake."

"It is firm," came from the headsman, who shuddered so that he could scarce hold the axe.

"I shall say a short prayer," the king said, as calmly as before. "When I hold out my hand, thus,—strike."

The king stood for a moment with closed eyes, his lips moving in prayer. Then he raised his eyes to heaven, knelt, and placed his head upon the block; and the headsman, with a single blow, severed his head from his body.

As the head rolled upon the scaffold, and the body recoiled from the block, a cry burst from the vast crowd,—shouts and weeping mingled.

Above the mass, thus agitated and moving to and fro, rose the scaffold, where the gray headsman, the associate of the wretched Brandon, held up the dripping head of the king, crying,—

"This is the head of a traitor!"

XII.

SO WENT THE KING WHITE TO HIS GRAVE.

I LEFT the scene of the king's execution, staggering in my gait like a drunken man, and for hours thereafter wandered about London, the prey to a species of nightmare which chilled and fevered me by turns. All objects which my dull eyes rested upon seemed unreal, like the shapes seen in dreams. I scarce knew where I was; could see nothing but that one fearful group on the terrible platform in front of Whitehall.

Night fell, and still I went to and fro like one who has lost his way. Then, I know not how, I found myself again in the neighborhood of Whitehall. The streets were deserted; the great crowd had vanished : save the light in a window on the ground-floor of the palace, I saw no evidence that London was not a city of the dead.

Towards the light a strange attraction drew me. Without any definite design, I went to the great door

of the palace : it was open. The hall was deserted. I
entered, approached the door of the apartment from
which the light shone, and, reaching the threshold, saw
before me a singular spectacle.

In a coffin, covered with black velvet, lay the body
of Charles I., the head replaced in its natural position,
the lips wearing a sweet smile.

Beside it stood three persons, and in shadow at one
corner of the room were a number of stern-faced hal-
berd-bearers, erect and motionless as statues.

The three persons were Colonel Axtel, dark, sombre,
and sullen; Sir Purbeck Temple, a friend of the king,
whom I knew well and at once recognized ; the third
personage was the now terrible General Cromwell.

General Cromwell was standing beside the coffin,
with his back turned to me; and I could not see his
face. His left hand was placed beneath his right elbow ;
the other hand supported his chin. As I reached the
threshold, Sir Purbeck Temple had drawn near to the
coffin, and was looking at the king's face with half-
suppressed sobs.

"My poor master!" he exclaimed; "and this is
all that is left of thee !"

"Did you expect to find him alive," growled Axtel,
"after the blow of the axe?"

Sir Purbeck was silent for an instant. Then he
faltered,—

"I know not what I expected, sir. But I have read
that a species of divinity and holiness hedges a
king !——"

He could say no more. Axtel growled: the word
best describes the sound he uttered. He extended his

O   27

hand towards the body; a smile of contempt curled his sullen lips, and he said, with a heavy frown,—

"If thou thinkest there is any holiness in kingship, look there!"

Sir Purbeck Temple made no reply. I could see the tears on his cheeks.

General Cromwell had meanwhile remained silent and motionless, gazing at the body, as he afterwards gazed at the king's portrait,—hiding his secret thoughts.

Suddenly he moved and drew near the coffin. For an instant he paused again. Then, reaching out his hand, he raised the head of the corpse, looked at it, and at the body, and said, in his deep voice,—.

"This was a well-constituted frame, and promised long life!"

As he uttered these words he replaced the head in the coffin, turned away, passed by me slowly, without appearing to be aware of my presence, and went out of the door of the palace.

In my turn I approached the coffin, and gazed long at the king. His lips were smiling: he had died, plainly, forgiving all his enemies. I bent down and pressed a last kiss on the thin hand. A growl from Axtel, and a harsh order to leave the apartment, followed. I left the room and the palace, and was again in the streets,—seeing nothing, as I went on, but the cold face and the smile of the king.

Let me finish the gloomy record.

The body of Charles I. was conveyed to St. James's Palace, where it was embalmed. It was then taken to Windsor Castle, Cromwell having refused sepulture for the king in Westminster Abbey ; and at Windsor it was committed to the earth. The pall-bearers were the Duke of Richmond, the Earl of Hertford, and the Lords Lindsay and Southampton. As the coffin covered with black velvet was borne from the hall,—the only inscription upon it, " Carolus Rex, 1648," cut with a penknife,—the snow began to fall slowly and tranquilly, as though it mourned the dead man.

By the time it reached the chapel, the pall of black velvet was entirely white.

"So went our king white to his grave!" said his weeping pall-bearers.

Not even the burial-service of the Church had been permitted to be read over the king's grave.

XIII.

AN OLD CAVALIER OF THE KING.

I MIGHT here terminate my memoirs: the great epic is finished, and the curtain has fallen on the tragedy. But some incidents remain to be narrated, which refer to my personal fortunes; and my children, if no others, will like to hear of these incidents and of what marked my last days in England.

On the night of the scene at Whitehall, I wandered about London, laboring under a sort of stupor of grief and despair. A new blow was, however, coming. Fate had not exhausted her malice.

I had entered a low tavern, worn out and seeking a

spot to rest. On the rude table, covered with beer-
stains, lay a newspaper, which I took up mechanically.
As my eye fell upon it, I saw my father's name; and
as I read, my heart sank within me. The paper gave
a list of estates belonging to royalists, which had been
confiscated. Cecil Court was among them, and the
name of Sir Jervas Ireton opposite indicated that the
estate had been conveyed to *him*.

This intelligence came near to unman me. Then
my dear and honored father would be turned adrift,
homeless, in his old age! The sworn foe of our family
had wreaked his utmost vengeance upon us! The
coarse Sir Jervas Ireton would rule in the ancient home
of the Cecils!

I rose, my head turning, nearly. Whither should I
go? To France, leaving this blow to fall upon my
father? I could not: I must first see him. But how
to get to Warwickshire? I had no horse: was penni-
less. I went out of the tavern with a fire burning in
my brain, and tottered rather than walked along the
deserted streets.

I was going along thus, the prey of a despair which
I could not resist, when, just as I passed beneath a
swinging lamp, I heard the clatter of hoofs. They
drew nearer. I raised my head, the light shone upon
my face, and I heard my name uttered.

A moment afterwards, a cavalier, whose horse's hoofs
had made the clatter, stopped near me, threw himself
from the saddle, and passed his arm around me.

"Cecil, you are ill!" he exclaimed.

The light fell upon the speaker, and I recognized
Colonel Edward Cooke.

"What mean you by wandering through the streets at this hour, friend?" he continued. "You are pale and woe-begone: you have seen all to-day, I doubt not. But come! you are ill, Cecil! Tell me whither you go."

In a few words I told him of the confiscation of Cecil Court, and of my resolution to see my father again before I left England forever.

"Well," the old cavalier said, "nothing is easier, friend. You know I live near London, and my stud is not yet seized. My horses are famous ones, as you know; and you shall take your choice. Come! my servant will give you his cob, and make the journey home on foot. Come, friend!—we poor forlorn cavaliers should help each other."

I responded by a warm pressure of the hand, and was soon in the saddle. Half an hour afterwards we had left London by a by-way where there was no sentinel, and two hours later reined in our horses in front of the old manor-house of Colonel Cooke. I had visited the house twice before, the reader will remember, —first to bear to the old cavalier the queen's note requesting him to be ready with his horses when she thought to fly with her children to France, and again to make arrangements for the king's escape from Hampton Court. The old house shone now in a bright moonlight, which lit up, too, the leafless and spectral trees; but within, in the great fireplace of an apartment hung round with portraits, roared a fire of logs, which revived our chilled limbs.

My host proceeded at once to produce flagons and cold meats. The food and rich wine warmed me and

brought back my energies.   Then, lighting a pipe, and
puffing clouds of smoke from beneath his gray mustache, Colonel Cooke began to speak of the terrible
event of the day just passed.

I have no space to repeat our conversation.   It
extended far into the night.   All over England, I
think, that night, poor cavaliers like ourselves were
conferring on the future and shedding tears over the
past.

At last Colonel Cooke rose, and the light fell full
upon his tall figure and his brave face, with its gray
mustache, and its sparkling eyes yet undimmed by
age.

"You must be weary, friend," he said; "and your
bed is ready.   At dawn my best horse will be saddled :
take him; I make you a present of him.   God bless
and prosper you!   And now a last cup!"

He filled my cup and his own, raised his above his
head, and, with flashing eyes, exclaimed,—

"Confusion to Cromwell and his gang, and God
save his majesty King Charles II. !"

With a close pressure of the hand, we parted, and I
retired to rest.

On the next morning by sunrise I was riding at a
gallop in the direction of Warwickshire.

XIV.

THE HOUSE BESIDE THE HIGHWAY.

THE animal which my host had presented me with was a superb hunter, in the finest condition. He plainly asked nothing better than to be permitted to go at top speed; and thus league after league fled from under his feet, every moment bore me nearer and nearer to Cecil Court.

I will not interrupt my narrative to speak of my thoughts and feelings, or to paint the gloomy picture of rural England in that winter of 1648. 'Twas terrible, what I saw as I went on my rapid journey. War had stamped its destroying heel on the lovely land of the past, and a curse seemed hovering over the once-smiling fields. I shall not speak further of my journey, save to relate one singular incident which befell me.

I was proceeding at a rapid gait in the direction of Oxford, when, raising my eyes, which had been bent upon the ground, I saw, beside the road I was following, a small house which seemed familiar to me. A second glance, and I had fully recognized it. 'Twas that to which I had been conducted by Gregory Brandon and his daughter, and where I had held the interview with the sick dwarf Geoffrey Hudson.

As I drew near, I saw that the house was uninhabited; but in front of the door stood a horse covered with

foam, apparently from a rapid journey. Who could
have thus stopped, I asked myself, to enter this deserted house? To whom could this animal, covered
with foam-flakes, belong? I determined to solve the
question speedily, dismounted, and entered the house.
Before me, seated on a broken chair, and leaning his
head upon an old table, I saw no less a personage than
the dwarf Hudson.

As my footsteps resounded on the creaking floor, he
quickly raised his head.

"Ah, 'tis you?" he said, drearily. "At first I thought
'twas a ghost. Whence come you, sir?"

"From London. And you, friend?"

"From London also."

"You have ridden rapidly."

"I set out at midnight."

"Then you saw all?"

"All."

I looked at the strange being, who had answered my
questions in his thin voice with an accent of sombre
indifference. The dwarf seemed to be laboring under
the crushing weight of a sentiment which resembled
despair.

"You were in the crowd yonder?" I said, at a loss
how to continue the conversation.

"Yes," he replied, in the same dull and dreamy
tone.

"You recognized——him; I mean the headsman?"

"Yes: 'twas Gregory Brandon."

"And his assistant?"

"Hulet: they paid him a hundred pounds to assist
at the execution."

" Hulet ! is it possible ?   The man in the gray beard Hulet ?"

" Yes, Hulet,—the man who had Brandon dragged from this place of concealment,—who persecuted to the death the woman I loved,—who has paid at last for all, and will plot no more."

" Paid for all ?"

" He is dead.'

" Dead ?"

" Killed· in a drunken brawl in a low tavern, at nightfall after the execution."

I remained silent at this strange intelligence.   Then I looked again at the dwarf.

"You say that Hulet persecuted to the death—— whom ?"

" Janet Brandon, of whom I knew as Janet Gregory here !   He was crazy about her,—harassed her with his importunities.   She fell ill, and that wretch stood beside her death-bed and taunted her."

The dwarf turned pale as he spoke, and uttered a low groan.

" All is ended for me in life," he added, in the same low dull tone.   " I have left courts forever, and go to my obscure home to hide my misery.   You were my friend, and here farewell !   We shall never meet on earth again,—but some day—I shall see *her*—yonder !"

He pointed to heaven, went out of the deserted house, mounted his horse, and disappeared.

Such was my last meeting with this singular being, of whom I never afterwards heard.

o*

XV.

HOME AGAIN.

I RODE on towards Cecil Court, lost in gloomy thought. The interview with the dwarf, who had thus informed me of the death of Janet Brandon and the man Hulet, had deepened the sombre mood which oppressed me.

But something still more tragic awaited me. I should probably arrive at Cecil Court to find it in possession of the foe of my family,—my father homeless, the name of Cecil replaced by that of Ireton! The memory of my poor brother Harry came to add poignancy to these gloomy reflections. Had he been spared, we might have borne up: leaning on his strong arm, my dear father might have gone forth again into the world. I was left; but I was nothing. Oh, if my brave strong Harry had not fallen!

Haunted by these sombre thoughts, I continued my way, and drew near Keynton. Near the village I met an acquaintance, a poor man of the place.

"Go not thither, Master Cecil," he said: "there be soldiers of the godly faction there."

"They would arrest me, then, friend?"

"Yes, master. See, the man yonder is moving this way."

It was necessary to avoid arrest above all things; and I turned into a side-road.

" A last word, friend," I said. "My father ?"

" The squire be well, master ; but look you !"

The trooper was riding towards me; and, setting spur to my horse, I followed a bridle-path which led straight through the woods towards Cecil Court.

In half an hour I emerged from the wood, and the old home of my family was before me. Oh, how my heart yearned towards it ! How my pulse leaped at sight of the dearly-loved roof! I put spur to my horse, went at full speed across the fields, drew near, passed through the great gate, then, galloping up the familiar old avenue, I threw myself from the saddle, and approached the broad door.

As I did so, a brilliant gleam from between two clouds fell upon the old portico. My heel clashed on the flags ; I heard a cry; the door opened, and I found myself caught in the arms of my father,—and of Harry !

XVI.

A FRIEND IN NEED, AND INDEED.

THERE are some scenes, reader, which the most eloquent chronicler shrinks from describing, feeling that words have not yet been invented adequate to convey his emotion.

My brother whom I thought dead was thus alive, and I clasped him in my arms ! The dear laughing face was there again before me,—the warm hand pressed

my own: it was Harry,—Harry! and, holding him
close to me, I laughed and cried like a child.

The history of this marvel was given me in few
words. Harry had been fearfully but not mortally
wounded on the day of Naseby. With the wounded
of both sides, he had been conveyed to an obscure hos-
pital in London, and only after long confinement to
his bed had he been able to rise again. He was then
conducted to prison: his obscure existence was unre-
corded. At last his prison-door had opened; and here
he was again at home.

"That's the whole, Ned," he laughed,—"except
something else. Shall I tell that too?"

"Speak, Harry."

"No; I'll think I'll let madam tell you in person."

"Madam!"

"Certainly. Do you remember our visit to my lord
Falkland's house 'Great Tew'?"

"Yes! yes!"

"And his handsome and most agreeable niece
Alice?"

I started, gazing at him with wide eyes.

"She has come to see *us*, now!"

And, opening an inner door, Harry called out,
laughing,—

"Alice!"

The beautiful girl hastened in, bright-eyed, laughing,
and holding up her red cheek.

"Welcome, brother Edmund!" she said.

I pressed my lips to the red cheek, lost in a maze of
wonder. As I did so, I felt two arms around my neck,
and Cicely's lips close pressed to my own.

"Oh, brother! God be thanked——!"

The child began to cry then, and only held me closer.

"My little Cicely!" I exclaimed, returning her embrace. Then I added, laughing,—

"You at least are not married?"

Harry burst into laughter.

"Ask Frank Villiers there if she's not!" he cried.

I turned, feeling as though I were in a dream. Before me stood young Frank Villiers, with his chestnut curls, blue eyes, and joyous smile, enjoying plainly my astonishment, my dumb stupor.

"Let me explain all, my son, in a very few words," said my father, in his mild sweet voice. "Harry and Cicely have just been married, and are about to leave me. They go beyond seas until the troubles of England have blown over. God has mercifully returned my dear Harry to me back from the grave, and now sends you too to add to the joy of my old heart!"

My father had scarce uttered these words, when hoof-strokes clattered up the avenue.

"Who comes so fast?" he said, going to the door, and opening it.

A moment afterwards I saw rush in the figure of young Jervas Ireton. He was covered with dust, and held a paper in his hand.

"Make haste, Mr. Harry, and Mr. Ned, and all!" he exclaimed. "They are coming to arrest you!—from Keynton!—the troopers!"

"To arrest us?" I said, coldly. "Doubtless 'tis your good father, sir."

"Father? Why, he's dead!" exclaimed the young

28

hopeful, without any exhibition of feeling. "Died of the quinsy,—furious because I'd married the game-keeper's daughter! Her name was Cicely,—she's a beauty! But hurry, Mr. Ned and Harry! I'm your friend; not one of the godly. I have no opinions of any consequence! Order your coach, quick, and horses too, and get to Charlecote with the ladies! Stay! the troopers are coming. See, yonder on the hill!"

A glance indicated that the warning was judicious. On the summit of a hill about half a mile from the house was seen a party of troopers approaching at a round trot.

"I'll see to the coach without a moment's delay!" Harry exclaimed; "and you, young ladies, gather up your jewels and laces and be ready! Ned, you and I will go on horseback. Your horse will await you in the shrubbery near the coach."

Cicely and the fair Alice were hastening out, when young Ireton caught the hand of the former.

"Do you remember old times, Cicely?"

"Yes,—oh, thank you, Jervas; but don't keep me."

"You are going away now, and I won't see you again, Cicely."

"Good-by, Jervas."

"One moment, Cicely. I am not of much conse-quence; but I'm not a bad fellow, and I will try to show you that."

He unfolded the paper in his hand.

"I loved you, Cicely," he went on, "and mar-ried the gamekeeper's daughter because she's named Cicely too! I love you still, and Mr. Ned, and Harry, and Mr. Cecil, and all of you. My father's dead, and

I'm the master, and this deed is mine. It is the deed to my father for Cecil Court, which they confiscated. Here, Cicely! that is my wedding-present. Now give me a kiss!"

He tore the deed in pieces, and presented it to her.

"Good, good Jervas! You are a true friend! Oh, thank you! you shall have a good kiss, indeed!"

And Cicely held up her lips quickly; the youth bestowed a resounding salute thereon: a moment afterwards, Cicely had disappeared, and the troopers were seen rapidly approaching.

"Go, my son," said my father. "I have seen you, and you must not run the risk of prison! God be thanked, my old eyes have looked again upon my children! Embrace me! God bless you!"

I threw myself into my father's arms, shook hands with Jervas, and ran to my horse, which stood in the shrubbery.

As the troopers thundered up to the door, the coach containing Cicely, Alice, and Frank Villiers disappeared in the wood behind the house.

Harry and I followed on horseback; and we gained Charlecote in safety.

On the next morning the coach with its gentlemen outriders set out for the coast. Fortune served us. We obtained passage on a vessel bound for Holland.

Three days afterwards our feet pressed the soil of the continent. We were beyond the reach of all our enemies.

XVII.

VIRGINIA.

A FEW pages more will terminate my memoirs.

I found her majesty the queen at the château of the Duchess de Montmorenci, in a hall hung with black ever since the execution of the great duke by Richelieu. And here in this funereal mansion the illustrious widows mingled their tears.

The queen scarce shed any when I gave her the king's letter and last message. A dumb despair seemed to have dried up the fount of her tears; and when I had finished my tragic narrative she simply dropped her head, fixing her eyes steadily upon the floor, and, seeing that she had forgotten my presence, I silently went out of the apartment, leaving the august mourner to herself.

Frances Villiers had remained with her, and now received me and soothed me. Need I relate what followed? The sole obstacle to our union had been the promise made to Harry. He was not dead now, but alive, and certainly would never more prove my rival. Thus I came to Frances, and took her hand and pressed it to my lips. An hour afterwards she had promised me; and in a month she was my wife,—the dearest and best wife man ever had.

Thus, friendly reader, whether of my own blood or

other, I have come to the end of my story. Would you have a few words more, and know how my life passed afterwards? The record will fill but a page, and I lay it before you. I remained on the continent, attached to the French court, until the summer of 1650, when I went with his majesty Charles II. on that ill-fated expedition that terminated at Worcester. I shared his perils and adventures thereafter, and may some day relate them. Now I will record only the fact that I escaped in safety and rejoined my wife in Paris.

The year afterwards I was in Virginia, and was building my house here on York River. Some old cavalier friends had preceded me, and told marvels of the country,—of the cheap and fertile lands, the stately rivers, and the charming climate. I therefore collected my resources, set sail from France, established myself on the great York, and have never revisited England.

The Cecils flourish there still,—Harry being the head of the house. My dear father is long since dead, —God rest him, and bless his memory! And Harry, the owner of Cecil Court, writes me at length by every sailing-vessel, filling his sheet with laughing comments on affairs around him, and memories of old times.

Just across the York resides Frank Villiers with his wife Cicely,—a well-to-do planter, surrounded by rosy-faced children. He and my dear friend Mr. Page of "Rosewell" are here constantly. And my old age thus passes serenely in the midst of my family and friends, beneath the sunshine of one of the most beautiful of all lands.

For all I am grateful,—chiefest of all for my dear wife and my happy children. God made the first portion of my existence stormy; he has mercifully sent the sunshine to bathe with its mild splendor my old age. I thank him humbly, and strive to love my fellow-creatures as I should. Old enmities have long since disappeared from my heart. The smiles of my dear Frances and my little ones shine brightly. And that cheerful sunshine lights up my life, blotting out all the sad memories of the past.

THE END.

www.ingramcontent.com/pod-product-compliance
Lightning Source LLC
Chambersburg PA
CBHW020944030726
47496CB00005B/1352